DEATH IN DOUBLE MOCHA

More books by Suzan Harden

(Each series is in suggested reading order)

Soccer Moms of the Apocalypse

Pestilence in Pumpkin Spice
Famine in French Vanilla
War in White Chocolate
Death in Double Mocha

Millersburg Magick Mysteries

Spells and Sleuths
Fae and Felonies
Magick and Murder

Solar System Services, Inc.

Alone Is Not Lonely
Halloween Harvest ("A Place at the Table")

Miscellaneous

Sword and Sorceress 31 ("Pig-Headed")
Sword and Sorceress 32 ("Unexpected")
Practical Witches
Revenge Served Hot
The Yule Switch
Chocolate for Dinner
Silver Shoes and Pigs' Ears

Bloodlines

Blood Magick
Zombie Love
Zombie Confidential
Zombie Wedding
Amish, Vamps & Thieves
Blood Sacrifice
Love, War & a Bulldog
Zombie Goddess
Ravaged
Sacrificed
Reality Bites
Ghouls in the Grocery
Resurrected
Bloodlines Shorts Anthology
Bloodlines: The First Boxed Set

Seasons of Magick

Spring
Summer
Autumn
Winter
The Seasons of Magick Anthology

Justice

Sword and Sorceress 28
("Justice")
Sword and Sorceress 30
("Diplomacy in the Dark")
Justice: The Beginning
A Question of Balance
A Modicum of Truth
A Matter of Death
A Touch of Mother
A Twist of Love
A Virtue of Child
A Hand of Father
A Measure of Knowledge
A Hint of Thief
A Cup of Conflict

The Justice Thalia Stories

Snowfall
Murder Most Fowl
The Sweetest Poison
A Granddaughter of Mine
Too Many Fish in the Sea

Tales of the Twelve

The Trickster Priestess and the Demon

888-555-HERO

Hero De Facto
Hero Ad Hoc
Hero De Novo
A Very Hero Christmas
Hero De Jure
Hero In Camera
Hero Amicus Curiae
A Very Hero Wedding
A Very Hero New Year
Hero Ad Litem
Queer Eye for the Super Guy

Crossover Worlds

Invasion!

For updates, news, and giveaways, joinSuzan's mailing list at:
suzanharden.blogspot.com/p/contact-me.html
Or visit her website at suzanharden.com.
You can also check her out on Facebook @ SuzanHardenWriter.

This is a work of fiction. All characters, organizations and events in this story are products of the author's imagination and are not to be construed as real. Any resemblance to persons, living or dead, is entirely coincidental.

DEATH IN DOUBLE MOCHA
(Soccer Moms of the Apocalypse #4)

ISBN-13 - 978-1-64918-020-9

Published by Angry Sheep Publishing
Findlay, Ohio

Interior Design by JW Manus
Cover Design by For the Muse Designs

Death in Double Mocha

SUZAN HARDEN

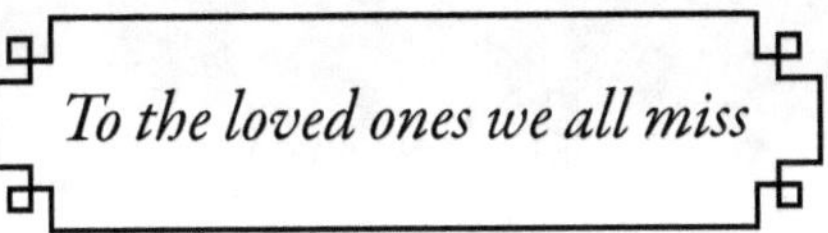

To the loved ones we all miss

Chapter 1

Irritated as hell, Dani Elante jabbed the button to open her garage door. Mark had forgotten to haul the garbage can out to the curb for tomorrow morning's trash pick-up.

Again.

Her normally conscientious son seemed to have totally lost his mind with the onset of puberty. He had barely acknowledged her presence when she marched into his bedroom and lectured him, his earbuds jammed in his ear canals and his nose firmly affixed to his phone screen as his thumbs typed messages to his friends. If her brother Marty hadn't put her and Mark on his family's unlimited phone plan, she would have had to take a second mortgage out on the house to pay for her son's excessive usage.

She should have grounded Mark, but guilt nagged her. He pretended to be okay with her being the avatar of Death, one of the Four Horsemen of the Apocalypse.

Or rather the Soccer Moms of the Apocalypse, as Wila had coined them.

But the four women's kids only had each other to talk to when it came to the weirdness of what was going on in Oakfield over the past couple of months. Deep down, she knew she couldn't take those relationships away from Mark. It was his only outlet for dealing with the madness.

A cold wind rattled the tree branches and the handfuls of dried brown leaves clinging to them in the dark. The bitter breeze also cut through her sweatshirt and jeans and raised goosebumps along her skin. She should have grabbed her coat before she came out.

The scent of smoke drifted in the freezing air along with the hint of the coming winter to Illinois. Someone in the neighborhood was fighting the chill with a cozy wood fire.

A sense of regret whispered through her. Maybe she shouldn't have sold the old Victorian she and Heath had started to refurbish before his accident. She loved the odor of pine and the crackle of real wood burning while cuddling with her husband in front of the flickering flames. But there was no way to pay two mortgages on just her salary, and Mark needed consistency with the loss of his father.

Dammit, Heath had been gone for six years. She was not going to wind herself into another depressive funk. Just because nearly everyone else she knew had family members rise from their graves, it didn't mean she'd get that lucky. Except the question was almost as nagging as her guilt. Had Heath not been righteous enough to deserve resurrection with the Second Coming of Christ?

Or was he still in his grave because she was Death?

Dani grabbed the handle of the garbage can and dragged it out to the curb before she went back for the recyclables container. She wheeled the blue can out to the curb and set it beside the pink trash can that promoted breast cancer awareness. Why did she miss Heath so much when she barely thought about Mom?

The better question is why hadn't either of them risen when half of the Oakfield Cemetery's residents had come back to life a few days before Halloween. They were both good people. Why did Penny get her mother-in-law and Wila get her grandmother back, and Dani was still alone? It wasn't fair.

But then, it wasn't fair she had been chosen as Death, one of the Horsemen of the Apocalypse, either.

A gust slapped her ponytail in her face. It was too damn cold to bemoan her luck in life outside. She'd make a hot cup of green tea and pout under her favorite blanket. Nope, she'd binge her favorite sitcom until she fell asleep. Marty would understand as both her brother and her boss when she called in sick in the morning. She turned to head back into the garage.

The oak tree in her front yard moaned, and a shiver ran down her spine that had nothing to do with the frigid wind. It was the same sensation of wrongness she felt around one of the newly risen dead. She whirled around, looking for the cause, wishing for the first time the city of Oakfield had installed more streetlamps in their subdivision.

A dark figure stepped out of the shadow of the fence-lined right-of-way running between the Cassadines' and the Jones's houses across the street. She was on the verge of summoning her scythe when the shape shuffled into the square of the light cast by the fixtures in her garage onto the asphalt pavement. The blonde hair was as dirty as the clothes and face, but the piercing blue eyes were the same as the first time she met him.

Her heart threatened to choke her. "Heath?"

"Hey, baby." He looked terribly confused. "I think I had an accident."

Chapter 2

"An accident?" Dani tried to catch her breath and calm her heart. Thank goodness, Mark was already ensconced in his bedroom. He would stay in his room until she forced him out of bed in time for school. "Are you hurt? I'll take you to the ER. Let me grab my coat."

What the hell was she thinking? She couldn't take Heath to the hospital. They'd call the police as soon as the admitting staff put his name in their computer system. Heath had coded in the Oakfield ER after the accident.

"I'm not hurt." Heath's frown deepened. "I'm just really confused."

"Honey, come inside. Let's get you cleaned up." She held out her hand. "We'll double-check to make sure you're okay. If you're still dazed, it may be a concussion. I'll call Wila—"

Heath's brow crinkled. "Who?"

Crap, she'd forgotten she didn't meet Penny, Wila, and Francine until after his death. The trio had become such an integral part of Dani's life it seemed like they'd always been there.

"Her son Derek is friends with Mark, and she's an EMT." She shivered. "Honey, it's dang cold out here. Let's go inside, and we'll figure things out."

"I-I woke up in the dirt," Heath said. "I couldn't find the car so I walked home."

"I'm so sorry, honey." Dani stepped closer, but he ignored her outstretched palm. "That must have been really scary. Come inside with me, and we'll deal with it."

He cocked his head and stared at something behind her. She glanced over her shoulder. The minivan. She had sworn up and down they were not going to be one of those couples when she was pregnant with Mark.

"Why is there a minivan in our garage?" Heath asked.

"I had a problem with my truck," she said. "Please come inside, honey. It's freezing out here."

He continued staring at the minivan. "Neal Astin couldn't give you a different colored loaner. Mark's going to be teased by the other first graders."

The scars on Dani's heart ripped. "Heath, Mark is twelve now."

That drew her husband's attention away from the damn minivan. "What?"

"Honey, you couldn't find your car tonight because you died in an accident six years ago."

The truth stunned Heath long enough for Dani to guide him into the house. Part of her was glad she hadn't moved though she'd thought about it after his funeral.

A lot.

She grabbed a clean washcloth out of the utility room, filled a bowl with hot water, and sat next to Heath at the kitchen table.

"I-I'm dead?" he asked while she washed the dirt from his face.

"Not anymore," she said as she rinsed the washcloth. "It's a rather long story, but the dead are rising from their graves because the Apocalypse has begun."

"What?" Heath stared at her. "If that's supposed to be a joke, it's not funny."

"I'm not joking," she murmured while she worked on his hands. "Are you hungry?"

"Yeah," he admitted. "But can we start this discussion over? I did have an accident, didn't I?"

"Yes." She focused on the dirt between his fingers. Heath's fingers. The last time she touched him was when she placed his wedding band back on his finger before his funeral. It was still there.

"Dani, look at me." He tilted her chin up until her eyes met his. "Please tell me what happened."

She swallowed the huge lump threatening to choke her. "You-you were hit head-on by a drunk driver going the wrong way on the interstate." Admitting the facts brought all the old pain back. Tears spilled over her eyelids and rolled down her cheeks. She'd been frightened of Heath coming back since that day nearly two months ago when Penny's dead mother-in-law showed up on the Hudson's doorstep.

"Oh, baby." He reached up and brushed away the wetness with the backs of his fingers. "I'm so sorry I left you and Mark alone. I never would have done that on purpose."

"I know," she whispered.

"And the Apocalypse stuff?" He cocked his head as he cupped her face.

She laid her hands on his and gently pulled them away. "There's no way for you to believe me without seeing for yourself. But promise me, you'll be quiet because Mark is asleep upstairs." At least, she prayed he'd fallen asleep while listening to his music.

He frowned. "Show me what?"

"What I've become." She slowly rose from her chair. "What I am."

Those big blue eyes remained locked on her. She released a deep breath, bowed her head, and let the power wash over her.

"What the—" Heath scrambled off the kitchen chair, knocking it over in the process. The wood clattered loudly against the ceramic tile floor. "Dani?"

"It's still me, honey." She hated the way her voice rattled when she was Death, but it couldn't be helped. "I'm one of the Four Horsemen of the Apocalypse."

"But you're not a man," he protested.

"That's why we call ourselves the Four Soccer Moms of the Apocalypse."

"The Four Soccer Moms of the Apocalypse?" He didn't look too sure, but he no longer wore the expression of insane panic.

"It's a long story, honey." She shrugged. "How about I make us some tea while I tell you about it?"

He cocked his head in the same adorable way he had when she told him she was pregnant, trying hard to reconcile reality with his preconceived notions. "Does this mean you raised me from my grave?"

"No," she said. "The Fifth Seal broke as foretold in the Book of Revelation."

"The Fifth Seal?"

"The Four Horsemen, or Soccer Moms in our case, are the first four Seals. The Fifth Seal is the dead believers rising from their graves."

"Aw, crap! Are demons running around town again?"

Dani whirled to find Mark standing in the doorway. She spread her arms in a desperate attempt to distract her son.

"What are you doing up?" she snapped. "It's a school night."

Mark crossed his arms. "I'm not the one banging around furniture. You woke me up. And you don't run around all skeleton-y if demons aren't causing problems again."

"Go to bed, young man," she ordered.

Instead, he marched over to the utility closet and pulled out his bright yellow and orange Super Soaker. "I can cover the demon while you interrogate him."

"Mark?" Heath stepped around Dani's left side. "Is that really you?"

"Dad?" Mark dropped his water blaster and ran straight into Heath's arms.

Chapter 3

Dani wasn't sure whether to be ecstatic or frightened. Mark devolved into a weeping mess. Heath held their son tight. Maybe it was finally sinking in he had been gone from hers and Mark's lives for six years because he kept murmuring, "I'm sorry, Mark. I'm so, so sorry."

"It wasn't your fault, Dad." Mark pulled away from Heath and looked up at him. "It was never your fault. You wouldn't have left us on purpose. I know you wouldn't. But you're back now." Mark looked at Dani. "Dad's back like Justine and Derek's abuelas, right?"

Dani didn't want to break Mark's heart or her own. "For now."

"What do you mean for now?" He glared at her. "You're Death. Aren't you supposed to know these things?"

Dani crossed her arms and glared back. "God forgot to send us the instruction books when He made me and your friends' mothers the Soccer Moms of the Apocalypse."

"Uh, Dani, are your eye sockets supposed to glow green?" Heath murmured.

Crap. She closed her eyes and concentrated on rainbows over Lake Michigan. The power flowed back into its hiding place in her heart. When she opened her eyes, she was back in her jeans and sweatshirt.

"Can Dad come to my game on Saturday?" Mark abruptly changed the subject. "It's our last game of the fall season."

"If you go back to bed—"

"But this is the first chance I've had to talk to Dad since I was in first grade," Mark protested.

"I know, sweetheart, but—" she started.

"Can't you call me in sick for just tomorrow?" Mark's tone switched to begging. "Justine got to stay home after she got kidnapped, and this is way bigger." He flung his arms wide to indicate how much of a deal this was to him.

"Mark—" Dani growled.

"But—" His voice cracked. For the first time, Dani realized exactly how much Heath's death affected their son.

"Mark," Heath said. "Listen to your mom. She and I need to talk, and I will be here in the morning."

"This is no different than Justine's or Derek's grandmothers, honey," Dani said. "Your dad's not going anywhere, and I will call you in sick tomorrow so you can spend some time with him."

Mark's shoulders slumped. "How do you expect me to sleep after this?"

He had a point. She knew she definitely wasn't going to get any sleep tonight. Not with her dead husband in the house.

She faced Heath again. "Why don't you take a shower, honey? Mark and I will make us some cinnamon toast and hot cocoa. We can cuddle on the couch like we used to and talk."

Heath's pale cheeks flushed red. "Um, do you have anything I can wear?"

"Your clothes are still in your dresser and in the closet," she said. "Towels are in the same place."

He blinked, but he didn't question why she'd kept his clothes. "Okay. I'll just be a couple of minutes."

Dani watched him stride out of the kitchen. Part of her wanted to chase after him and kiss him senseless. The rest of her wanted to scream in agony. And he had the same weird vibration all the risen dead in Oakfield had. Why the hell did God rip him away from her and then bring him back? What had she done to deserve this special kind of torture?

"It's going to be okay, Mom." Mark hugged her.

She couldn't remember the last time her son had hugged her. But she remembered the last time she hugged Heath before tonight.

It was the morning before the day he died. He had to spend a couple of days at a client located on the north side of Chicago. She suggested rather than wasting the time on the four-hour round-trip commute, he should stay at a hotel for the night near the client's office. She'd hugged Heath that morning and told him to be careful of the crazy Chicago drivers.

Little did she know it would be an Oakfield resident driving drunk on the freeway, and Heath would die only a couple of miles from their home.

Mark released her. "I'll make the cinnamon toast while you make the cocoa."

"Sounds like a plan." Dani sniffed and wiped her nose on her sleeve.

"Geez, Mom." Mark rolled his eyes. "Use a tissue like a real person. You want to impress Dad, don't you?"

"Since when did you start worrying about appearances?" she teased as she reached for the box of tissues sitting on the table. The box that never made it upstairs to be put away in the linen closet. She had been a better housekeeper when Heath was still alive.

"I don't," Mark grumbled. But the deep rose blush on his cheeks said just the opposite. He glanced at the kitchen doorway and lowered his voice. "Maybe you should call one of the other Soccer Moms and let them know what's going on. You know, just in case."

Mark was only making sense. Like the other demon hunters assigned to protect the Soccer Moms' immediate family members, Father Rodriguez only stayed at the Elante home when Dani was out. He'd gone back to the rectory hours ago.

Dani nodded. "You're right. If I put the ingredients in the pan, could you—"

"Mom, I'm almost thirteen." He scowled at her. "I think I can handle a pan of cocoa, especially since you premix the cocoa and sugar in a jar."

She held up her hands. "I didn't want you to think I'm dumping chores on you."

"Shit."

"Marcos!"

"I'll take the garbage and recycling bins out first—"

"Already done." Dani tried very hard not to smirk at the guilty expression on her son's face. She reached into her pocket for her phone, but it was already ringing when she pulled out the device. Dad.

Why on earth would he be calling this late?

She thumbed the icon to answer. "Hey, Dad! What's up?"

"I need a Soccer Mom over here right now!" In the background, there came a sound of glass shattering. "She's already whacked Pierre with a frying pan and knocked him out!"

If the demon hunter guarding her father was already down, he was in deep, deep trouble. "Dad! Grab a cross and get into the bathroom!"

"Carmen's already locked herself in there!" The way Dad huffed and puffed, he was running. "I need help now!"

Across the kitchen, Mark had pulled out his phone and texted someone. He looked up at Dani. "Penny's on her way to Papa's house."

"Dad, Penny's on her way to your house." Dani's heart thudded in her chest. "Can you get to the basement? Lock yourself in the extra bathroom."

"Penny's coming? I need *you* here, Daniella!"

"Daddy, listen to me. Are you wearing your cross? The demon can't possess you if you're wearing your cross."

"Demon? What demon?" There was another crash of breaking glass, followed by some Spanish invectives. "It's your mother who's trying to kill me!"

Chapter 4

"Mom?" Dani couldn't catch her breath. She couldn't deal with both her husband and her mother coming back from the dead on the same night. At least, Penny's mother-in-law Laura had the grace to climb out of her grave and arrive at the Hudsons' home during daylight hours.

"*Hijo de puta*!" Yep, that was definitely Mom screaming in the background.

"Dad! Tell Mom I want to talk to her!"

Mark dropped the saucepan he'd retrieved from the dishwasher and stared at her.

"Dani, you need to come get me." Mom sobbed through the receiver. "Please, I beg of you. I cannot believe your father brought a whore into our marriage bed."

"Mami, listen to me," Dani said. "I need you to walk away from Dad. Go to the living room and sit down."

"Dani, please come get me." More sobbing. "He tried to kill me."

"Was he the one throwing things at you?"

"He left me in a grave!" Mom wailed.

Could this night possibly get any worse?

"Mom, I can't leave Mark alone at home." Dani sucked in a deep breath. "I'm going to call my friends Penny and Francine. Do you remember them?"

"Y-yes," Mom said between hiccupping sobs.

"Hold onto the phone. I will call you right back. I promise."

"O-okay."

Dani clicked off the call and took another deep breath.

Mark picked up the saucepan. "Is that really Abuelita?"

"I'm afraid so." Dani released the air from her aching chest. "However, I can only deal with one dead family member at a time, kiddo."

She punched the speed dial icon for Francine's number. After four rings, the signal rolled over to voicemail. Nope, she couldn't let this one go. Mark had done the right thing by sending Penny over to Dad's, but both Penny and Wila were already overloaded with their own dead family members at their houses. She tapped Francine's phone number again.

This time, Francine picked up on the second ring. "I was asleep. The Devil himself better be on your doorstep."

"It's almost as bad," Dani said. "Heath showed up at my house tonight."

Francine muttered an obscenity. That girl had developed a potty mouth over the last two months, but becoming one of the Four Horsemen was bound to drive the sanest person crazy.

"That's not the big problem," Dani added. "Mom showed up at Dad's tonight, and she's trying to kill him."

"As bad as Penny's in-laws and the girlfriend?"

"Worse. Mom knocked out Pierre. Mark texted Penny, but—"

"Gotcha," Francine said through a yawn. "You need a place to stash Olivia since Heath's already at your house. Let me get dressed and grab a spare demon hunter from Saint Michael's if Pierre's down for the count."

"Thank you, Francine."

She laughed. "You owe me a couple of boxes of Long John's for this, girl."

Dani ended the call and collapsed on the closest kitchen chair. She couldn't deal with any more insanity.

"Is everything okay?"

Dani looked up. Heath stood in the doorway to the living room. His short blond hair was damp from the shower and curled around his ears. He wore his old sweatpants and his favorite UC-Oakfield jersey.

Dani's heart threatened to quit beating. She wanted to seize this moment and not let go. Heath standing there was like the last six years had never happened.

"I dropped the pot, Dad." Mark carefully scooped Dani's homemade cocoa mix with the measuring cup and dumped it into the saucepan. "Mom, maybe you should call Uncle Marty. Francine can turn a little scary if Abuelita loses it with Papa again."

Heath frowned. "What's going on with your parents?"

"Mom went to their house tonight." Dani blinked rapidly to keep the tears from falling. "Just like you came here."

"Olivia . . . died, too?" Disbelief darkened his blue eyes.

Dani swallowed hard and nodded. "Last January. She had a heart attack."

"Do we need to go over to their place?" Heath asked.

"Penny and Francine can handle Mom, but Mark's right about Marty helping them." Dani picked up her phone and tapped the icon for her brother's home number.

"Hey, little sis! What's up?" came Marty's cheerful voice over the receiver.

"Can you go over to Dad's?"

"Now? It's almost eleven."

"Mom showed up at the house tonight."

There was a long pause before Marty said, "She came back?"

"Yeah. Unfortunately, Carmen is there, and Mom went ballistic. She knocked out Pierre with a frying pan."

A suspicious snort came through the receiver that sounded more like her brother stifling a chuckle. "No offense, but wouldn't this be a Soccer Mom matter?"

"Penny and Francine are on their way, but Mom could use a friendly face."

"Dani, what's going on? This isn't like you to avoid—"

"Heath's here," she blurted.

"Oh."

"Yeah." She looked at her husband. She wanted to laugh and cry at the same time, but she couldn't. Not in front of Mark. Her son needed her to keep her own shit together.

"Is Wila on her way to your house?"

"No. I've got this. Don't worry about me."

"I'll always worry about my baby sister."

"I need you to worry about our parents, Marty. Call me when things are settled over there."

"No, I'll call you in the morning. And you're taking tomorrow off."

"But—"

"No arguments," Marty bit out. "I'm the boss." His voice gentled. "Let me do this for you, Dani. You've got enough on your shoulders."

She sniffed. "All right. Thanks." After she ended the call, she reached for another tissue.

"I'll do the cinnamon toast." Heath sauntered across the kitchen to the counter where Mark had already laid out plates, and he picked up a knife.

For a spit second, Dani had the urge to grab Mark, carry him out to the garage, and toss him into Verde. She sucked in a deep breath. *It's just a table knife.*

Maybe she should ask Wila about accompanying her to the Buddhist meditation classes she took.

Heath eyed her as he spread butter over a slice of bread. "So, who are Carmen and Pierre?"

"Pierre's a demon hunter," Mark said enthusiastically. "He's awesome!"

"Demon hunter?" Heath's right eyebrow rose as he looked at Mark, then Dani, and back to Mark.

"He's a risen dead like you." Mark set the burner on low and stirred the milk and cocoa mix. "He was part of the Vatican taskforce in the eighteen-hundreds. He died during the Franco-Prussian War. Now, he's Papa's bodyguard."

"Bodyguard?"

"All of the immediate family members of the Soccer Moms have one." Mark shrugged. "Father Rodriguez is mine. He picks me up after school and stays here until Mom gets home from work. Besides, having a bodyguard is way cooler than having a babysitter."

"I take it the father isn't as cool as Pierre?" Heath asked.

"He's . . . depressed is the best thing to call it." Mark stared at the contents of the saucepan. "Father Rodriguez would never admit it to me, but Father McAvoy said he was tortured and executed during the Spanish Inquisition."

Dani frowned. This was the first time she'd heard Mark say anything remotely derogatory about Father Rodriguez. And why hadn't Father McAvoy mentioned Father Rodriguez's past to her before assigning him to Mark? She needed to look into the matter tomorrow since she had the day off.

Heath glanced at Dani before he said, "If you're uncomfortable with Father Rodriguez, I'm sure your mom would make arrangements for a different bodyguard."

"Father Rodriguez isn't bad." Mark waved the spoon for emphasis, and Dani winced at the chocolate milk splattering all over her clean backsplash and countertop. "If I had a choice, I'd want Justine's grandparents, but she needs them way worse than I need a different bodyguard."

"Who's Justine?" Heath asked.

"She plays on the Tiger Sharks with me." Mark continued stirring the hot chocolate. "Her mom is Pestilence. Her dad's parents were demon hunters before they had kids."

"Wow." Heath automatically reached in the same spot in the cupboard she'd kept the sugar and cinnamon shaker since they moved into this place. There were a few times in those early years cinnamon toast was all they could afford for breakfast besides eggs.

"They sound like pretty cool grandparents," Heath continued.

"Oh, they definitely are." Mark nodded emphatically. "They've been teaching us all kinds of stuff about how to hurt and kill demons."

"Let me guess," Heath said. "Your water soaker is filled with holy water?"

"Yep." Mark laid the spoon on the spoon rest, turned off the burner, and set aside the pan of hot chocolate. "And I'm learning the exorcism prayer. Grandpa Ed says I've got the best Latin pronunciation."

Dani clenched her teeth to keep from saying anything. She didn't like the fact Mark and the other kids had to learn this stuff. Edward Hudson was adamant the kids not take on a demon themselves. In fact, he told them bluntly to run and call their moms when they found a safe haven if they spotted someone they suspected was possessed.

The guys chatted while Mark carefully poured the hot chocolate into three mugs and added mini marshmallows and Heath stuck the bread slices in the toaster oven.

At a knock on the front door, Heath frowned. It was terribly late for anyone to drop by unannounced, but their house was warded against demons. Dani manifested her scythe and charged into the living room.

After a quick check through the peephole, she put away her scythe and jerked open the door. "What are you doing here?"

White teeth flashed against Wila's dark skin. "I got tagged for babysitting duties. And if Mark and the guy behind you spray me with holy water, I will shish kebab them both with my flaming sword."

Chapter 5

Dani looked over her shoulder. Mark had given Heath his extra water soaker. While her son had relaxed at the sight of Wila, suspicion marred Heath's face.

The *ding* of the toaster oven interrupted Dani's introductions. After locking the front door, Wila followed the rest of the Elante clan into the kitchen. Since she wore her paramedic uniform, she must have been on the way to work when either Penny or Francine called her.

"You didn't have to come over," Dani said while Heath pulled their treats out of the toaster oven.

Wila shrugged. "After the meltdowns Penny and I had when our relatives showed up on our doorsteps, Francine was a little worried about you. Especially since you got a twofer tonight."

Dani crossed her arms. "You mean you guys were worried I couldn't tell the difference between my husband and the Prince of Hell."

"Have you checked him?"

"Checked me for what?" Heath said.

Dani glared at Wila.

"Checked me for what?" Heath repeated.

"Checked to make sure you had your soul," Mark offered. "Mom and Wila already know you're not possessed because they can see the demon under the human, but they don't like looking at someone's soul because that person can see theirs, too."

Heath set the plate of cinnamon toast slices on the table. "Why wouldn't I have my soul?"

"So far, all the resurrected have them, but with Lucifer running around Oakfield, we're extra cautious," Wila said.

"Would you like some cocoa, too, Wila?" Mark asked. "And we have plenty of bread to make more cinnamon toast."

"No, thank you, but I'll take you up on it the next time you and Derek have a sleepover." Wila smiled gently at the pre-teen. She'd mellowed quite a bit since Crucifer's death. Dani knew her sister Horseman would never admit she developed feelings for the fallen angel, but it was very obvious his loss had affected her.

"Maybe cinnamon toast is what we should make for my party instead of cake," Mark suggested.

Dani's heart lurched. Mark's birthday was next month. He'd officially be a teenager. Maybe Heath came home to them just in time for Mark to become a man.

Wila leaned close to Dani's ear. "I'll examine Heath if you don't feel comfortable."

"No. You're right." Dani sighed. There was a time when she hadn't been so easily distracted. "We have to know for sure, but I'll do it." She rounded the table and looked up at Heath. "I'm sorry."

"You had my heart and soul from the first day I saw you." He took her hand and smiled.

She twisted her focus.

And relief flooded her. His soul glowed with the same intense blue as his eyes. Energy threads of the same color connected his soul to his body. He was her Heath.

She blinked the tears from her eyes, and her vision returned to normal.

He tightly hugged her. "I knew your soul was beautiful. I never dreamed it would look like what I imagined."

Mark joined them in a group hug.

Wila chuckled. "Thank you for making sure, Dani. I'll leave you folks to your night."

"I'm sorry Francine and Penny made you come over." Dani released her husband and son. "But you're right. I needed a bit of a reality check."

"Call me if you need anything."

"As long as my mother doesn't knock out any more demon hunters, I'll count my blessings." Dani smiled.

She walked Wila to the front door, hugged her friend, and locked up before she returned to the kitchen. Her family sat at the table and munched on cinnamon toast.

Her family. Another wave of joy rippled through her. Her family was together again.

Heath eyed her. "So, Mark tells me that's War. I was picturing her in armor, not an Oakfield paramedic uniform."

"That's her day job. The only thing worse would be me all boney while I'm trying to sell a life insurance policy."

Mark chortled, but Heath obviously didn't find her joke funny. She wouldn't have either if she just crawled out of her grave.

She slid into the chair next to Heath's. The mini marshmallows had congealed into a gooey layer from the heat of her hot chocolate. She took a sip from her mug and licked the sweet fluff from her upper lip.

"When did you meet her and the other Soccer Moms?"

Of course, he was curious. She had a totally different set of friends when he was alive. None of whom knew how to deal with a twenty-eight-year-old widow.

"The day Mark returned to school, I went to Java's Palace after I dropped him off." She tore off part of the crust from one of her slices. "I didn't know what to do. I didn't have a job. I didn't know how I would finish my degree—"

Heath's eyes widened. "What about the life insurance? Or the Victorian we were restoring?"

"I wasn't thinking straight at the time, honey," she said gently. "Penny owns Java's Palace. She noticed me and sat down at my table. We started talking. She and Francine helped me get our finances in order."

Dani swallowed the growing lump in her throat. "I'm sorry, but I had to sell the Victorian. I used the excuse it was the money, but I couldn't bear walking inside that house without you. Wila's son Derek is the same age as Mark, so she watched him a lot while the other two helped me deal with all the legal matters. You have no idea how much paperwork is generated when someone dies.

"I started working at the insurance agency. It was supposed to be a temporary thing while Marty took over the day-to-day operations so Dad could retire. But almost seven years later, I'm still there."

Heath whistled. "Chuck was okay with you working for him? No offense, honey, but Chuck can be a, um . . ." Apparently, Mark's presence sunk through Heath's fresh-from-the-grave brain, so he aborted whatever not-so-nice thing he was about to say.

"It's okay, Dad," Mark said. "Mom knows Papa is old-fashioned like Justine's Grandpa Edward."

"That wasn't what I meant," Heath protested.

"Yes, it was. And Mark's right. Dad wouldn't have let me work at the insurance agency if you were still around." She sipped her hot chocolate.

"But Uncle Marty can't handle everything without Mom," Mark stated.

"That's not true." Even as she said it, she wondered if that was the real reason Marty kept giving her raises so she wouldn't quit and go back to school. Granted, numbers weren't his strong suit. He was a lot like Francine's husband Neal. Sales were both men's superpower. And she had learned a ton about money matters from Penny and Francine.

"I'll explain it to you later," Mark pseudo-whispered to Heath.

"Mark!" she snapped.

"Mom, when you had the flu last year, Uncle Marty called every ten minutes, and that was after I got home from school."

She lowered her face into her hands. It had been a very long day before Heath showed up. She stole Wila's technique of counting to ten in a foreign language in order to calm down. Chinese through a phone app helped Dani. Once she was a hair calmer, she looked up at her son.

"Mark, whatever happens between me and my brother—"

There was a sharp, rapid knock on the front door.

She pushed to her feet. Wila probably left something here.

Dani marched into the living room and checked the peephole.

In time for Penny to beat on the door again.

Dani jerked it open. Mom rushed into her arms and grabbed her tight. "Daniella! Your father needs to burn in Hell!"

Chapter 6

Dani hugged Mom in return. Despite the filth covering her and her Sunday best outfit, the fragility of her flesh and bones from the last month of her life was gone. Her arms held the same loving strength as they did when Dani fell off her bike, she was teased for speaking Spanish, or a boy in school broke her heart.

However, as much as she dreamed of seeing her mother again, this whole situation was turning into a nightmare.

Dani glared at Penny over Mom's head and mouthed, "Why'd you bring her here?"

Before Penny could answer, Mom shrieked in Dani's ear, "*Espectro*! *Espectro*!"

Dani glanced over her shoulder. Sure enough, Heath stood behind her with Mark.

"Mom, Mom—" When she continued screaming, Dani shook her and said in Spanish, "Mami, that's not a ghost!"

Mom looked up at Dani, over at Heath, and back at Dani. "But we buried him."

Dani switched back to English. "We buried you, too, Mom."

"Carlos—" She gulped. "Carlos was telling me the truth?"

Dani breathed a little sigh of relief Mom was listening to her. "Yes, Daddy was telling you the truth. He wouldn't hurt you that way, I swear."

"Th-that woman? In-in our bed?" Tears glistened in Mom's eyes.

Her pain ripped at the scars of Dani's heart. Mom had been the strong one in her parents' relationship. To see her broken when this should be a joyous time . . .

Dani sucked a deep breath. "Mom, you know Dad has problems being alone. You told me that yourself before my own wedding. Do you remember?"

Mom nodded.

"He couldn't handle life after you passed. He was so lonely. He never wanted to admit it, not even to me and Marty. I'm so sorry you saw him and Carmen together. You know Dad would never intentionally hurt you."

"But Penny said the dead started coming two months ago. Surely, he, you—didn't you expect me to come home?"

"I—" Dani's shoulders sagged. "After I learned Penny's mother-in-law had been resurrected, I was afraid of you and Heath coming home. Then as time passed, I wondered if I'd done something wrong that kept you from coming back."

"You?" Mom cupped her cheek. "Only God has that power, my love."

Dani glanced at Penny who shook her head.

The dang lump in Dani's throat was back, threatening to suffocate her. She swallowed hard. Nothing could have prepared her for the reality of this moment, no matter how many times she imagined it. But with everything that had happened tonight, the knowledge her daughter was one of the Four Horsemen might be the thing to break Mom's psyche.

"Mom, it's very late." Dani smiled gently. "At least, it is for Mark and me. Would you like to take a bath or shower before bed?"

"I suppose I should." Mom plucked at the mud caked on her dress sleeve. "Though I didn't bring any clothes with me."

"You can wear some of my sweats to bed for tonight, and I'll get you something to wear in the morning," Dani promised.

Heath stepped to her side. "Olivia, is it all right if I go upstairs with you to get the clean clothes and a fresh set of towels?"

"B-but—" Terror crossed Mom's face.

"You and I are in the same boat." He smiled at her. "And Dani and Penny need to talk without us dead people around."

"I'll come up and help, too," Mark said. "I outgrew the leather slippers you got me for Christmas last year, Abuelita, but they'll fit you. And I'll make sure you and Dad don't eat each others' brains."

"Marcos Emmanuel Elante!" Dani shrieked. Why the hell would he make everything worse while Mom was having her own breakdown?

"Ah, that's my grandson." Mom stepped back from Dani to turn and hold out her arms toward Mark.

Like earlier with Heath, Mark rushed into Mom's hug and squeezed her tightly.

"That's my grandson," Mom repeated as she patted him on his back. "Just one question. Who's going to make sure we don't eat your brains?"

"*Un momento, por favor*?" He whirled and strode into the kitchen. A few seconds later, he returned with water soaker in his hands. "Locked and loaded. You and Dad try to eat my brains, holy water will fry you."

Mom broke out into a grin and looked at Dani. "Good to hear Father Perez is teaching the children the old ways."

Dani groaned. They were all messing with her. Under normal circumstances, she'd handle it with more good humor, but whatever nerves she had left after becoming a Soccer Mom had died this day with her husband and mother's return.

Heath and Mom compared notes about coming out of their graves while they climbed the steps. Mark tagged along behind them.

"I'm so sorry, Dani," Penny murmured. "After Francine took Carmen and Pierre to the hospital, I couldn't get her to calm down."

"You left Dad alone?"

"Give me a little credit," Penny said dryly. "Marty, Lane, and Brother Giuseppe are with him."

Good, Marty listened to Dani and drove over to Dad's. Brother Giuseppe was one of the resurrected demon hunters. Lane Manewell was

Giuseppe's trainee. She understood Penny's reasoning though. As much as Mom doted over Marty, she never trusted him with the really important stuff.

"Is Carmen okay?" Dani asked.

"Possible broken wrist from the frying pan." Penny made a face. "Your dad only had a few bruises and scratches. I swear. The black eye Courtney Lasser gave me looked worse."

Sudden exhaustion dragged on Dani, and she flopped on her couch.

Penny perched on the couch next to her. "I'm more worried about you."

"I was beginning to believe they weren't coming back." Dani stared at the ceiling.

"The good news is the Devil doesn't have them."

"True." Dani looked at Penny. "Any word about Pence?"

Officer Miles Pence of the Oakfield Police Department was a racist jerk, but no one deserved getting possessed by the Devil.

"Not yet." Penny scowled. "For all we know, the Devil possessed someone new, killed him, and dumped his body in another state."

"I doubt it," Dani said. "All of us have had run-ins with Pence over the years. He knows us too well for Lucifer to throw away an asset like him. Even with the ability to teleport, he's not going too far from Oakfield as long as we're here. He needs to destroy us to win the war."

"You're beginning to sound all tactics and strategy like Wila." Penny grinned.

"I want this war over with and Earth and the human race intact," Dani said wearily.

"How about instead of playing poker Wednesday night, we all go get massages?" Penny suggested.

"I'd love to, but—" Dani waved wearily in the direction of the staircase.

"Girl, we need a break. We all need a break." Penny sighed. "Before we actually break."

Dani giggled. "Is that you talking or the shrink you're married to?"

"Both."

"Sounds like a wonderful idea to me."

"I'll make reservations at that spa Francine is always raving about—" Penny grimaced at the ringing of her phone. She tugged it out of her jeans pocket and thumbed the control. "Hey, Chief Wright."

For once, Dani really wished she didn't have enhanced hearing as a Horseman, but his problem wasn't something the OPD could handle by themselves. Penny rubbed her right temple with her free hand as she said, "It's going to be twenty minutes before Death and I get there."

"I can't leave Mark, Heath, and Mom alone here," Dani protested.

"I know." Penny scrolled through her contacts and tapped one. "Hi, Chief O'Leary. It's Pestilence. Two of Death's resurrected family members showed up tonight." She chuckled. "Nothing like that, but Chief Wright needs us, and we—" The resurrected former chief of the Oakfield Police Department assured Penny he'd dispatch a team of demon hunters to Dani's place immediately.

Her power cloaked her head and shoulders like the warmest, fluffiest blanket. "I guess I'd better let Mark know." But her voice sounded like one of those wind-up chattering teeth toys.

Penny, still in her street clothes, tried not to smirk. "You might want to let me do it—"

Mom shrieked.

Dani turned in time to see Mom's dirty calves and feet as she ran back up the stairs from the landing. Worse, Mom was still shrieking.

Dani shook her head. "I think it's been taken out of both of our hands."

Chapter 7

Pride filled Dani upon hearing Mark gently talk Mom down from her hysterics. It didn't help that upon seeing Dani as her avatar, Mom believed Santa Muerte had come to reclaim her and Heath. This wasn't how Dani wanted Mom to find out she was one of the Four Horsemen, but Mark explained it better than she could.

Dani turned to Penny, who inclined her head toward the street right before someone knocked on the front door.

"Could you answer it?" Dani couldn't deal with any more insanity. She had more than enough in the last—

The clock sitting on the entertainment center said it had only been an hour and a half since she took out the trash and recycle bins.

Penny crossed to the front door and peeked through the side window. "Don't worry. It's the cavalry." She unlocked the door and opened it to reveal Father Rodriguez and three other demon hunters.

After nodding at Penny, the father crossed to Dani while the other men entered her living room. "Chief O'Leary said you had family members show up. Are you all right?"

Dani laughed weakly. "Don't I look all right?" She shook her head. "My mother thinks I'm Santa Muerte come to reclaim her."

"Santa Muerte?" The priest cocked his head. Of course, he wouldn't know any of the New World religious figures.

"I'll explain it to you later, Padre," Hank Eastwood said. "If Chief Wright requested the ladies, then they need to get going."

"Thanks for watching Mark, Heath, and Olivia, guys," Penny said.

Dani winced. Maybe she wasn't handling the situation at all if she couldn't remember her own manners. "Yes, thank for coming over this late. Hopefully, we won't take too long."

"Don't worry, Ms. Elante," Hank said. "We brought air mattresses and sleeping bags in case."

"And Mark can do the introductions," Penny added. As if to confirm her statement, the water pipes rattled to life, which meant Mark talked his abuelita into getting that shower.

"There's plenty of milk and juice in the refrigerator. Father Rodriquez knows where the coffee, tea, and cocoa mix are kept," Dani said.

"Ooo! Do you have mini marshmallows, too?" Barry Wayne asked.

"Nearly a full bag in the cupboard next to the cocoa mix," Dani said.

"Awesome!" Barry grinned. "Between that and video games, we'll keep Mark occupied until you get home, Ms. Elante."

"Mark has school tomorrow," Father Rodriguez said with a frown.

"I already told him he could stay home tomorrow to visit with Heath, Father," Dani said. "It's not every day your dad comes back from the dead."

"As you wish, Ms. Elante." The priest inclined his head.

"We'll see you later." Penny's clothes flowed and faded into her white leathers and fur cloak. "Thanks for coming, guys."

"Yes, thank you," Dani added as she followed Penny out her own front door. Part of her hated leaving Heath and Mark behind like this, but Chief Wright wouldn't call them unless the police force couldn't handle a problem. And it sounded like they were severely outnumbered.

Dani and Verde raced after Penny and Silver toward the Herrington Hotel near the interstate exit for Oakfield. With Crucifer's death and Lucifer roaming around the greater Chicago metropolitan area, the low level demons had stepped up their harassment of the populace. But possessing the members of a bridal party took the cake.

Yep, it was pretty bad when a possessed lady in a beige suit was trying to stab the obvious groom with the wedding cake knife in the Herrington's parking lot. Dani nudged Verde in the groom's direction and shifted her scythe to her left hand. She leaned over like she and her mare were playing polo. A quick swipe through the woman in beige ignited white sparks along her skin. The demon died, and the remaining human collapsed on the parking lot asphalt.

"What the hell did you do to my mother?" the groom shouted.

Dani looked over her shoulder at him. "Saved her soul and your life."

He blanched beneath the super-white halogen security lights in the parking lot. Her fleshless skeleton and her green glowing eye sockets tended to have that effect on humans.

A loud *crack* sent the non-possessed ducking for cover. The police in the lot grabbed their sidearms and prepared to return fire. The dozen or so members of the Vatican taskforce scrambled to get the unpossessed guests out of harm's way. A demon had possessed the proverbial crazy uncle, a middle-aged man with one rifle in hand and two more hanging from the gun rack in the back of his pickup.

"Death!" Penny shouted from across the parking lot. She had her hands full with the possessed bride in a blood-soaked wedding gown, wielding carving knives from the prime rib table.

"On it!" Dani shouted back. Verde pivoted and galloped toward the possessed man. The demon took aim and fired at them. Dani heard the bullet tear her robes and whistle through her rib cage. As gross as she looked as Death, there were definite advantages.

The possessed man tossed his rifle aside, and with a bellow of rage, he raced toward Dani. Verde's haunches tensed beneath Dani's ass as the mare prepared to defend her rider.

"No!" The word sounded like rocks in a clothes dryer. Verde listened and dodged to her right. Dani swung her scythe. Once again, a demon died in flashes of white light, and the human crumpled to the pavement.

Dani killed the demons possessing three bridesmaids and using hairspray as flamethrowers. Penny handled the bride herself and shot the two possessed grandparents trying to play wishbone with the flower girl.

Verde circled, looking for more demons, but it looked like the police and demon hunters had things under control.

"Pestilence!" Dani shouted.

Penny waved from the other side of the parking lot. "All clear over here."

Chief Wright waved his hands over his head. "Death, we've got a dozen over here in handcuffs," he yelled. "Can you check them?"

Dani didn't have to nudge her mare or tug on the reins. Verde automatically trotted over to the police chief. Dani dismounted and examined the twelve people cuffed and sitting on a series of parking blocks under the watchful eyes of Oakfield's finest.

The majority of people were possessed, the demons inside finally realizing who Chief Wright had called over to them. One tried to leave its human, and she thrust her scythe through the woman. White light flashed, and the woman slumped over. One of the officers caught her before she hit the asphalt.

"Here's the deal," she said addressing the remaining eleven prisoners. "Tell me where the Morningstar is, and I'll let you leave your human intact. Any of you try to leave without permission—" The faint creak of Penny's bow came from behind her. "—well, you won't get very far."

The demons exchanged looks with each other. All except the one unpossessed man in the middle of the group. Salt and pepper hair. A little hefty but it was due to age. An off-the-rack blue suit. But somehow, he felt . . . wrong.

Dani leaned closer to Chief Wright. She had to give him credit. He didn't flinch at her appearance or her nearness to him.

"Why is the man in the middle with the blue and gray paisley tie handcuffed?" she asked.

"We weren't sure about his status," he murmured. "We caught him attempting to abuse the ring bearer, but he didn't have any of the markers Famine or the sister taught us. Plus, we ran out of holy water, which was why I called Pestilence."

Dani gritted her teeth at Wright's unspoken truth. Of course, the bastard in front of her thought he could get away with raping the child with all the madness going on around him. Then, he would cry and say a demon made him do it.

She stalked over to the man and crouched in front of him. "You realize the police called us here to sort out who is and isn't possessed, don't you?"

"You don't understand!" he wailed. "I was possessed!"

"I can check," Penny said from behind her.

"This one's mine," Dani stated grimly. She cupped his face with her boney fingers and peered at his soul. Instead of a bright jewel, a chunk of crumbling coal stood in its place. The ring bearer wasn't the first child he'd violated.

She released the man, a little thankful she didn't have her internal organs at the moment. No cop deserved having to haul this piece of work in their patrol vehicle while their prisoner was covered in her vomit.

For the first time in Dani's life, she wished she could beat the crap out of someone. Maybe there was a reason she was chosen as Death. She'd been swallowing her anger for too many years.

"Death?" Chief Wright murmured.

"He wasn't possessed." She straightened, keeping her attention on him. "The boy tonight wasn't his first victim either."

"But I was possessed!" the man cried again. "I would never—"

"You can't be possessed," she spat out. "Your soul is so corrupt you are practically a demon yourself. And if you succeeded in your plan tonight, I could kill you because you would no longer be human. Remember that in the time you have left on this planet."

He started weeping, but none of the police had any sympathy for him. Oddly, neither did any of the demons as two cops dragged him toward one of the police SUVs.

Her gaze swept over the ten demons. "Anyone going to tell me where your prince is?"

The one on the far left screamed defiantly, "We will defeat you, Horseman—"

An arrow pierced the possessed woman. White light flashed again, and a policewoman caught the victim as she fell backward off the parking block.

"Let's try this again." Dani twirled her scythe. "Same deal. Whoever talks gets to smoke out of here alive. You have one minute."

The nine remaining demons remained silent, glaring defiantly at her.

Chief Wright watched the timepiece on his wrist. "Forty-five seconds."

"I thought demons were supposed to be smart," Penny mocked.

At the back of the parking lot, the paramedics dealt with the injured. Dani caught a glimpse of Wila's partner Brian, but at six-five and with his nearly platinum blond hair, the man stood out in any crowd.

"Thirty seconds," Chief Wright said rather loudly.

The demon inside a teenage boy twitched.

Dani stepped closer to him. "All I need to know is where he's staying."

The demon opened his mouth, but the demon inside the woman next to him nudged him with her shoulder. "He'll kill all of us," she hissed.

"And I won't?" Dani said dryly.

"Bitch!" The demon in the woman lunged for Dani. A quick swipe of the scythe took care of that problem.

"He's at the Waldorf Astoria in Chicago," the demon in the teenage boy blurted.

The other seven demons stared at him with appalled expressions.

"Idiot!" a demon in an elderly woman cried. "The Horsemen have no reason to keep us alive!"

"True." Dani eyed the kid. "But unlike your boss, I keep my word. Go."

The demons all hesitated, shooting each other confused looks.

"Go now before I change my mind," she added.

In a rush of black smoke, the demons exited the last seven humans. As soon as the demons disappeared into the night, the surrounding officers caught the unconscious humans and carefully lowered them to the pavement. Chief Wright radioed for more ambulances.

Dani backed out of the way to stand next to Penny. "Did I make a mistake?"

"No." She slid the arrow she held back into her quiver. "But that means we need to go downtown tonight. Can you hold it together?"

"Of course."

"Really? Because usually Wila's the ruthless one when it comes to demons."

"I let them go like I said I would," Dani grumbled.

"I'm not talking about them. You're not the type to swing the scythe first and ask questions later."

Dani clenched her jaw. She didn't like the idea of Penny being right. Because if her best friend was right, Dani had thrown away everything she ever believed in.

And she was no longer the person Heath fell in love with.

Chapter 8

At the clopping of hooves behind her, Dani turned to find Francine astride Sable. In some ways, she scared regular people more than Dani did. With Francine's emaciated frame, she resembled the starving kids in the commercials for aid to third world countries.

"Why aren't you—" Dani started.

"Pierre's at the hospital under guard," Francine reported. "The ER released Carmen after they set her arm. Chuck's x-rays came back clean. They are spending the night at my place. Karen sent extra security to all of our houses, including Marty's." She glanced around the Herrington's parking lot. "It looks like you have things under control here."

"How do you feel about a trip to Chicago tonight?" Dani asked.

"We got a tip on the big guy. He's supposedly at the Waldorf." Penny chuckled. "Death would make an excellent Bond villain the way she interrogated the demons."

Dani pushed away the wave of guilt. They may have been demons, but there was a time when she'd capture spiders and crickets and release them outside instead of squishing them like Marty did. "We should be at full strength if we're going to confront him. And War is a little busy."

As she said the words, Scarlett galloped into the parking lot alone and toward their little group.

"Maybe we are going together." Penny jutted her chin at the figure in a scarlet balaclava and red fatigues striding toward them.

An ambulance tore out of the parking lot as Wila joined them. "What else is going on?"

Penny laid out Chief Wright's call for assistance, Dani questioning the demons, and the tip they received.

Wila eyed Dani. "Remind me not to piss you off."

"Do you think the demon lied?" she asked.

"Sometimes, the best lies are the truth." Wila shrugged.

"It's a trap," Francine said. "But I vote we take the chance."

The three of them turned to Penny. She pursed her lips for a long moment before she nodded. "I don't like walking into an obvious ambush, but I don't think the demon was lying either. We need to take the opportunity that's been presented to us."

"What opportunity?"

Dani whirled around to find Captain Wright scowling at them like they were teens plotting to vandalize the high school. It unnerved her that she hadn't heard him approach.

"What opportunity?" he repeated.

"We're going after Lucifer," Penny stated.

"That demon would have said anything to save its life," Wright growled.

"Because they're more afraid of their prince than they are of us," Dani said. "I know how this sounds as a practicing Catholic, but I want to earn their trust. If we do, they'll turn against him because right now they think they have nothing to lose."

And for the first time since this craziness with the Apocalypse started, she realized she had more to lose than her son.

Chapter 9

The Four Soccer Moms of the Apocalypse raced through the suburbs of the greater Chicago metro area straight for the Gold Coast. It made sense the prince of Hell would hole up in the most exclusive area of the city. Chicago's rich and powerful didn't care about the regular populace anymore than Lucifer did.

Her robes whipped around her skeleton with the speed of their horses' passing. Through backyards, over train tracks, and across highways, they galloped.

With the breaking of the Fifth Seal and the rising of the dead, more and more people noticed the Four Soccer Moms while they passed through the night. Cars pulled over on the roads. Cameras came out. Families burst from their homes, the adults in fear and the kids treating the Soccer Moms like heroes. It was . . . sacrilegious. They were on a mission from God.

Dani learned not to say that around Penny and Wila. Her friends would recite lines from *The Blues Brothers*. Francine was the only one who seemed to understand how much the four of them being chosen as the avatars of Pestilence, Famine, War, and Death bothered Dani. What if they were no longer human after they saved the world?

Her sisters' children still had their fathers. She had no idea where Heath fit into hers and Mark's lives now. A twinge of guilt plucked her nerves. As much as she wanted her husband back, she wasn't sure she could trust him alone with Mark.

Yet, she trusted Mark's wellbeing every day with Father Rodriguez. He'd also risen from the dead. How was that any different than Heath?

But her own self-doubts weren't something Dani could lay on her sisters as they rode into battle for what she prayed was the last time.

As their horses turned onto the Magnificent Mile, traffic was fairly light due to the late hour until a CPD interceptor they passed performed a U-turn and started following them, complete with sirens wailing and lights flashing. Another patrol SUV, then a third, joined the first vehicle chasing after them.

Penny glanced over her shoulder and muttered an obscenity.

"Why don't they bust into the damn hotel and announce our presence to Lucifer?" Wila said.

At Penny's signal, all four riders and their steeds slowed and stopped. The CPD vehicles did the same. Penny walked Silver back to the lead interceptor. Dani pulled her hood lower over her skull. Last thing, the Soccer Moms needed was some nervous cop shooting wildly on the street.

Penny dismounted and approached the driver's side window of the interceptor. "Is there a problem, officer?"

"No, ma'am." The cop's tone was ultra-serious. "We've been instructed to assist the Four Horsemen if you showed up in the city."

"While we appreciate the backup, could you please not announce our presence to everyone in Chicago?" Humor filled Penny's voice.

A fourth police SUV caught Dani's attention as it approached from behind the other three CPD vehicles. However, its lights and siren were off, and it was not slowing down one bit.

"Pestilence!" she screamed.

Penny spotted the oncoming SUV and flung herself over the hood of the interceptor. Silver reared to protect her mistress. The fourth police SUV missed the horse and sideswiped the interceptor in an attempt to crush Penny between the two vehicles.

There was no mistaking the demon possessing the human cop behind the wheel.

Verde danced out of the way of the careening SUV as it sped toward them. With a nudge of Dani's knee, her mare whirled and galloped after the vehicle.

"Death, no!" Wila shouted behind her.

All bets were off if any demon knew the Soccer Moms were in town. Dani hunched low over Verde's neck, her scythe in hand.

The demon deliberately clipped cars on the street, ran red lights, and tried to mow down a handful of pedestrians in an effort to slow down Verde, but the mare nimbly sidestepped or leapt over any obstacles.

"C'mon, girl," Dani whispered in Verde's rotting ear. "We've got to stop that *hijo de puta* before he kills someone."

Her mare's hooves barely touched the asphalt as she flew even faster down the street. In two blocks, Verde pulled even with the police SUV. The demon glanced at Dani and her horse and tightened his grip on the steering wheel.

"Jump!"

At Dani's command, Verde leapt over the SUV as the demon tried to clip her. Dani leaned to her left and sliced her scythe through the roof and the demon as she passed over the top of the vehicle. White light exploded inside the cabin, and the SUV veered out of control. The vehicle slammed into a fire hydrant and stopped.

Only their supernatural grace kept Dani in her saddle and Verde on her hooves. The horse pivoted to face the police SUV. The odor of gasoline and ash filled the air an instant before flames burst from the engine compartment.

"Oh, shit." Dani jumped down from her saddle and raced over to the SUV. Roiling black smoke that wasn't demon-related filled the interior. How the hell could she get the cop out? Her scythe only worked on demons. It phased through normal matter. She dropped her scythe, wrapped her boney fingers around the door handle, and yanked.

Only to have the handle come off in her hands.

The sound of horseshoes clipping the pavement nearby came to a halt. Wila launched herself off Scarlett and yelled, "Break the window!"

Dani struck the driver side glass with her fists. A couple of cracks appeared, but that was it. The flames from under the hood grew and licked at the holiday decorations hanging on the corner streetlight.

"Use your elbow!" Wila raced toward Dani.

Dani slammed her right elbow into the glass. It shattered, and smoke poured out of the opening. By the time she got the door unlocked and open, Wila reached the vehicle. Dani ducked into the cabin and unbuckled the cop since she didn't technically have lungs as Death. Together, she and Wila carried him away from the burning vehicle.

"Uh, girl," Wila murmured. "Your cloak's on fire."

"Crap!" Dani shed the flaming garment and flung it into the water spraying from the hydrant.

Which prompted screams from people exiting a nearby nightclub.

Wila laughed and shook her head as she check the vitals of the unconscious officer.

Dani looked down and realized she was naked. "Oh, my god! I'm going to get arrested for public nudity!"

"You're a walking skeleton," Wila said. "You're not going to die of exposure and you're not going to get arrested. Wring the water from your robes."

She pulled her phone from her pants' pocket and tapped in 9-1-1. "This is Wila Ardale. I'm an off-duty paramedic from Oakfield. A CPD vehicle struck a hydrant on North State Street."

She peered down at the sign at the north intersection while Dani retrieved her robes. "The closest cross street is Chestnut. The vehicle is now fully engulfed in flames. My friend and I got the officer out of the vehicle." There was a long pause before Wila added, "Smoke inhalation and first and second degree burns. Respiration is ten and wheezy. Pulse is seventy-two." Another pause while Dani squeezed water from her tattered, sodden robes. "Thanks."

Wila looked up at Dani. "Paramedics are on the way."

"Is he going to be okay?" She asked while she dressed.

"Depends on the damage to his lungs. Please tell me you got the demon."

Dani nodded. More people were coming out of the nightclub across the street, pointing and staring at the burning vehicle. Sirens came from every direction.

With all this attention, there was no way she and her sisters could quietly enter the Waldorf Astoria and deal with Lucifer. She hugged herself. God help her, she screwed up good tonight.

Chapter 10

Dani tried to stay out of the way because there wasn't a damn thing Death could do in this situation without making things worse. Penny, Francine, and the other three police vehicles caught up to them about a minute before the fire trucks and the ambulance arrived. Unfortunately, while Wila updated the Chicago paramedics on their patient's status and they began treatment, the news crews started to arrive.

More pictures and video of the Soccer Moms were taken. The reporters shied away from Dani and Francine, but they had no problem asking Penny questions since she was the only Soccer Mom who didn't look like something out of a horror film.

"I'm going to head home," Dani said to Francine.

"I get wanting to spend some time with Heath, but don't leave by yourself."

"Why not?"

Francine shifted to face Dani. "Look over my right shoulder. Do you see what I see?"

One. Two. Four demons were scattered through the crowd. None of them looked happy.

"Well, you said it was a trap." Dani twirled her scythe. Dang, she was really going to need tomorrow off. With everything that happened in the last few hours, she dangled on her last strand of nerves.

"'Scuse me, Miz Death?"

Dani stopped twirling her scythe and looked over her shoulder. A little boy around eight or nine stood behind her. She turned around to face him.

His jeans and shoes had seen better days, but his blue, zippered parka was fairly new. She knew from experience how rough a kid could be on their clothes, and that was assuming they didn't outgrow anything before they wore it more than once.

"Yes?"

The boy held up a spiral notebook and a Sharpie. "Can I have your autograph, please?"

She knelt before him on the sidewalk and rested the wooden end of her scythe on the concrete. "Why do you want my autograph?"

"My preacher said you and the other Horsemen, ur, Horsewomen weren't real, but I want to show him you exist."

His earnestness was so damn adorable, but she didn't want be in the middle of a battle between a minister and their flock.

"You have a camera, kid?"

Somehow, his eyes got even wider as Wila approached them. He shook his head.

"Not old enough for a phone?" Wila asked.

"I have a phone." The boy grinned.

"Hey, Pestilence!" Francine called.

Penny and the cop she was talking to joined them. "What's up?" she asked.

"Officer, would you mind taking a picture of this young gentlemen with us?" Wila asked.

"Certainly." The cop grinned, displaying white, straight teeth. He was maybe five-ten at the most, but broad and muscular. Dani's senses said he was one of the guys who actually believed in protecting and serving. "As long as I can get a photo, too. My wife and kids will kill me if I tell them I met the Four Horsemen tonight and didn't bring home proof."

"Soccer Moms," Wila and Penny automatically corrected.

"I beg your pardon?" The cop pushed his hat back and scratched his forehead.

"We prefer being called the Four Soccer Moms of the Apocalypse," Francine said. "Because our kids play on the same soccer team, and it doesn't have the same negative connotation as the Horsemen."

Dani stared up at her sisters. Had they totally lost their marbles?

The little boy pulled out his phone, unlocked it, and handed it to the officer before he scampered over to Dani and slung his right arm around her shoulders. Wila knelt on the kid's other side. Penny's fur-lined cloak brushed against the singed portion of Dani's robes as she stood behind Dani.

"What's this black stuff coming off you, D?" Penny asked.

"It's soot. I caught on fire while getting the injured policeman out of his car."

"You rescuing him was totally awesome!" The boy grinned at Dani before he looked up at Penny. "She broke the window and carried him out and her robes went whoosh—" He threw up his hands. "—and she threw them in the hydrant and then she was just a skeleton dancing around and—"

"Hey, kid, what's your name?" the officer called out.

"Keenan."

"Keenan, you and the Four Soccer Moms say cheese!"

The phone camera flashed. Reds spots danced in Dani's sight. She couldn't even blink them away.

"One more." The officer held up his index finger to indicate everyone should hold their positions. Another flash left more scarlet orbs dancing in Dani's sight.

The officer handed the kid's phone back to him. Keenan grinned with delight at the photo on his screen. The cop unlocked and handed his own phone to Keenan.

"Think you can handle it?" The officer grinned.

Keenan rolled his eyes. "It's the same model as mine. I can deal. What's your name?"

"Officer Hayes."

"No, your first name," the kid insisted. If he were Mark, Dani would have demanded her son treat the officer with respect.

However, the officer didn't seem to mind. "My name's Jason."

"Like Jason and the Argonauts?" Keenan asked.

"Sure," Officer Hayes said, but he didn't seem to recognize the boy's mythological reference. He knelt on one knee between Dani and Wila. Unlike Keenan, he rested his forearms on his thigh.

"Say pizza!" Keenan yelled.

Dani didn't say the word. Another round of red blotches marred her sight. But not before she noticed the change in the crowd observing them across the street. As much as she hated attention on her, the crowd calmed down upon seeing the Soccer Moms interacting with Keenan and Officer Hayes. Maybe Francine was right about the sisters controlling their media image.

Dani started to stand when several other police and firefighters approached about getting pictures of the Soccer Moms as a group or selfies with their favorites. And it shocked the crap out of her when she was by far the favorite of the first responders who put their lives on the line every day.

She graciously submitted to yet another selfie when a woman across the street screamed, "Keenan!"

Thankfully, the cops closed off this block. The woman didn't even look before she sprinted across the street in obscenely high heels and a sequin-covered mini dress that would have given Dani's principal, Sister Mary Bernadette, a heart attack.

"Keenan!" The woman grabbed the boy and pulled him tight. "What did I say about staying in my dressing room?"

"But Mom!" he wailed. "I just wanted an autograph of one of the Soccer Moms of the Apocalypse. I was coming right back!"

"Don't you ever leave like that again!" Tears smeared mascara down the woman's dark cheeks.

"Ma'am?" Dani carefully approached the pair, but terror filed the other woman's face. She dragged Keenan a couple of steps back.

"Stay away from him!" Keenan's mom spat. "It's not his time!"

"I know," Dani said softly. "I can't do anything to him because it's not his time and he isn't a demon, Ms.?"

The woman trembled, her fear overwhelming her. Thankfully, Officer Hayes walked over to them.

"This your mom, Keenan?" he asked.

"Yes, sir, Officer Jason." The boy nodded solemnly.

The cop eyed the woman. "May I see some ID, ma'am?"

"Officer Hayes?" Dani stepped between him and the little family. Keenan's mom wasn't only afraid of Death. Dani recognized the other trigger. Single moms got ten times more crap from public employees. It wasn't fair. It didn't matter why a woman was single, but the assumptions, stereotypes, and condemnation were always there. "She is Keenan's mom. He took off without permission, and she's been looking for him. Please don't make her night worse than it already is."

"If you're sure, Ms. Death?"

"I am."

He nodded. "Keenan, don't be disobeying your mom anymore."

"I won't, sir."

He pulled out a business card and held it out to Keenan's mom. "I'm part of the Chicago Big Brother program. Give me a call once we all get a good night's sleep. I'm off this weekend."

Dani recognized the excitement in Keenan's eyes, the glow of male attention in a fatherless boy. Her non-existent heart skipped a beat. She wouldn't be able to bear the anguish on Mark's face if he lost his father again.

"Th-thank you." Keenan's mom accepted the card, but her suspicion switched back to Dani.

Officer Hayes touched the brim of his hat. "Later, ladies." He sauntered back toward one of the patrol SUVs.

"W-why—" Keenan's mom gulped. "Why did you stand up for me?"

"A favor from one single mom to another." Dani waved the boney fingers of her free hand at the business card. "Call Jason. He's serious about helping you." She turned to the boy. "And Keenan, don't ever take off from your mom like that again. That kind of fear a parent has when their child is missing makes them vulnerable to demons." She tapped her ribs. "I want you and your mom to stay safe."

Keenan swallowed hard. "I won't run off again, Ms. Death. Cross my heart." He made the requisite sign.

"Good." She nodded. "Have a good night."

Dani started to turn back to her sisters when Keenan's mom clutched the sleeve of her robes.

"M-mya Th-thorpe."

Dani faced her again. "Excuse me?"

"M-my n-name is Mya Thorpe." Her shaking seemed to fade. "Is it true? What you said about fear? It makes us vulnerable to demons?"

"Yes, but love is the antidote. Just remember that."

Mya nodded before she and Keenan crossed the street. The boy looked over his shoulder and waved.

Dani waved back. Even with all of her self-doubts, maybe that was a lesson she needed to heed as well.

Chapter 11

While the Soccer Moms rode home, Dani asked, "What were the damn photos all about, Francine?"

"We agreed to a PR campaign," she said. "Did you change your mind?"

"That's right," Dani ground out. "A PR campaign. Not selfies with kids and first responders."

"Speaking for my people, we need the first responders on our side," Wila stated.

"But Penny's face wasn't covered like yours is." Dani glared at Wila. "It's not going to take much for the reporters to identify her. And when they figured out who Pestilence is, it's only a matter of time before they discover who the rest of us are."

"It's not like Lucifer and his demons don't already know where we all live," Penny snapped.

"And I was outed before Halloween," Francine added.

"So the rest of us should give up our privacy?" Dani stared at her friend. "I don't live in a gated community like you do."

"Girl, we knew it was a matter of time when Francine's perfect teeth ended up all over the internet after she was filmed at the cemetery," Wila said. "It happened, and that's why we all agreed to film the PSA tomorrow afternoon."

"But—"

"Or are you jealous the rest of us have fans, too?" Wila mocked.

"Of course not! But there's other factors to consider." A shiver rattled Dani's bones. "Did you or Penny spot the demons in the crowd of onlookers?"

"I saw four," Francine said. "What was everybody else's count?"

"Four," Wila confirmed.

"Five."

Dani turned to look at Penny at the same time Wila and Francine did.

Penny shrugged. "A possessed human dressed in a business suit followed Keenan's mom out of the nightclub. When he realized I spotted him, he took off down the street."

"To tattle on us," Dani spat.

"With the witnesses and the crash, there was no way we were getting close to Lucifer tonight." Penny scowled at her. "I'm not the one who let a bunch of demons run off after what they did at that wedding reception, and I'm not the one proposing we team up with them!"

"Can we please stop this squabbling?" Francine said. "We need to focus on Lucifer, not fighting amongst ourselves."

Dani focused on the freeway Verde and the other three horses traveled. Very few vehicles were on the road, mainly truckers hauling freight into and out of Chicago. Earth still spun around the sun, and the human race still existed.

But who knew for how long?

The Soccer Moms took the same exit for the Herrington Hotel. The parking lot was silent. Debris from the wedding reception was still strewn across the area, and a few of the damaged cars were gone.

Two patrolmen remained in their SUV. They nodded as the Soccer Moms passed by. Everyone waved except Wila who saluted the officers.

At Main Street, the horses started to turn in the direction of their own homes when Francine said, "Wait."

Dani shot Francine what should have been a dirty look, but she didn't have any skin on her face to convey her irritation.

"Please?" Francine asked. "Are we still doing this PSA?

Penny and Wila both looked at Dani.

"It's your call, Dani," Penny said. "None of us are going to force you into something. If we do, we're no better than Lucifer."

"But kids like Keenan expect us to save them," Wila added. "We've got to get the adults on board. This PSA may be the only way to keep them from being possessed. There's no way we can do a worldwide public relations tour before the next seal breaks."

The next seal. The Sixth Seal. A massive worldwide earthquake.

Dani's invisible heart squeezed. Her sisters were right.

Or maybe the real truth was worse. She was afraid to go home.

"It's late," Penny murmured. "Why don't we talk over breakfast?"

"You forget I have guests?" Dani asked.

"I'm sorry." Penny actually sounded contrite. "I did."

"So we should reschedule the PSA?" Francine asked. "We don't want to intrude on your time with Heath and Olivia. You've been super supportive when Penny and Wila had dead family show up."

"I seem to recall you drove Gammy straight to my house, Francine," Wila teased.

"No," Dani said more strongly than she felt. "We've blown off Andy too many times as it is. Just don't be surprised if they come with me to Gleeson and Associates tomorrow."

"No problem at all." Penny grinned. "Why don't you bring them to Java's Palace in the morning? Breakfast on the house."

"And my living room full of demon hunters, too?" Dani tried to interject a teasing note in her voice.

"Sure," Penny answered. "The more the merrier."

"I appreciate the offer, but can I please get some sleep tonight?" Dani said.

"Sure," Penny said again, but this time she didn't sound so positive.

"Are we good?" Francine asked.

Penny and Wila nodded their heads, so Dani did as well.

Except she wasn't. Nor could she drag down the rest of the Soccer Moms.

Her sisters said their goodbyes and headed for their respective homes.

Verde turned toward their neighborhood without Dani saying a word. Her mare wasn't as talkative as the other three horses. She let Dani stew in her thoughts.

Which she did until a half mile from her house, Verde abruptly stopped and stamped her right front hoof.

Someone stepped out from behind a minivan parked on the street. A possessed human.

Dani tightened her grip on her scythe. It had already been a long night, and the last thing she needed was another fight.

"I was the demon who told you where you could find the prince." This time, the demon wore a plump older woman in a huge, fluffy pink bathrobe and matching slippers. "The prince respectfully asks for an audience with you."

"I'm sure my sisters and I would be delighted to meet with your prince."

"Not the other three Horsemen, just you, Death."

Confusion and suspicion warred for dominance inside her soul. "Why me?"

The demon shrugged. "He wishes to make a deal."

"What kind of deal?"

"He did not entrust me with the specifics, Lady Death. He only stipulated you and he have a private conversation."

Dani wished she could read the demon's mind. On the other hand, Verde whickered softly. Her horse didn't like the terms one bit.

"And what guarantees do I have your prince will honor his word?"

"He will meet you tomorrow at noon on the sidewalk in front of Saint Michael's Church."

"Demons can't pass the sigils on the grounds and buildings—"

"He's an archangel, Lady Death." The demon's breath steamed in the frigid night air. "He's not a demon despite his current position as ruler of Hell."

"All right." She nodded. "Tell him I agree."

The demon turned to leave.

"But first—" Dani stared at the demon. "You put that lady back in her bed, safe and sound, and no nightmares. *Comprende, amigo?*"

"Yes, Lady Death."

The fuzzy pink woman marched into the house the minivan was parked in front of. Lights inside winked out, showing her progress back to her second floor bedroom. A few seconds after the last light was turned off, a smoky black cloud shot out of the chimney and flew in the direction of Chicago.

Verde twisted her head to regard Dani with one baleful, rotting eye.

"I know, my sweetling." She patted Verde's neck. "It's a stupid plan, but you will be there with me."

Verde snorted. A hunk of mucus and gray matter splattered on the blacktop before she set off in an easy canter toward home.

It didn't take a genius to realize her horse was pissed, but Dani prayed Verde wouldn't tattle on her to the other horses until she discovered what new mischief Lucifer was up to.

Chapter 12

Dani ducked low on Verde's back as her horse phased into the garage. Within a second, the mare transformed back into a puke green minivan. As much as she hated it, the color was starting to grow on her.

She entered the kitchen, only to have a paint ball pellet explode on the chest of her hoodie. Thankfully, it was only holy water, but dang, it was cold. She dabbed at the splotch before she glared at Heath.

"Sorry." He winced. "I didn't mean to shoot you, honey."

Mom sat at the kitchen table and snickered. The entire room smelled like cinnamon and vanilla. Dani slowly took in the dirty pans and mixing bowls as well as the buns sitting on the cooling racks and dripping with vanilla glaze.

"What have you been doing? And where are your guards?"

"We couldn't sleep." Mom shrugged. "We tried. Maybe the years in our graves are the issue. Mark finally passed out on the couch after playing video games with all the hunters. Two of the Vatican men are sleeping on air mattresses up in Mark's room. Father Rodriguez and Mr. Wayne have been patrolling the yard."

As if Mom's words summoned them, the two demon hunters entered from the enclosed back porch.

"Are the rolls done yet?" Father Rodriquez asked.

Mom jumped up. "Let me get you gentlemen plates and forks. Heath will pour you some coffee."

Dani took the opportunity to duck into the utility room and strip off her soaked hoodie. She spread it on the edge of the laundry sink to dry before she retrieved a t-shirt and a flannel overshirt from the dryer. Finally comfortable and presentable, she entered the kitchen.

"Would you like a cinnamon roll, Daniella?" Mom asked.

"Yes, please."

Heath set a cup of chamomile tea in front of the chair next to the one he claimed. Dani's heart skipped a beat. She missed the little things he used to do for her.

"Thank you." She sat next to him and squeezed his hand. What she really wanted to do was kiss him, but there were too many other people in their kitchen.

Mom sat a plate with a cinnamon roll in front of her. Dani took a bite. No matter how many times she tried, her cinnamon rolls never tasted like Mom's. Now was her chance to ask about the recipe. She swallowed and opened her mouth.

"You've had a busy night, Ms. Elante." Barry Wayne's grin distracted her from her maudlin thoughts.

"Yes." But when his grin widened, a shiver ran through Dani. "What do you mean?"

"It's been all over the internet and the early morning newscasts." Barry pulled out his phone and swiped it before he handed it to her.

In full living color, the video showed her talking to Keenan and then Officer Hayes taking their pictures. The female voiceover stated, "But all wasn't roses for the Horseman Death. According to security cameras at several businesses, she slashed her scythe through the police vehicle before it crashed into the hydrant."

Grainy black and white video rolled. Dani winced at her actions. She may have killed the demon possessing the cop, but he passed out from the demon dying inside him. The newscaster was right. The injuries to the cop were totally her fault.

"In addition to the incident on the Miracle Mile, the Four Horsemen assisted the Oakfield Police Department in breaking up a riot at a wedding reception in the Herrington Hotel off Exit 270 on Interstate 55. According to an official statement, only one arrest was made, but twelve people were transported to the hospital. Minor injuries were treated at the hotel by paramedic teams."

"Thank you for that report, Heidi." The male anchor turned to his female co-anchor. "If they're ladies, shouldn't they be called the Four Horsewomen?"

The woman's perky smile made Dani want to stab the reporter with her fork. "According to witnesses at the site of the police vehicular accident, they refer to themselves as the Four Soccer Moms of the Apocalypse."

"Speaking of soccer, let's go to Jim with the scores of last night's regional high school playoffs—" The clip ended, and Dani carefully handed the phone back to Barry.

"You okay, honey?" Heath watched her with concern. He hadn't even touched his own cinnamon roll.

She glanced at the clock on the wall. Heath bought it for her after she insisted he return the rather expensive watch he bought her for their first Valentine's Day. It was a black and white cat with a tail that swished and eyes that darted back and forth with each tick of the second hand.

"The problem is I've been awake for nearly twenty-four hours." She shook her head. "Christ may have chosen me as one of his Soccer Moms, but he didn't take away my human vulnerabilities." Her stomach growled, but it was normal hunger, not her anxiety.

Dani forced a laughed. "Speaking of which, I really miss your baking, Mom. But I need you to help me with this recipe. I never seem to get it right." She dug into the rest of her cinnamon roll.

About the time everyone in the kitchen finished their treats and cleaned up, Hank Eastwood and Sonny Larkin came downstairs. Mom insisted on making them a full breakfast since she wasn't tired.

Somehow, Father Rodriguez woke Mark and guided him up to his room. Barry shook his head and followed them. Out of sheer habit, Dani began straightening the living room.

Heath took the blanket from her hands and tossed it back on the couch before he cupped her face. "Honey, go to bed. You're barely upright."

"I-I—" She wanted him with her. She was scared to have him in her bed again.

"If you're afraid of being with me, I'll stay down here," Heath said gently.

Her vision blurred. "I'm more afraid I'll wake up, and you'll be gone again."

"Has that happened to any of your friends' family members who've come back?"

She shook her head. "Not yet, but it doesn't make the fear go away."

"I won't leave you again," he whispered fiercely. "Not for anything in the world."

Dani couldn't help herself. She kissed him, and that touch was everything she remembered. He tasted like the best present of Christmas morning. His strong arms wrapped around her, and he deepened his exploration, reminding her of everything she'd lost.

But Heath was back. Her husband was home again.

She reluctantly broke contact and smiled up at him. "Let's go to bed."

And if God dared to take him from her again, he'd learn the true wrath of Death.

Chapter 13

Dani woke up late Friday morning with Heath's body spooning her back and his right arm around her waist. She stroked his long fingers and the fine hair on his arm, hardly daring to believe any of this was real.

"Good morning, sunshine," he whispered against her hair.

She reached for her phone, wondering how much longer she could stay under the covers with him. The time was twenty to twelve. She was supposed to be somewhere at noon. Meeting up with the girls to do the PSA wasn't until two—

Crap, the deal she made last night with the demon to meet with the Prince of Hell.

What would Lucifer do to the people at Saint Michael's if she didn't show up at noon? Demons took their deals very seriously. It only stood to reason their prince would, too.

"Crap!" She jumped out of bed and grabbed the jeans she'd been wearing last night.

"What's wrong, Dani?" Heath looked so damn adorable with his blond hair tousled. His bedroom eyes watched her sleepily.

"I forgot I have an appointment at noon at the church." She yanked her jeans up her legs. "And the Soccer Moms hired a PR firm to help us do a public service announcement. We're supposed to meet with him at two."

"Let me get dressed." Heath flung back the comforter and blankets. "I'll come with you."

"Not to these meetings, honey." Now where did her bra land last night?

She fished it out of the trashcan. Luckily, she'd emptied it last night before she took the garbage bin out to the curb.

"What's really going on, Dani?" He stalked over to the closet and pulled out a pair of his jeans.

The ones Mom washed after she found them in Dani's bed shortly after the funeral. Dani had flipped out on her mother. It wasn't like her to lose her temper with anyone, but it was the last thing she had that still smelled like Heath. The woodsy scent of her husband was the only thing that helped her get to sleep during that first week without him.

"One of us Soccer Moms checks in with Father Perez every day. Today's my turn." She pulled on her t-shirt. A shower would have been preferable, but she didn't have time. Not if she wanted to find out what Lucifer was up to.

"Who's Father Perez?"

"The new—well, I guess he's not so new anymore." Dani gave Heath a weak smile as she shrugged on her flannel overshirt. "He's been Saint Michael's parish priest for almost three years. He also acts as our liaison with Oakfield's religious leaders."

"So I'm just supposed to sit around the house and do nothing?" His disbelieving expression tore at her heart.

"I'm not trying to put you down or hold you back." She paused in buttoning her shirt. "But life went on after we lost you. Life had to go on. And my sisters and I are trying to make sure life keeps going for a long, long time."

"But—"

"Spend the day here, and get to know your son." She smiled gently. "Mark's not the six-year-old you remember."

"Yeah, I got a hint of that last night." Heath rubbed the back of his neck.

Dani chuckled. "He takes after his father."

"Really?" Heath said dryly. "I would have said he takes after his mother's side of the family."

She wasn't sure what to say next. Her family could be stubborn at times. But she didn't want to fight with Heath. She just got him back.

"Look, we really didn't have much of a chance to talk last night." When he opened his mouth, she added, "I mean really talk, and I know that's on me and my new job. Can we try again tonight?"

He nodded.

She slipped her boots on and grabbed her keys and phone. But when she kissed him goodbye, the contact had none of last night's passion. Neither Gene nor Neal had issues with what their wives were. Why did Heath resent it so much?

That wasn't fair. Gene had left for a hotel when he found out about Penny. At least, Heath shared Dani's bed last night.

Dani checked on everyone in Mark's room. Her son, Father Rodriguez, and Barry snored with equal vigor. At least, Mark wouldn't blab to Penny about Dani leaving the house early.

When she entered the kitchen, Mom puttered around the counters again. Last night's dishes had been washed. From the delicious odor, she found the pork tenderloin in the freezer Dani had been saving for Christmas dinner, and the meat simmered in her crockpot.

She hugged Mom and kissed her cheek. "Mom, I appreciate you trying to help, but please don't cook everything in my freezer and cupboards. I still have to make Christmas dinner."

Mom looked like she was about to argue. Instead, her shoulders sagged, and she slowly lowered herself into the closest chair.

"I'm sorry, Daniella." Mom picked at her cuticles. "I'm afraid to stop doing things. Because when I do, then I remember—" She shuddered.

Dani crouched next to Mom. "It's no different than being born."

"How would you know such things—" Mom choked off whatever she was about to say, though Dani had a pretty good idea what it was.

"I hoped I'd been hallucinating when I saw you last night," Mom whispered.

"And I prayed I wasn't dreaming when both you and Heath showed up on my doorstep." Dani stood. "We will talk, really talk, later tonight. However, I have an appointment I cannot miss."

She whirled and charged out the door to the garage before she totally lost it. As much as she wanted to fall into both Heath's and Mom's arms for comfort, she couldn't. This was something she had to handle on her own.

Dani climbed into Verde and opened the garage door. When she punched the start button, her minivan shuddered to life.

"Is everything all right, *mi amora*?" She stroked the dashboard.

And realized she had five minutes to get to Saint Michael's according to the digital clock.

As if responding to her rider's distress, the minivan stretched and squeezed and shifted until she was the pale, rotting corpse of a mare she should be. Instead of human hands gripping the steering wheel, Dani's skeletal fingers held reins and a scythe.

"Let's go, girl." Dani reached over and tapped the garage door button with the tang of her scythe. Verde phased through the garage door as it lowered and galloped down the street.

After trial and error over the last two months, Dani discovered most of the public couldn't see her as long as she and Verde were alone. And the person in question wasn't dying.

A demon attack at the Oakfield Retirement and Rehabilitation Community had proven that point. She had been the first Soccer Mom to arrive. The staff ignored her, but several of the dying residents and their guardian angels screamed for her to take them before the demons did.

Angels.

Dani really needed to get two of those for herself and Mark.

Maybe Heath and Mom, too.

Verde galloped into Saint Michael's parking before she slowed her stride. Angels perched on the roofs of the sanctuary, the community center, and the rectory. A few sat on branches, conversing among themselves.

Dani's heart would have been pounding if it still rested in her rib cage. She'd never seen so many balls of eyes and wings at one time before. Did they know something she didn't?

Of course, they did.

After Dani dismounted, Verde sauntered to her parking spot the parishioners had assigned her, but she didn't turn into a minivan. Plus, the spot allowed her to keep her rider in sight.

Dani strode to the front sidewalk where a lone gray, older-model sedan sat at the curb. The passenger window rolled down, and a familiar face grinned at her.

Former Oakfield policeman Miles Pence.

AKA Lucifer, the Prince of Hell.

Chapter 14

Dani resisted the sudden urge to slice the archangel out of the human with her scythe. Pence may be a racist, misogynistic jerk, but no one deserved being ridden by Lucifer.

"I'm surprised you came without your sisters, Death." He eyed the roof of the church. "I guess I should have been more specific about no backup whatsoever."

"That's funny considering you have a buddy with you." She pointed her scythe at the demon in the driver's seat. "But then, I'm surprised you haven't found a better host than the asshole you're currently inhabiting."

"At least, I didn't make a fool of myself on the Magnificent Mile." He laughed.

She shrugged. "I don't consider saving lives making a fool of myself. And if all you really want is to mock me, there's no reason to stay."

Dani took one step toward the church parking lot when he said, "Wait." She took a second step when he added, "Please."

She faced him again but said nothing.

Lucifer rolled up the window, climbed out of the sedan, and took two steps toward her.

Her grip tightened on her scythe, but he halted. Even the angels stopped their whispery sing-song commentary.

"Believe it or not, you and I have something in common—" Lucifer faltered.

One of the smartest things Papa ever taught her was when to stay quiet in negotiations. And the nice thing about only having a skull was no one could read her expressions, micro or otherwise. Maybe the glowing green eye sockets bothered the Prince of Hell as much as they did humans.

Lucifer sucked in a deep breath. "Look, we both got screwed over by the big guy. I lost my home and my family. You lost your husband."

Except she just got Heath back. And Mom. Why wasn't Lucifer mentioning Mom?

"If you and your sisters stop the Apocalypse, I'll never go home, and you'll lose Heath again, Daniella," Lucifer murmured sadly.

"I'm supposed to believe the Lord of Lies?" She cackled, and the noise sounded like dice in a cup.

"I'm not lying," he said with the same sad tone. "If you don't believe me, go ask the Kid. He's inside your church."

"The kid?" She played dumb though she knew exactly to whom he referred.

"Acting ignorant doesn't become you, Death." Lucifer shook his head. "Think about what I said. Ask him for the truth. I'd like to see us both get what we want. What we deserve. Think about joining forces. We can stop the bullshit our way and still win. I'll be in touch."

Lucifer climbed back into the passenger seat of the sedan. A second later, the vehicle roared to life and pulled away from the curb.

His words bothered Dani as she watched the car until it turned onto one of the side streets and disappeared from view. His implicit threat about losing Heath was bad enough. Why didn't he mention losing Mom again?

The dead going back to their graves wasn't something Dani and her sisters had really considered. They'd been so focused on stopping Lucifer and his demons they hadn't discussed the total ramifications. On the other hand, if one of the Seals were fixed, didn't that mean all the Seals could be?

As much as her abilities freaked her out, Dani was becoming accustomed to them. What would happen if they were gone and everything went back to normal?

She'd probably back her minivan through the garage door, forgetting it was just a minivan again. The idea of trying to explain the situation to the insurance adjustor made her chuckle. And her laugh sounded normal. Without the presence of Lucifer, she'd unconsciously shifted back to human form.

Suddenly cold since all she wore was a t-shirt, flannel, and jeans, she turned and trudged toward the entryway of the church. She needed to find a certain carpenter and ask him a few questions.

Ten minutes later, Dani sat in the front pew, her fingers wrapped around a mug of coffee for warmth. Jesus Cordero strode into the sanctuary through the door to the church's offices.

Dark curls framed his face, and he wore the circle beard that was popular among men these days. Like her, he dressed in jeans, flannel, and boots, the common Midwestern blue collar uniform of winter. And as always, a warm smile filled his face and eyes.

"Maria said you wanted to speak with me?" He sat next to Dani on the pew.

"I've got a question, and I really need an honest answer, Jesus."

"I'll try to."

Dani shook her head. "Try isn't good enough."

He exhaled and leaned against the back of the pew. "What did Lucifer say to you?"

Dani stared at him. "How did you—"

"I felt him outside of the church grounds."

Dani snorted at the half truth.

"Also, Maria saw you talking to him through her office window."

"He said if the Soccer Moms stop the Apocalypse, I'll lose Heath." She watched her son's soccer coach carefully.

"If you ladies do stop the Apocalypse, all of the dead will return to their slumber," Jesus said gravely.

"So, my mom, Penny's mother-in-law, Wila's grandmother, everyone will return to their graves?"

Jesus nodded. "Unless you allow the last two Seals to break."

"W-will we stop being the Four Horsemen if we stop Lucifer?"

"I don't know."

Dani cocked her head. "What do you mean you don't know? You just said the breaking of the Fifth Seal would heal itself."

He shrugged. "Humans and free will. You are the great unknown factor."

"B-but—" She waved at the carved Christ on the cross hanging from the wall behind the pulpit, and for the first time, she wondered what it was like for Jesus to see his past displayed in such a manner. "The Lord made you human. You have the same free will as I do."

A wry smile tilted the corner of his mouth. "Yes, I do. In order to understand you better. Why do you think Lucifer resents me so?"

"It seems to me he's exhibiting a lot of free will, too."

Jesus shrugged again. "Humans aren't the only beings who blame their parents for what they decide to become."

"Do the angels on the roof of the church and its facilities and in the trees on the grounds blame the Lord for what they are?"

His eyes widened. "You can see them?"

It was her turn to shrug. "I'm Death."

"You would have to ask them."

"They don't seem the talkative type. At least not to us humans."

Jesus chuckled. "You need to sing your question, not speak it."

Dani's phone vibrated, and she jerked at the sensation. She pulled the device from her pocket and check the message from Penny.

Wanna meet for lunch @Java's?

Sometimes, Penny spouted off without thinking like she had last night, and she obviously felt guilty about pushing the PSA. Her decisiveness was one of the things that made her a good businesswoman and a leader, but it made her rather pushy in her personal relationships.

Well, Gene did leave Penny for a couple of nights over the whole Soccer Mom thing. Maybe Heath's reaction to Dani's alter ego wasn't totally unprecedented.

"Everything okay?" Jesus asked as Dani tapped in her reply.

"Yeah." She shoved her phone back into her front jeans pocket. "We're supposed to film the PSA today."

He made a face.

"Look, I know you don't think it's a good idea." She sipped her coffee. "Honestly, I'm not even sure it's the right move, but we need to do something to quell the fear around the world."

Jesus chuckled. "Free will, remember? My opinion means nothing, but you ladies can't make people unafraid of the future."

"But we have to try to calm them," she said. "Too many folks are getting possessed. And too many are letting their fear and hatred turn them into demons."

Jesus nodded. "You and your sisters need to do what you must."

Irritation sparked along her nerves and threatened to become a full-blown bonfire of rage. "You are the Messiah. Can't you come up with a suggestion that wasn't a cross-stitch on my mother's kitchen wall?"

"You want a few of the sayings from my wife's throw pillows?"

Dani stood. "This isn't funny."

"No, it's not," Jesus admitted. "But you want answers I can't give you."

"Can't or won't?" Yep, those sparks flared into raw anger.

"I cannot tell you what to do, Dani." Jesus shook his head. "Free will, remember?"

"Even my father will offer advice if I ask him," she spat.

Jesus chuckled. "And yet, you complain every times he override your decisions. Like buying Verde."

"You're blaming my father for triggering the Apocalypse?"

He shrugged for a third time. "You've been blaming me and my father."

If it wasn't a waste of good coffee, Dani would have thrown the remainder of her cup in his face. Instead, she stalked out of the sanctuary, and she headed back to the church's kitchen.

What pissed her off the most was that Jesus was right. Ever since Heath died, she'd let everyone else around her call the shots. It was time to take matters into her own hands.

Chapter 15

Dani's heart still pounded when she pulled into the parking lot of Java's Palace. Snow flurries fluttered in the wind while she parked next to Wila's minivan. She should have grabbed a coat before she left the house.

On the other hand, the brisk cold and ice crystals felt good against her hot skin when she opened the van door.

"You girls play nice," she said to Verde. The minivan's shudder could be attributed to the wind, but Dani felt her mare's laughter at the back of her brain. Dani strode into the café. The rich aroma of freshly roasted beans mixed with the savory odor of frying bacon.

Penny's manager Valerie Simmons grinned at her and waved her toward the pickup area at the opposite end of the counter. "Penny said to go ahead and make your usual. But if you want something else—"

"No, that's fine." The fire inside of Dani burned a little hotter. Penny meant well, but in some ways, she was as bad as Papa and Marty about making decisions for other people. The realization she'd let everyone around her make her life decisions sat like hot coals in her gut. But it wasn't fair to take her anger out on Valerie who was merely obeying her boss's orders.

Dani pulled out her phone case from her jeans pocket, withdrew cash for her lunch and double mocha, and held out the bills to Valerie.

The manager held up her hands. "No charge. The boss insisted it's on the house."

"Then put it in the tip jar, Valerie," Dani said. "I'm not taking charity."

"Whoa, girl!" Valerie cocked her head. "It's not like you to take your bad mood out on other people. Is the husband expecting things to go right back to the way they were?"

Dani's cheeks grew even hotter. "Penny told you about that?"

"Dani, we're all worried about you." Valerie shook her head. "Dana and I still remember the first time you came in here."

So did she. A week after the funeral, and she'd been so numb she could barely function. Valerie was right though. She couldn't be taking her frustration with Lucifer and Jesus out on everyone else.

"I'm sorry, Valerie." Dani smiled weakly. "The real problem is I've been running around town when I'd rather be home with Heath."

"Yeah, the accident on the Miracle Mile was all over the morning news."

Dani groaned. "I'm sure they left out the footage of the possessed cop's attempt to run Penny over."

"She's okay, right?"

Dani and Valerie both jumped. Courtney Lasser stood next to them. Dani had been so wrapped up in her own worries she hadn't noticed the president of the Oakfield Parents Association approach them.

"It's been a while, Mrs. Lasser." Valerie's customer service smile didn't reach her eyes, but the old Courtney had made a lot of enemies in town. "What can I get you?"

"Thank you, but Melody already took my order."

Dani and Valerie exchanged glances. Courtney usually referred to all of Penny's employees as "Hey, you!" with an added snap of her fingers.

Courtney peered intently at Dani. "Penny is okay, right?"

"She's fine." Dani forced a polite smile. "How's the renovations going on your house?"

"Getting there. The contractor has the framing, exterior siding, and insulation installed." Courtney shrugged. "They won't be done with the interior before Christmas, but we're just grateful we're okay."

"Here's your cinnamon macchiato, Courtney." Melody slid the large cup across the counter.

"Thank you." Courtney flashed a smile at Melody.

Dani peered at the OPA president closely. Nope, Courtney wasn't possessed.

"Um, Dani, could I talk to you privately?" Courtney inclined her head away from the counter.

"Sure." Dani handed the cash still in her fist to Melody. "Put that in the tip jar, please. I'll be back for my lunch in a second." She moved over to the community bulletin board Penny had installed when she first opened the coffee shop.

Courtney followed, but she wouldn't meet Dani's gaze.

"What's going on?" Dani asked softly. "Are you or Kenny having nightmares about what happen?" It wasn't every day that the Devil took hostages and wrecked a house in a gated community.

"No." Courtney started to shake her head, but she stopped. "Well, yes, we are, but that isn't why I wanted to talk to you."

"What's wrong?" Dani frowned. It wasn't like Courtney to act coy unless she was setting someone up to take a fall.

"I'm not planning to run for the OPA president's office in January." She took a sip of her macchiato and licked her lips. "I'd like to nominate you for president."

"You wanna what?"

"I want to nominate you for president. You have the organizational abilities. You have the intelligence, and Helen pointed out you—" Courtney sighed. "—have the emotional quotient."

"Emotional quotient?"

Courtney finally met Dani's gaze. "We all know I was a bitch. I just wish it hadn't taken me nearly losing my son before I learned my lesson. And I'm glad you and the rest of your . . . sisters didn't ignore my phone call."

"Why did you call Wila when Lucifer showed up at your house?"

Courtney blushed. "She was the first person on my contacts list."

Dani bit her lower lip to keep from laughing at her. Courtney was trying to be civil after all.

"I need to spend more time with my kids while I can," Courtney continued. "And you would do an excellent job."

"If I agree to this—" Dani held up her right hand when Courtney opened her mouth. "Hear me out first. I'm not going to put up with backseat driving from you or anyone else. I'm not anyone's bitch."

"You never were," Courtney said softly. "That's why you were chosen by the Lord. I'm sorry it took me so long to see that about you and your sisters. And it's why I think you would do an excellent job as president."

"I need to think about it," Dani responded. "I've got my hands full at home. My husband Heath and my mom came back last night."

"At the same time?" Courtney's eyes widened.

"Yes." And her statement reminded Dani she hadn't checked on Dad, Carmen, or Pierre. Too much. There was just too much on her plate right now. "Unfortunately, I have an appointment this afternoon. Can I talk to you after the game tomorrow?"

Courtney nodded. "Thanks for taking me seriously, Dani." She pivoted and walked out of Java's.

Dani crossed to collect her lunch and coffee.

Of course, Valerie had been watching the whole exchange with Courtney. Her eyes narrowed. "What kind of trouble is that woman trying to cause now?"

"She's not." Dani picked up her tray. "The last soccer games of the season are tomorrow thanks to the delays when the dead started rising back in October. Talk to you later, Valerie"

Dani didn't wait for a reply. She stalked toward the back booth the other Soccer Moms had already claimed and sat down across from Wila.

"You okay?" Penny asked.

"Yeah, why?" Dani picked up her BLT with cheddar and took a bite.

"We saw you talking to Courtney," Francine said.

Dani swallowed her first mouthful of real food today and laid her sandwich back on her plate. "I'm not in the best of moods because I didn't get enough sleep last night. And not that it's any of your business—"

"You don't have to regale us with stories of resurrected penises," Wila grumbled.

Dani glared at her. "I wasn't going to."

Francine lifted her cup of French vanilla to hide her face, but not before Dani saw her smirk.

"Courtney's not going to run for OPA president again. She asked if she could nominate me."

The shock on her sisters' faces was worth it.

"What the hell is she up to now?" Penny poked at her salad.

"Maybe being taken hostage by Lucifer and having the Four Horsemen and two archangels destroy her home made her re-evaluate her life's priorities," Dani shot back.

"Keep it down, girls," Francine hissed.

"We should come clean in this PSA." Dani picked at the cheese hanging out of the two slices of bread.

"What do you mean?" Penny watched her.

"Like give out our real names?" Wila's eyes threatened to pop out of her skull.

"It's not like everyone doesn't already know mine." Francine swirled a baby carrot through her little plastic cup of ranch dressing.

"I'm tired of dancing around everything," Dani murmured. "Heath and Mom need some stability. Mark, too. You guys have had the last six weeks to get used to your dead family members. I'm essentially working two full-time jobs. I haven't gotten my Christmas decorations put up yet. I haven't started on my Christmas shopping. And to top it off, my mother cooked the pork loin I had in the freezer for the holidays."

"That's not what Christmas is about, Dani."

She looked up at the smiling face of Father Perez. He grabbed a chair from an empty table and placed it at the end of their booth before he eased out of his black wool coat and sat down.

"Hey, Padre!" Wila grinned at the priest. "What's up?"

"I came to check on my parishioner." He faced Dani. "Maria said you were pretty angry when you left the church this morning."

Dani could feel the eyes of her sisters boring through her flesh. "I asked Coach Cordero a few questions." Any time she mentioned his first name, the other three Soccer Moms got squirrelly enough though she used the Spanish pronunciation because it reminded them he was far more than their kids' soccer coach.

"About?" Penny prompted.

"What would happen to the dead if we stopped . . . ?" Dani waved her right hand helplessly.

The other three exchanged looks.

"You didn't like His answer," Father Perez surmised.

"No, I didn't," Dani snapped. "What am I supposed to say to my son? He just got his father and grandmother back." She slid out of the booth.

"Wait, where are you going?" Penny said.

"Why? Do you need to tell me where to go? Like I'm a little kid and I need you to order my damn lunch?" The embers in Dani's mood flared back to life.

Penny's mouth hung open, but nothing came out.

"That's what I thought." Dani whirled and stomped out of the café.

Chapter 16

Dani climbed into her minivan, started the engine, and cranked up the defrosters to deal with the snow before she leaned her head back and closed her eyes. She should have known Jesus would blab to Maria, who in turn would blab to Father Perez. The priest was probably ratting her out to the other Soccer Moms as she sat here.

The passenger front door clicked, and a frigid blast filled the minivan. Her eyes popped open to find Father Perez climbing into the passenger seat. He slammed the door shut. Verde whined via the heater fan.

"What do you want?" she snapped.

The priest switched to Spanish. "I'm worried about you, Daniella. The Lord has laid a huge weight on top of your human responsibilities. While I haven't known your friends as long as I've known you, I do know it's unusual for you to bite people's heads off over minor matters."

"Minor matters?" She stared at him. "Everyone in my life tells me what to do! God didn't even bother to ask if I wanted to be a Soccer Mom of the Apocalypse. No one asks what I want."

"What do you want?" His sincerity made her want to unleash the tears she'd barely kept in check over the last fifteen hours.

Her rage rushed out of her and left her trembling. "That's the problem. I don't know what I want anymore."

"How are things with Heath and Olivia?" he asked.

She sucked in a shuddering breath. "I don't know. We've barely had any time to talk."

"Do they know about—" Father Perez motioned to indicate both Dani and Verde.

"I was able to tell Heath, but Mom found out accidentally." She shook her head. "She did mention she was afraid to go to sleep. She's been up all night cooking."

The priest pursed his lips and looked at the snow melting on Verde's windshield. "Would it be all right if I call on Olivia and introduce myself to Heath?"

"You'll have to compete with Mark, Father Rodriquez, and whoever else Karen has assigned to watch my family."

Father Perez chuckled. "Unless you want me to guard you at your video recording this afternoon?"

The minivan engine coughed like it was about to die.

"Verde, be nice to Father Perez," Dani chided.

The engine returned to idle mode.

"It's okay if she laughs." He grinned. "I was making a joke." His expression faded. "Do you want me to go with you?"

"No." She shook her head. "Thank you though."

"If you need to talk—" he said.

She eyed him. "What did Jesus tell you?"

"He didn't say anything to me. However, Maria said you were talking someone in a car at the curb who upset you, and you were angrier after you spoke to her husband."

"I'm scared we'll lose, and Lucifer will destroy the world." She turned and watched the falling snow. "And I'm scared of what we'll lose if we win."

"You mean the resurrected dead like your husband and mother?"

"Yes." She clutched the steering wheel. "And don't give me any lectures on humans having free will. The resurrected aren't intact humans. That's the reason God is jerking them around."

"What makes you say that?" No condemnation, only curiosity in his voice.

"I can see their souls. They aren't connected to their bodies properly. And because there's not a proper connection, the demons can eat their souls." She looked at him again. "That's why angels are guarding Saint Michael's."

"Angels?" After a long pause, Father Perez finally shook his head. "I don't know why I'm surprised. One of the Four Horsemen, Christ, and Mary Magdalene attend mass at the parish I'm responsible for. Of course, there're angels at my church."

"Soccer Moms," Dani corrected.

"Fine, Soccer Moms, but I think you're all being sacrilegious out of spite." He sighed. "I don't think the Lord is jerking around anyone."

"Really? So if Heath wants to stay, he can?"

"I can't guarantee that, Dani." His eyes narrowed. "Why don't you want your mother to stay?"

Verde's engine roared, and her tachometer ratcheted into the red for a second before she went back to a normal idle. Dani peered out the windshield. The other three Soccer Moms exited the café and walked toward their own minivans.

"Unless you want to be in this stupid PSA, you might want to get out of my minivan, Father." Dani sure as hell didn't want to explore why she wasn't more concerned about her mom. They had a good relationship.

Didn't they?

He opened the passenger door. "All right, I'll leave, but you need to be honest with yourself in order to make the right decisions, Dani." He closed the door.

As soon as he was clear, everything shifted around her, and power rushed through Dani. Her pelvic bones settled into Verde's saddle. Instead of the steering wheel, she gripped her scythe and her mare's reins.

Wila looked up at her and laughed. "You were serious about going public, weren't you?"

"Don't we need to be our Soccer Mom personas for this stupid commercial?" Dani shot back. But the other minivans were already transforming into horses while their riders turned into their alter egos.

"I said you didn't have to do this." Penny glared at Dani from atop of Silver.

"And I said I would," Dani snapped.

Wila heaved herself into Scarlett's saddle. "Then there's no reason to keep Andy waiting." Scarlett tore out of the parking lot and headed for downtown Oakfield.

Francine gave Dani an odd look before she and Sable galloped after Wila and Scarlett.

Silver walked closer to Verde.

"You want to tell me what's going on?" Penny asked. "I get being thrown off when the dead show up on your doorstep, but Francine usually owns the acting like a royal bitch trophy. It's even weirder that you're making nice with Courtney and treating us like we're demons."

"I know," Dani said softly. "There's some things we need to discuss. Can we do it after we finish this PSA?"

Penny nodded solemnly. "Thank you. I don't like bickering with my best friend."

The warmth in Dani had nothing to do with anger this time. "Neither do I."

"Ready to ride?"

Dani nudged Verde with her heel bones and yelled, "Race you there!" Her hood and robes flapped around her as Verde raced Silver through the snow.

Chapter 17

Dani dismounted along with her sisters at the back of the Oakwood Building that housed the Gleeson and Associates offices. Their horses lined up in parking spaces before they shifted back to their minivan forms.

The four women trooped into the building's foyer. The two security guards stared at the Soccer Moms, as did everyone else in the lobby. A couple of folks surreptitiously pulled out their phones and took pictures. Francine ignored everyone's looks, headed straight for the elevator bank, and pressed the up button. The lights showing the floors counted down to one. The doors slid open.

And the older woman standing inside the car locked her eyes on Dani before she screamed bloody murder. The two security guards raced over to them.

However, the man in the business suit standing behind the screaming woman scowled. "For the love of God, Mother! Death isn't here to claim you!" He looked at Dani. "Are you?"

The older woman paused her screaming to hear Dani's answer.

"No, we have an appointment on another floor." She would have smiled if she could. It didn't help that Wila snickered behind her. "We're just waiting for you to clear the elevator. Unless there's something you forgot upstairs?"

"No." The man had to push his mother out of the car and past the Soccer Moms.

The quartet entered the empty car, but Dani held the door for the three people who obviously wanted to use the elevator. One of them was Helen Chow.

"Going up?" Dani asked.

"N-no, thank you." Helen shook her head. "W-we'll wait the next car."

"Okay." Dani released the door and pressed five on the control panel. The two sides slid shut, and the car inched upward.

She looked at Francine. "How did Helen not recognize my voice?"

"Because you sound like dice in a Yahtzee cup when you're channeling Death," Wila said.

Penny chuckled. "She definitely recognized me."

"Maybe you need a mask like the Lone Ranger," Francine suggested.

"Or a balaclava like mine," Wila added.

"This is what I mean about outing ourselves and being done with it," Dani grumbled.

"Andy is one of the folks who helped get the reporters off my case." Francine swung her scales like they were a kid's fidget toy. "Do the rest of you want reporters camping on your lawns? You don't have the protection of living in a gated community."

"Don't you mean the privilege of living in a gated community?" Wila said.

"Po-tay-to, po-tah-to," Francine shot back.

Dani groaned. "Can we please not do this today? I already have enough stuff on my plate at home."

The elevator slid to a stop, and the doors parted. This time, no one was waiting to board the car.

Francine took the lead. The other three Soccer Moms followed her down to a corner office suite. Inside the reception area, the silvery light from the overcast sky and falling snow gave the glass and polished chrome an ethereal quality.

A receptionist sat at her desk. She appeared to be in her mid-fifties. She wore a sweater set and a string of pearls.

A polite smile graced the woman's mouth though fear shone from her eyes. "Hello, ladies. Mr. Gleeson will be here in a moment to escort you back to the video stage. Per your request, the office is clear of all the staff except me and our cameraman Joey. Can I get you anything to drink in the meantime?"

Dani couldn't stop her laughter. Her guffaws sounded like the time she forgot to check Mark's pockets while she did the laundry and he had stuffed a collection of rocks in his jeans. The noise of the stones during the spin cycle had been horrendous.

She parted her robes and flashed the receptionist. "I don't think I want to mess up your carpet, but thanks anyway."

"Oh, um, I'm sorry," the receptionist mumbled.

"Death, be nice," Penny chided. "The poor lady is just doing her job."

"Ask stupid questions, win stupid prizes," Dani shot back, but she let her black tattered robes fall back into place.

"What the hell is wrong with you?" Wila snapped. "Didn't your dead husband put out last night?"

"Like that's any of your business, bitch." Dani stepped into Wila's personal space.

Wila's eyes narrowed. "It's my business when you're acting like a rude Karen."

"Stop it, you two." Francine pushed them apart. "You both promised Karen Longstreet you wouldn't use that term again. Frankly, we need her whether you want to admit it or not."

A tall man entered from a side door, interrupting their spat. In addition to the custom-tailored navy suit, he definitely dumped a pretty penny into dental work from his white, wide grin.

"I'll give you this, you ladies are definitely punctual. Why don't you follow me?" He gestured at the hallway beyond the door he held open.

"Thank you, Mr. Gleeson." After shooting nasty glances at Dani and Wila, Francine strode toward him.

"Move it, you idiots," Penny hissed under her breath.

Dani pushed past Wila and stalked toward the open door.

"*Puta*," Wila muttered, followed by a loud, "Ow! Hey!"

"Next time, I'll slice off that finger," Penny said.

Dani didn't need to turn around to know what was happening. And she sure as heck wasn't going to give Wila the satisfaction of seeing her reaction.

"Thanks for meeting with us, Mr. Gleeson," Dani said.

Like his receptionist, Andy Gleeson's professional smile didn't reach his eyes. She could see her reflection in his pupils. The skeleton was bad enough, but the green glow in her eye sockets was the proverbial cherry on top. No wonder Mom freaked out last night.

Was the glow caused by her own soul? The effect wasn't something any of them had questioned. Maybe she should have Penny check her soul to see what it really looked like.

Andy took the lead in the hallway, and they followed him into a small studio. Lime green curtains lined two of the walls. Professional cameras and other equipment sat in the opposite corner. No other people were in the room.

"Okay." Andy clapped his hands. Dani recognized the nervous gesture for what it was. "Francine and I have been messaging about the potential script, but there's one matter I need to address."

He sucked in a deep breath. "I protect my professional reputation by knowing who I'm working with. While I trust Francine, and my staff frequents Java's Palace—"

"Not just your staff." Penny grinned. "Triple shot espresso with a dash of cream."

Andy chuckled. "And Pestilence is a respectable business woman. But I need to know War and Death don't have records."

Dani looked at Wila. "I think *ese* here just dissed us brown chicks."

Wila glared at him. "I don't think. I know."

"That's not what I meant." Andy waved his hands frantically. "I can't even see Death's skin!"

"Lighten up, man." Wila shook herself, and her fatigues shifted into her street clothes. "Wila Ardale. Paramedic with the Oakfield Fire Department."

Dani took a deep breath and relaxed, letting her power fade away. "Daniella Hernandez Elante."

"You're Chuck's daughter, aren't you?" Andy asked.

"And your limited liability company bought your business and liability insurance from the Hernandez Agency," Dani responded.

"Thank you for showing me who you really are, ladies." Andy nodded.

"What would you have done if you didn't know most of us or we were criminals?" Wila asked.

"I wouldn't be having this conversation with the Four Horsemen of the Apocalypse—"

"Soccer Moms of the Apocalypse," Dani said in unison with her sisters.

"Excuse me?" Confusion took over Andy's face.

"Do we look like men?" Francine pointed out.

"But the Bible—" Andy started.

"Is notoriously misogynist," Penny said.

"Not to mention the deliberate mistranslations," Wila added.

"Call the Pope if you don't believe us," Dani finished.

Andy rubbed the back of his head. "I guess I'm a little out of my league here."

"You and eight billion other people." Dani sighed. "Not to mention all the billions of dead rising from their graves."

"Are you sure you ladies want to do this?" Andy asked. "You saw Maggie's reaction to you."

"Just like we saw yours," Dani said. "But after last night's incident in Chicago, we really need some positive publicity."

Andy crossed his arms. "You're saying the cop crashing into the hydrant wasn't your fault?" Of course, he had watched the news clips about the incident on the Miracle Mile.

Dani matched his pose. "The police officer was possessed by a demon, who was attempting to kill innocent pedestrians, motorists, and other police officers. Should I have let the demon continue until it succeeded?"

"No, I suppose not." Andy eyed her. "If you all live here in Oakfield, what were you doing in downtown Chicago last night?"

"We got a tip about Lucifer's location," Penny said.

Andy's eyes widened. "Y-you mean the Devil? Like the real thing? The Prince of Hell?"

"Yep," Wila affirmed.

The door to the studio opened slightly, and the receptionist Maggie looked around the edge. "Andrew?"

Someone's fingers were wrapped around her neck. Dani drew her power about herself. Wila did the same.

The person holding Maggie pushed her further into the studio. He was twenty-something, wearing jeans and a University of Chicago sweatshirt. A slightly messy man-bun contained his medium brown hair.

"Joey, what the hell are you doing?" Andy stared at the pair with a mix of horror and confusion. "I said I'd get you when I was ready."

"That's not Joey." At Dani's words, her sisters drew their weapons. "That's a demon."

Chapter 18

Dani reached for Andy's arm and dragged him away from his employees. The other three Soccer Moms spread out to surround the demon.

"Let Maggie go," Francine demanded.

"You think I'm going to let you bitches get away with what you did at that wedding reception last night?" The demon sneered. "And you call us murderers."

What the heck was going on? Had Lucifer reneged on his offer already? Or had Dani made things worse when she questioned the demons the police collared last night?

"If you want revenge, I'm the one you want." Dani stepped forward. Wila automatically retreated to protect Andy.

The demon laughed. The ugly sound bounced off the walls of the studio. Not even the green curtains muffled the horrible cackles.

Maggie trembled in its grip. Her face had a sickly paleness beneath the sheen of fright sweat. If she passed out, the demon would strangle her.

Dani wanted to do something. Anything. This was as bad as the standoff in Miles Pence's house.

When a demon ate the soul of Pence's resurrected grandmother.

At least, a demon couldn't eat a living soul, but Dani and her sisters needed to play this cool. They'd seriously screwed up at Pence's house. As a result, Lucifer used the police officer's pain to possess him. She rested the butt of her scythe on the floor, leaned on the handle, and examined the distal bones of her left hand.

The nasty laughter died. "What is wrong with you Horsemen?"

"Soccer Moms," Dani and her sisters corrected.

"What?" The demon stared at each of them in turn. "Are you all insane?"

"Did your precious prince send you here?" Penny asked. "Because we cut a deal with him. If he's reneging, we have no reason to keep you alive. And if you're going behind his back, he has no reason to keep you alive."

What? Dani couldn't even properly breathe as Death, but Penny's words felt like a punch in her gut. Had Lucifer approached her sisters in addition to her? Or did the Prince of Hell rat her out to the other Soccer Moms?

"I don't believe you." But the demon's voice shook.

"It's true," Francine added.

Dani piled on. Just in case because Penny could bluff like heck when they played poker on their girls' nights. "So you can let Maggie go, or we drag you back to your prince because he's way more creative with punishments than we are."

The possessed human jerked, and Maggie broke free. The poor receptionist must have had enough because she whirled and kneed him in the balls.

"You bastard!" Maggie shrieked as Penny yanked her away from the black smoke poring from Joey's orifices. The young man dropped to the floor now that the demon no longer controlled him.

Dani rushed forward in step with Francine. Their Heaven-gifted weapons sliced through the wisps of smoke. White lights flashed. A gray, powdery ash drifted over the unconscious Joey and the floor.

"Nice bluffing, ladies." Wila pushed past Francine and Dani. "Good to know our poker nights have come in handy."

Wila rolled Joey onto his back and checked his vitals. While she tended to the poor kid, Francine pulled out her phone and called 9-1-1. Penny walked Maggie out of the studio, murmuring softly in the older woman's ear.

Dani shed her power and walked backed to Andy, who looked like he was about to go into shock himself. "Why don't you have a seat while we wait for the paramedics?" She guided him to a box covered in plush fabric, and he gingerly lowered himself onto the prop.

"Is-is Joey going to be all right?" Andy couldn't take his eyes off his employee.

Francine handed her phone to Wila, which meant the 9-1-1 dispatcher had patched the call through to the responding squad.

"It really depends on the person," Dani said softly. "Has anything major happened in Joey's life over the last year or two? Loss of a close family member or friend?"

"Oh, god," Andy muttered. "The accident." He swallowed hard. "A minivan t-boned him over by the mall last Christmas. The accident wasn't his fault. The father ran a red light. Both parents were above the legal limit. They didn't put their kids in their safety seats, and the baby died at the scene."

Andy released a deep shuddering breath. "The accident investigation cleared Joey, but he told Maggie he's been having nightmares since the dead started rising that the baby shows up on his doorstep."

Dani couldn't stop the shiver that ran through her. She hadn't admitted to anyone she'd had the same nightmare about Heath. They had a closed casket at his funeral because the funeral director couldn't conceal all the horrific damage. And when he showed up at their house last night—

She whirled and seized a nearby trash receptacle as she lost what little of the BLT was in her stomach.

Chapter 19

Dani was reduced to dry heaves by the time Francine wrestled her into Andy's private bathroom. She leaned her head against the cool glass of the shower door while Francine ran a pristine white washcloth under the running faucet.

France wrung out the washcloth, knelt next to Dani, and gently wiped her face. The cool terrycloth felt damn good against her overheated skin.

"All this stress isn't good for you," Francine murmured. "Have you seen your doctor since the Apocalypse started?"

"No," Dani admitted. "I didn't know what to say to her."

"Yeah, but you're the one of us with the closest relationship to one of the resurrected." Francine flipped the cloth to the cleaner side, folded it, and held it against the back of Dani's neck. "You've been terrified Heath wouldn't appear. You've been terrified he would. None of this has been easy, but you've taken the emotional brunt."

"I don't get it." Dani looked up at her sister. "I thought you were going to break first, but you've blossomed under the pressure of being a Soccer Mom."

Francine shifted to sit down next to her. "Penny had to smack me upside the head and point out I was the one who's been holding me back all these years. For the first time, I'm doing what I want, what I'm capable of doing, and not worrying about what other people think."

"You think that's what I'm doing?"

"Yes and no." Francine smiled. "You're doing what you think is best for Mark. But maybe it's not best for you."

Dani groaned. "Are you going to get on my case about going back to school?"

Francine chuckled. "First, we've got to make sure you've got a school to go back to, if that's what you want, but that's your decision. Not mine or Penny's or anyone else's."

"I don't know what to do." Dani rested her head on her knees. "I know I need to make some decisions, but I'm so worried I'll make the wrong decision."

"And what happens if you do?" Francine asked.

"I don't know. That's part of the problem."

The ridiculousness of her statement sunk through her fried brain. Dani burst out laughing at the same time as Francine.

"Damn, girl." She shook her head. "You need to spend some time on Gene's couch. That view is seriously messed up."

Dani pulled the damp cloth from the back of her neck. "I guess the grief counselor he referred me to didn't help as much as I thought."

And what the heck would Doctor Morgenstern say if she waltzed into her office with a very much alive Heath?

🔥 ☠ 🔥

After the ambulance left with Joey, the Soccer Moms and Andy retreated to his office to review the script one last time. Drafts had been shooting between them and Andy over the last few weeks.

Maggie turned out to be made of sterner stuff than Dani first gave her credit for. She brought in soft drinks for everyone, along with some healthy snacks. Rather than avoiding the Soccer Moms after witnessing them in action, Andy's receptionist rolled in a chair to join the conversation.

"I don't know how you girls do what you do." Maggie shook her head.

"You aren't so bad yourself," Penny said. "Most people who've encountered a demon can't keep their cool in such a situation."

"I still feel bad about kneeing poor Joey in the crotch," Maggie said mournfully. "The kid has been through so much."

"You did what you had to do," Dani murmured. "Trust me, the demon felt the pain way worse than Joey would have because they aren't used to physical sensations."

"But will he be okay?" Maggie asked. Andy stared intently at Dani, waiting for her answer.

"That depends on him," Dani said softly. "On whether he's willing to fight for his soul."

"What can we do to help him?" Andy asked.

"Exactly what this script says." Penny tapped the papers in her lap. "This is the whole point of our PSA. To prevent people from being possessed, and for family and friends to know what to do if a loved one is taken over by a demon."

Two hours later, everyone seemed satisfied, if not happy, with the result. It turned out Maggie wasn't Andy's receptionist as Dani had first assumed. She was actually Andy's sound engineer. Andy handled the camera.

"I'll add the background by computer tomorrow," Andy assured them. "Do you want me to e-mail the video to you for final approval?"

Francine shook her head. "Let me know when it's ready and load it onto a flash drive or a memory card. I'll pick it up. We don't want this leaked before we release it."

"I don't like the idea of you being here working by yourself tomorrow, boss." Maggie wore a worried expression. "Not after what happened with Joey."

"I think our clients gave me all the tips I need to stay safe." Andy smiled.

"Speaking of staying safe—" Wila yanked on the Velcro on one of her pants pockets and pulled out a little plastic bottle. She handed it to Andy. "Holy water. All you need is a few drops in any kind of spray bottle. Fill the rest of the way with tap water."

"Our kids prefer Super Soakers," Dani volunteered. "But any bottle with a pump spray or a squirt top will work."

"Thanks for the tip." Andy's smile turned into a full-fledged grin. "I'll talk to you tomorrow."

🔥 ☠ 🔥

The Soccer Moms left Andy's office and took the elevator to the main floor. This time, only the two guards were in the lobby. They nodded at the Soccer Moms, and they all nodded in return. Outside, only a dim glow lit the western horizon. It got dark too fast at this time of year. When the quartet rounded the corner of the building, their minivans had already transformed into their horses.

"Are you guys going to the post season party at Rusty Rat's after the game?" Dani asked as she mounted Verde.

"Is there any reason we shouldn't?" Penny asked.

"Mark wants Heath at the game." Dani hesitated for a moment. "And probably Mom, too. It's not that I don't want them to go—"

"You don't want all the questions," Wila said.

Dani shook her head.

"You've got three bodyguards right here," Francine assured her. "And Neal and Gene can head off any issues."

"Actually, so can Grammy," Wila volunteered.

"And my in-laws," Penny added. "You're not the only one with resurrected family coming to the games the last half of the fall soccer season."

Heck, the season should have been over before Thanksgiving, but thanks to the three weeks of delayed games when the dead started rising in October, they were playing well into December.

"I know," Dani said. "It's just with demons popping up everywhere lately—"

"Girl, you know Karen will have half the demon hunters there to keep an eye on things," Wila pointed out.

"Go home and get some sleep, Dani," Penny said. "In fact, I could go to bed early myself after last night's extracurricular activities."

The women said their goodbyes, and they split up to head for home.

Five minutes later, Dani was about to turn into the main entrance to her subdivision when Verde jerked to the right and nearly unseated her rider in the process. Dani clung to the pommel and pulled herself upright.

"What is it, girl?" she whispered. Verde sent her a mental image of a demon hiding behind the six-foot wooden fence to their left.

"I know you're back there," Dani shouted. "You might as well come on out."

A possessed human stepped from behind the sound-blocking fence. He appeared to be in his late teens and dark-skinned. He wore a black hoodie and jeans. The demon inside the boy glared at her.

"The prince believed he had a temporary truce with you while you considered his offer, Death. Why are you killing demons?"

Chapter 20

Dani regarded the demon confronting her. It could be lying. On the other hand, Lucifer was noted for fooling people by telling the truth.

"I thought we had a truce, too, until he sent a demon to kill me and my sisters this afternoon," she finally said.

"That was not authorized."

"And yet, you are here, accusing me of breaking the truce." Dani twirled her scythe. "And your prince, who should be apologizing to me at the moment, is nowhere to be seen."

A sly smile crossed the demon's face. "What? No demand to apologize to your sisters, too?"

"I'm not going to argue semantics with the Devil's stooge," she said coolly. "Leave the human you currently possess."

"Or what?" It sneered.

Dani nudged her mare with her heels. Verde charged. With a swing of her scythe, Dani took out the demon. The young man dropped to the dormant grass.

Verde pivoted sharply and trotted back to the unconscious kid. She whiffed at his hair while Dani slid down from the saddle. She knelt beside him and laid her boney hand on his chest. He was breathing, but his heartbeat was elevated. She needed to play it safe and take him to the hospital.

"What the hell do you think you're doing!" a man shouted behind her.

She rose back to her feet and turned to face the person. He was clean-shaven with his dark hair in a conservative style, and he wore a gray wool overcoat over his charcoal suit. A running pickup sat on the asphalt behind him, but it was the rifle in his hands and pointed at her that worried her most. More people would be coming to their homes in the neighborhood. This was a good way for any innocent person to get hurt.

Or worse.

"He was possessed by a demon," she said.

The man paled when he got a good look at her skull. "Wh-what are you?"

"I'm Death, the fourth Soccer Mom of the Apocalypse."

As expected, her answer befuddled the stranger.

"I don't recognize you," she added. "Did you just move to this neighborhood?"

"Why?"

"Because I live here, too." She shrugged. "I don't normally meet the new neighbors looking like this. I'm assuming your family are the folks that moved into the Thomson place."

At his nod, she gestured at the young man on the ground. "If you don't mind, I need to get this poor guy to the hospital. After being possessed, most folks need a sedative when they wake up."

The man audibly gulped and lowered his rifle. "B-but if you're Death—"

"I killed the demon possessing him. I don't kill humans." She pointed at his truck. "Why don't you go on home? The Soccer Moms are releasing a public service announcement with tips on keeping demons out of your home and keeping your family from getting possessed. I'll swing by your house on Sunday afternoon. I bake a killer banana bread."

"O-okay." He retreated to his truck with frequent glances at her over his shoulder. But he sat in the driver's seat until she lifted the unconscious man onto her shoulder and mounted Verde. She shifted her demon victim until he was cradled in her arms before she waved at the man in the pickup. Verde wheeled and took off for the hospital.

Luckily, Officers Graham and Simmons were leaving the emergency room when Verde slowed to a gentle stop in front of the main doors.

"What do we got, Death?" Graham asked as he and his partner grabbed the unconscious young man and lowered him to the snow-damp pavement.

"Demon possession." Dani dismounted. "I'm no paramedic, but his heartbeat was rather fast. It seemed best to bring him here."

"Dave, go grab a gurney, and let Annie at registration know what we've got out here," Graham said.

"On it." Simmons jumped up and raced for the ER doors.

"I can carry him inside," Dani said.

Graham chuckled. "We just brought in a kid on meth. He doesn't need to catch sight of you looking like this, my dear."

More white, fluffy flakes started to drift down as the ER doors hissed open again. A nurse ran toward them. Simmons and an orderly followed with a gurney.

The nurse barked orders, and Dani found herself obeying along with the police and the orderly. Graham stayed outside with Dani while Simmons and the medical personnel got the kid into the much warmer ER. It was a little funny how she was more comfortable out here. She always hated the cold. Dad claimed it was her Mexican blood.

"What's going on?" Graham murmured. "I heard Longstreet assigned extra demon hunters on all the Soccer Moms' homes last night." He was the first police officer who had taken the Soccer Moms seriously, even before the dead started to rise last October. His only fault was what Penny referred to as his 1970's porn moustache.

"In the last twenty-four hours, my husband and my mother rose from their graves, there was a demon-inspired brawl at a weekday wedding reception, and we got a tip of where Lucifer was holed up in Chicago only to be jumped by a demon wearing a police officer."

Graham whistled. "That is definitely a handful. How are you doing with the family coming back?"

Dani chuckled. Surprisingly, Graham didn't flinch at the awful rattle.

"Honestly, I haven't been home long enough to deal with them."

Graham grunted an acknowledgment. "What about this kid?"

"The demon confronted me at the entrance to my subdivision. I killed the demon, but then, my new neighbor confronted me with a rifle because he thought—" She shook her head. "Oh, heck, I'm not sure what he thought. I was crouched next to the young man, checking his vitals. It probably looked like I was mugging him."

"Why did a lone demon confront a Soccer Mom?" Graham asked.

The only thing that would appear worse than mugging a kid would be admitting she was in the process of cutting a deal with Lucifer. So she took a tactic from his book—the best lie was a portion of the truth.

"We were at an advertising agency to do the PSA we've been talking about," Dani started.

Graham nodded his head to encourage her.

"The cameraman, a guy named Joey, was possessed. His demon threatened to kill Maggie, the sound engineer."

"You ladies saved Maggie and killed the demon inside Joey?" Graham cocked his right eyebrow.

Dani nodded. "The demon inside the kid I brought in wanted revenge."

Graham grunted again. "It probably tried your house and couldn't get in. So it thought it could ambush you on your way home."

"Do you need anything else from me, Officer?" she asked. "I've got a houseful of people to take care of."

"Go on." He smiled. "I've got your number if anything else comes up."

"Thanks." Dani climbed into Verde's saddle. The mare arrowed for home, but Dani had the distinct impression her horse was not happy with her.

"I couldn't tell Graham the whole truth," she whispered.

Verde snorted in disagreement.

Maybe Dani's mare had a point. She'd been the one who wanted to give the demons a chance to redeem themselves. Yet, she struck at them first lately without a thought. What the hell was going on in her head?

Normally when she was this troubled, she'd go to confession. However, Father Perez had bent over backward to help the Soccer Moms. She couldn't jeopardize the relationship between her sisters and the priest. God knew how such a confession right now could damage the partnership between the Soccer Moms and the Vatican taskforce. Nor did she need Edward Hudson crawling up her ass. He gave his own daughters-in-law a rough enough time, though he'd lightened up since he learned Penny was Pestilence.

Of course, her racing thoughts could totally be due to the lack of sleep. Four hours was simply not enough anymore. She needed to go to bed early with Mark's last soccer game of the fall season in the morning. And she found herself looking forward to cuddling with Heath the entire night.

She would have whistled the rest of the way home if she had lips.

Chapter 21

Dani ducked when Verde phased into their garage. She rather appreciated her mare's ability considering her driveway was full of cars. None of them were demon hunters' cars either.

Those were parked along the curb in front of the house, but they consisted of Karen's blue Charger along with Edward Hudson's black Accord. The vehicles in the driveway were Dad's pickup, Marty's SUV, and Father Perez's little electric car.

Add in the fact this was Marty's weekend with his kids, and Dani could feel the tension behind her eyeballs.

She dismounted Verde, who shifted back into minivan mode, and shrugged off her power before she entered her kitchen. For a split second, the years dropped away. Savory odors filled the house, especially slow-cooked pork and poblanos. Mom stood over the stove while she also directed Edward's resurrected wife Laura in making homemade tortillas at the counter. The weird part was Mom wore a dress Dani swore she had packed into a box Dad had allegedly taken to the homeless shelter.

"Hello, sweetie!" Mom smiled at her. "Go wash up. Dinner is almost ready."

"Okay," Dani said. "Where did you get that dress?"

"You're not the only packrat in the family." Mom retrieved a wooden spoon from the ceramic jar that held Dani's cooking utensils she used most often. "Your father brought over a couple of boxes of my clothes he'd kept."

Dani breathed a sigh of relief that she didn't need to take Mom shopping after tomorrow's soccer game. For the first time in ages, the extra leaves had been inserted in the Elantes' kitchen table. Marty's two daughters sat the table while Father Perez entertained a toddler Dani didn't recognize. The buzz of additional conversation came from the living room.

Dani didn't escape the kitchen without warm hugs from her nieces. When she entered the living room en route to the bathroom, Karen and the rest of the men paused talking long enough to greet Dani. But the most surprising thing was the presence of Dad's girlfriend, Carmen. The bright pink cast on her left arm said everything.

"Ah, crap." Dani leaned over to hug Carmen. "I'm so sorry Mom broke your arm."

"It's a hairline fracture just above the wrist." Carmen awkwardly returned the hug with her good arm. "The doctor said he'd normally put the patient in a sling, but with me being so close to seventy, he didn't want to take any chances."

They parted, and Carmen grinned up at Dani. "Besides, I probably would have done the same thing if I were in your mother's position."

That wasn't a subject Dani wanted to touch.

"I'll be right back. I need to wash up." She jogged up the stairs and headed straight for the master bathroom. Footsteps came from behind her. She turned to find Heath following her with a concerned expression on his face.

"Are you mad at me about this morning?" he murmured.

"What? No," Dani protested.

"You didn't kiss me hello," he said. "I thought after last night, well, that . . ." His expression turned sheepish. "I'm sorry about what I said this morning. You were right about me spending today with Mark while you ran your errands."

"I'm sorry for not greeting you properly." She stepped closer to him, wrapped her arms around his neck, and thoroughly kissed him. When they parted, she smiled. "Is that better?"

"Definitely." He grinned.

"And I owe you an apology." She sighed. "I've tried to keep Mark out of this Apocalypse business, but you're a grown-ass man. I had no right to treat you like a child this morning."

"And I owe you another apology," he murmured. "I should have put my foot down about everyone coming over tonight."

Dani laughed. "It's my family. How did you plan to stop them? Seriously, let me clean up. It's been a long day."

"Mind if I talk to you in the bathroom?" Heath asked.

There had been a time when he would have simply followed her into the bathroom while they were discussing something and perched on the edge of the tub. He was trying so hard to be respectful given the weirdness of the situation. As much as Dani dreamed of having Heath back, the reality was so much harder than she imagined.

"Come on." She inclined her head and continued into her bedroom.

Their bedroom, she corrected herself silently.

She entered the connected bathroom. He followed and settled on the edge of the tub, but he didn't say anything.

She pumped liquid soap into her palm. "If having the family here is overwhelming for you—"

"Have you told my parents?"

Dani watched Heath in the vanity mirror. "Honestly, I haven't had two seconds to even text them."

"I thought about calling them." He sighed and raked his hands through his blond locks. "But I didn't know how they would react to hearing my voice."

"It's probably a good thing you didn't call them, honey." She nudged the faucet lever to the warm water position and scrubbed her hands. "Not that I think they'd go off their rocker like Mom did, but I wouldn't want to give them a heart attack or stroke."

"Are they still living in Corpus Christi?"

Dani nodded while she rinsed her hands. "Audra and Case moved to Corpus three years ago. Maybe it would be better if we call them first." Heath's sister and brother-in-law had bought a house near the senior Elantes for the same reason Dani had stayed in Chicago. Sometimes, family needed to rally around the senior members as age caught up with them.

"You didn't answer my initial concern," she said as she reached for the hand towel. "Do I kick the family out for tonight?"

Heath chuckled. "You couldn't kick your brother and parents out if you tried."

"You'd be surprised what I can do these days." She smiled before she rehung her hand towel.

"I already am." His eyes sparkled with the familiar mix of humor and love. "No, I can't do that to your parents. Olivia is struggling with what's going on. Mrs. Hudson, Ms. Longstreet, and Father Perez have been a huge help. Plus, the father came over to talk to you about an argument you had this morning with another parishioner."

Dani crossed her arms and considered her options. She hated all the lying she'd been doing for the last twenty-four hours. On the other hand, would she end up in Hell for outing Christ Himself?

"Honey, whatever it is you don't think I can handle, it can't be any wilder than learning you're one of the Four Horsemen—"

"Soccer Moms," she automatically corrected.

"Sorry, Soccer Moms of the Apocalypse," he amended before he chuckled again. "The only thing crazier than that would be if you were arguing with . . ." His eyes widened. "Please tell me I'm wrong."

"He's been hiding in plain sight for the last thirty-three years." She smiled at the shock on her husband's face.

Heath cocked "Should I ask what your argument with Him was about?"

"Same old, same old." She shook her head. "Whenever we ask Him for advice, He claims He can't interfere with human free will. I can't get a straight answer out of any angels either."

"Angels?" Heath repeated.

"Don't bring it up to anyone." She dropped her arms to her sides. "The other three can't see them. I think it's because of which Soccer Mom I am."

"Daniella! Heath!" Mom's voice echoed up the stairs.

"Coming!" Dani yelled back. "By the way, who's baby was Father Perez holding in the kitchen?"

"If I got everything straight, he's Marty's girlfriend's son."

"Which girlfriend?" Dani demanded.

"He didn't say, and I didn't ask." Heath grinned. "It's nice to know some things haven't changed."

Dani rolled her eyes. "C'mon. We need to get downstairs before Karen runs up here to kick some ass."

Chapter 22

The odor of spice mixed with cilantro, and citrus filled the kitchen. There was nothing like homemade barbacoa with rice and black beans. As Dad always did, he complained it should be made with goat like his abuela's recipe. As always, Mom told him to find her some goat in Oakfield, and she would. And as always Heath claimed Cuban cuisine was better than Mexican. For once, he had an ally in Carmen.

While family and friends dug into the food, Mom and Laura Hudson gossiped over dinner like old times. The toddler Luca belonged to Marty's newest girlfriend Abigail. She had begged him to watch Luca while she attended her sister's wedding.

Unfortunately, that wedding happened to be the one last night at the Herrington Hotel. Her new brother-in-law's mother had stabbed her. Poor Abigail was still in the hospital. Her surgeon said her prognosis was excellent, but no one in her family was healthy enough to take care of Luca at the moment.

Dani eyed her brother. "So, you're babysitting Luca to score points with Abigail?"

"No! I'm not!" Marty protested.

All four of his kids chorused, "Yes, you are."

"Whatever happened to wooing a woman with flowers and dinner?" Edward asked.

"That wasn't how you wooed me." Laura snickered.

"Not every lady thinks premium lockpicking tools are an appropriate courting gift." Edward scowled.

"Lockpicking tools?" Mom stared at the pair in total confusion.

"Haven't you wondered why Karen is the only Vatican taskforce member here now?" Laura said.

Karen rolled her eyes. "Oh, God, please leave me out of this."

"No one takes the Lord's name in vain. No matter who you work for," Mom lectured sharply before she turned back to Laura. "You were a demon hunter?"

"Ed and I both were back before the kids were born." Laura smiled.

"I thought you came over to see me." Disappointment filled Mom's face.

"I did, Olivia," Laura sad gently. "Because you're my friend and we're in the same boat."

"But why didn't you ever tell me?" Mom's bottom lip quivered.

Damn, Laura had accidentally trampled Mom's already fragile feelings.

"Mom, not even Gene and Theo knew about what their parents did," Dani said. "And Edward didn't come clean until he found out about the Soccer Moms." She eyed Edward, who smirked. "Of course, if we'd known, Penny would have told him she was meeting with a demon so he didn't blow up our interrogation of the enemy."

Edward's smirk melted into a nasty scowl. "It wasn't my fault. Based on my experience, I assumed a couple of demons were trying to take advantage of my daughter-in-law."

"My point was—" Dani shot Edward a dirty look. "—Laura is being honest with you now, Mom."

"If it's any consolation, Olivia, I didn't know about the Vatican taskforce either," Father Perez said. "But I understand the Church's need for secrecy when it comes to demons. Especially after seeing the fear in Oakfield with the start of the Apocalypse."

"Mom and the rest of the Soccer Moms will end it, and we'll all be safe," Mark said with a surety beyond his twelve years. "You keep talking about having faith on Sundays. Don't you have any, Father?"

"Marcos Emmanuel Elante!" Mom glared at Mark. "We do not speak to our guests in such a manner. Especially a man of the cloth!"

"Mom—" Dani started.

However, Mark roughly shoved his chair back and jumped to his feet. Rose tinted his cheeks and ears. "No, Abuelita. I will not be quiet. These demons kidnapped Justine by using her father. Others attacked Brittany and her family at their house. Derek and I aren't stupid. We know we're at risk, too. But I have faith in Mom and her friends. And after Penny saved Father Perez's ass from some demons, I don't get why he doesn't have any faith at all considering who our soccer coach really is." He whirled and raced from the kitchen.

Mom turned to Dani. "Daniella! Are you going to allow your son to speak to his elders in that manner?"

Dani lifted her chin. "Yes, I am. Because Mark is right." She pushed to her feet. "Both you and Heath have been pouting because things aren't the way they were." She turned to Father Perez. "I understand your allegiance is to God, Father, but His Son called the Horsemen forth, and He is supposed to be our general in this fight, but He's sitting on the sidelines. At this moment, the only person in this house who has any faith that I and my friends can stop the Apocalypse has left the room." The anger coursing through her threatened to bring forth her avatar, and that would be the worst thing she could do. "I will follow his good sense and leave, too."

She stalked out of the kitchen, through the living room, and up the stairs. At Mark's bedroom door, she hesitated.

"Come on in, Mom," Mark called.

Dani turned the knob and pushed open the door. Mark sat cross-legged on his bed and had his phone in his hands, obviously texting someone.

"You okay?" she asked.

He swallowed hard and laid the phone face down on his navy comforter. "No, not really. And I'm not going to apologize to Abuelita or Father Perez, if that's why you came up here."

"It's not." She crossed the carpet and sat at the foot of his bed. "Actually, I owe you an apology. I've been so wrapped in Apocalypse stuff I wasn't being the mom you needed. I am so sorry for that."

"It does suck at times, but we understand." Mark gave her a wry smile.

"We?"

"Me, Justine, Derek, and Brittany."

"I guess they are the only ones who do understand what you're going through," Dani admitted.

Mark nodded before he added, "Can I tell you something?"

"Of course."

"You can't tell anyone," he said.

"I promise," Dani assured him.

"I used to dream Dad and Abuelita came back to us." Mark frowned and rubbed his palms nervously on the denim covering his knees. "The reality isn't what I expected."

"It isn't for me either," she said.

"But I'm glad they're here," Mark continued. "Especially Dad." Unshed tears glimmered in his eyes. "I was beginning to forget him. I look at the old picture albums, and it feels like I'm looking at a stranger."

Dani pulled her son into a tight hug. It wouldn't do Mark a damn bit of good if she confessed she'd been feeling the same way about Heath before the Apocalypse started.

Chapter 23

Dani jerked awake to the sound of angels screaming. She could feel Heath snoring softly next to her, but the angels drowned out the actual sound of it.

She threw back the comforter, swung her legs over the side of the mattress, and felt around for her slip-on athletic shoes. Once her feet were safely ensconced, she stood and crept out of her bedroom. The racket on the roof continued while she checked on both Mark in his room and Mom in the guest room. Thank goodness, sheer exhaustion had finally claimed Mom, and she was sound asleep.

The living room was dark and silent, but a dim glow came from the kitchen. When she reached the door, she found Karen and Sister Clare talking quietly over tea at the kitchen table.

"What's wrong?" Karen immediately jumped to her feet.

"I don't know yet," Dani grabbed her coat from its hook and put it on. "Stay in here. Something's got the angels riled up."

"You can hear the angels?" Sister Clare stared at Dani in amazement.

"Do I need to call the rest of the Soccer Moms?" Karen already had her phone out.

"Give me ten minutes to do a circuit around the neighborhood before you call in the cavalry." Dani shrugged on her power over her coat. "Whatever you do, don't leave the house until I come back or my sisters get here."

"Or the demons set the house on fire?"

Dani knew the American demon hunter was joking, but the French nun paled. Sister Clare had been burned at the stake, ironically accused by a demon-possessed monsignor of practicing witchcraft. "Karen, shut it," Dani hissed.

Karen immediately realized her mistake. "I'm sorry, Clare. That joke was in poor taste."

"Very poor," the sister said with a sniff.

"I mean it, you two. Stay inside." Dani strode through the mud room and out the back door.

It was still snowing. Close to two inches carpeted the backyard.

The angels stopped screaming the moment she stepped on the stone path from the house to the storage shed. Dani realized why.

Lucifer stood in the middle of the yard, and this time, he brought friends. She counted five demons, but none of them possessed humans. Instead, they inhabited two feral cats, two gigantic great horned owls perched in the oak tree, and the Ravenwoods' Doberman Pinscher Rocky. The weird thing was no footprints appeared in the pristine blanket of snowflakes.

Dani grasped her scythe in both hands. "Here to do your own dirty work?"

"You have that backwards, Death." His eyeballs literally glowed red. "You could have simply said no when we met rather than resume assassinating my demons without warning."

"Really?" The entire backyard looked like someone had crazy taste in Christmas lights between his burning red eyes and her own sockets' phosphorescent green. "After one of your little friends attacked me and my sisters this afternoon at the Oakwood Building and another one ambushed me on my way home."

"I did not authorize any demon to attack you at the Oakwood Building."

"And you're known as the Prince of Lies." She twirled her scythe. "Whatever you want to say, make it fast. I have a couple of trigger-happy demon hunters watching us through the back door window."

Lucifer looked over her shoulder, and the Doberman demon growled.

The Prince of Hell ignored his lackey before he looked up at the roofline. He frowned at the feathers and eyeballs perched on the shingles.

"So, you tattled to the Kid after we spoke," he accused.

"I didn't have to," Dani answered. "The Watchers don't answer to me. Yet, you made a point of meeting in front of them in front of Saint Michael's. It's not like you didn't notice them when you pulled up to the curb."

Which led to the question of why the dang angels were perched on her roof tonight. But she didn't dare say that in front of Lucifer.

"Let's walk and talk," he said. "Away from your house."

"Tell your buddies to get out of the animals first."

His jawline twitched before he said, "Go find some humans."

Black smoke poured from all the critters, and the demons darted off into the night. The cats and owls followed suit. Rocky ran to Dani and huddled against her leg, shivering. Strange how the dog still trusted her even though she was boney.

"After you." She gestured at the gate to the front yard.

"So you can stab me in the back with your blade?" he mocked.

"You're the one who lured me out of my nice, warm house," Dani said. "You're the one who wants to go for a walk in the snow. Just me and you. I'm the one who should be worried. Don't you think?"

Lucifer scowled at her.

She waited.

"Fine," he snapped and stalked toward the gate. At least, he was leaving footprints in the snow.

She followed as did Rocky, though she was pretty sure the dog was coming along so she'd protect him. Maybe she needed to give in to Mark's request for a puppy. He'd protect a new pet, and it would give him some normal companionship. And if she focused on normal stuff, she wouldn't freak out over the angels staying at the house instead of covering her butt.

Stop it, Dani castigated herself. Focus on the devil who's in front of you.

Lucifer strolled along the sidewalk for a block before he spoke. "Someone's playing both of us. I didn't send anyone to kill you or your sisters. If my messenger threatened or assaulted you, he acted against my orders."

She brushed the snow from her shoulders while she considered his words. Rocky padded at her side. "I suppose you believe Jesus is behind our . . . misunderstanding."

"No." Lucifer stopped, so she and the dog halted, too. "Frankly, it's not the Kid's style. He's honest to a fault."

"So it's another demon or one of the Fallen," Dani murmured. Rocky whined softly.

Lucifer snorted. "You're making assumptions. There are both angels and humans who wish to see the end of the world, too, not just demons."

She ground her teeth in frustration. There were humans who wanted to see this war happen. Would there be angels who wanted to finish off the Fallen?

Of course, there were. It would be the perfect excuse to get rid of both demons and those humans they found troublesome. In a way, both Jesus and Lucifer were right. The only way for everyone to survive was to keep the war from happening. "How about the next time you want to talk to me, call or text me instead of sending a messenger?" she suggested. "Or better yet, call me at my place of employment so it doesn't raise suspicions."

"Are you ashamed of consorting with me, Death?" He leered at her.

"Why do you have to be so weird?" She shook her head. "If you're correct, and the being screwing with us is on the heavenly side, do you want them to know I cut a deal with you before we're ready? God or Jesus could replace me with someone else as Death. Then where will you be?"

Lucifer watched her with new respect. "I apologize. You're right."

"So, what is it you actually propose we do?" she asked.

"I want you and the other Soccer Moms to stay on the sidelines." The red glow of his eyes died down. "Protect your families. I don't expect you to do otherwise. But stay out of our way."

"That's it?" She cocked her head. "We don't lift a finger?"

"Yes."

"At least, Crucifer wanted us to fight along with him."

Lucifer looked away from her at the mention of the fallen angel he himself had murdered when he held Courtney and Kenny Lasser hostage.

"Which brings me to the question of why do you expect me to go along with your plan?" Dani watched him carefully.

His attention shot back to her, and his eyes narrowed. "You want to keep your husband Heath, don't you? What do you think happens if Heaven wins this battle? Do you really believe you will go to Heaven with him after the things you've done as Death? Thou shall not murder."

He hit her own doubts dead center.

She lifted her chin. "Demons are no longer human."

"You sure about that?"

"You need to give me something more to work with other than do nothing," she said.

"What do you want then?" he asked.

"The demons stay down in Hell for the rest of eternity, and the Soccer Moms will leave them be." Dani would have smiled if she wore her skin. "You abdicate from the throne of Hell and assign one of the Fallen as your successor. I'll negotiate your return to Heaven, but you know dang well that part of it will require you to apologize to your Father."

Lucifer's jaw muscles twitched. She tightened her grip on her scythe, half-expecting him to strike her. He shoved his hands into his coat pockets while he regarded her.

"You don't ask for anything easy, do you, Death?"

"If you have a counter-proposal, then let's hear it." she said.

"Can I think about your proposal for a day?" He seemed serious.

She hoped he was serious. Meanwhile, Rocky gave himself a vigorous shake to shed the snow collecting on his fur.

"I'm busy tomorrow, so take two days to consider my idea. But—" She gently poked Lucifer in the chest with her free boney forefinger. "—if you decide not to accept my offer, you need to come up with another idea. One I can actually sell to my sisters."

He exhaled, but his breath didn't steam in the frigid air. "All right. Will you be at your office on Sunday?"

She chortled. "Technically, it's already Saturday morning. Give me a call on Monday."

Behind Lucifer, flashlights bobbed along the side street. The falling snow muffled the people's shouts and whistles.

"You need to get out of here, and I need to return Rocky to his family," she said.

"You think you can dismiss me?" His expression of incredulousness would have been funny under different circumstances.

"I'm not the one wearing a corrupt officer the Oakfield Police have a BOLO on," she responded. "Or do you want witnesses who have seen us together?"

"I can take care of the humans."

"If you want my help, we're doing things my way."

Lucifer literally popped out of sight. Rocky whimpered. Dani extended her senses to confirm he and any other demon was gone.

All clear. She shed her power.

"Come on, Rocky." She petted the dog's head, and they both headed toward his family who were searching for him.

But Lucifer's visit still disturbed her. What if someone was trying to make sure the Apocalypse happened? And worse, what if it was someone she knew?

Chapter 24

The morning dawned cold and clear. All the soccer league families arrived early to the park. The city plows had taken care of the roads and public parking lots, but the parents and older kids needed to clear the two fields by hand. It helped when Rick Courtney and Tom Mercer showed up with their snow blowers in Tom's landscaping trailer. Penny brought urns of coffee, hot chocolate, and hot water for tea, and Helen Chow helped her to set up and serve the warm beverages. Meanwhile, Dani, Wila, and two other mothers supervised the younger kids in sweeping snow off the stands.

Introducing Heath to the other parents wasn't as bad as Dani had feared, and everyone recognized Mom. Given the strangeness in Oakfield since the start of the Apocalypse, no one batted an eye. Besides, Mom and Laura Hudson weren't the only resurrected grandparents in attendance.

Despite needing to clear the two and half inches of snow that fell during the night, the last games of the season began as scheduled. By the time the eleven and twelve division started, a quarter of the stands was filled with the Soccer Moms, their families, and a good chunk of the Vatican task-force. And nearly everyone had brought blankets or seat cushions to insulate themselves from the ice cold aluminum seats.

The starting lineup didn't shed their sweatpants until the last minute. Dani had tried to talk Mark into wearing thermal leggings, but he was ad-amant he wasn't going to wear girly clothes in front of the other players. Instead, he doubled his soccer socks and put on a black long-sleeved t-shirt beneath his league shirt. However, Derek was wearing insulated runner leggings under his uniform shorts.

Dani leaned over and whispered to Wila who sat on the bench in front of her. "How'd you get Derek to wear something warm under his uniform?"

Wila shot a wry grin over her shoulder. "It wasn't me. Gammy pointed out Brittany was too smart to be impressed by someone too dumb to take care of himself."

Francine and Penny snickered. Heath chuckled, too.

"I should have thought of that," he murmured. "Is there anyone Mark is interested in?"

Dani took Heath's hand in her mittened one and grinned at him. "More the other way around I think. I wish you'd been here to give him the talk on what to do when a girl likes him because I accidentally left that part out."

"Well, I am here now," Heath teased. He started to stand.

Dani giggled and yanked him back down. "Now is not the time."

The referee set the ball between Brittany and the Muskrats starting forward and blew his whistle to start the match. With the sun out, the formerly frozen pitch quickly turned into a mud pit. It didn't stop the kids one bit, though there was a few unintentional slide tackles.

The intentional one by a player on the opposing team knocked Justine off her feet. But it wasn't the redhead who lost her temper. Mark charged out of the Tiger Sharks' goal and probably would have whaled on the Muskrat player if fellow Tiger Sharks Derek and Kenny Lasser hadn't grabbed him.

Coach Cordero welcomed a limping Justine back to the player bench and subbed Nancy Chow as the replacement forward. Gene climbed over the demon hunters surrounding the Soccer Moms and their families and headed down to the field to check on his daughter.

"Why is he going down?" Heath whispered.

"Gene acts as the unofficial team doctor when he attends a game," Dani whispered back. "The advantage of having a medical degree even though he's a shrink."

"You don't have to whisper," Edward barked. "There's nothing shameful about being a psychologist."

Laura elbowed him in the ribs. Most of the surrounding spectators laughed. Dani felt her cheeks heat in embarrassment despite the cold December day. Heath leaned over to face Edward.

"I meant no offense, Mr. Hudson," Heath said. "There's a lot of new people in my family's lives, and I'm still working on keeping everyone straight."

"It's all right." Edward waved his gloved hand.

It wasn't like Penny's father-in-law to drop a subject. Or maybe he did because Heath was a man. It would explain why he gave Penny so much crap, and why Laura had a few regrets about acceding to Edward's wishes during her first lifetime.

From the other soccer field, Dani could identify Marty's distinct voice whooping it up as Cory's team played. Dad was trudging back and forth between the two fields since two of his grandsons were playing at the same time. She had a feeling Carmen was with Marty's other three kids and Luca in the other set of bleachers. At least, Dad's latest girlfriend would make sure the baby was appropriately dressed for this weather. Marty could be an idiot at times, as his two ex-wives and numerous girlfriends would attest.

The Muskrats star forward broke away and raced for the Tiger Sharks' goal. Mark quickly scanned the field to make sure there wasn't another Muskrat player the oncoming pre-teen could pass the ball to. Nope, the opposing player wanted the glory despite his coach's shouts to the contrary. Mark's instincts were on. The Muskrat player foolishly launched the ball dead center at the goal. Mark caught the ball despite slipping in the mud and landing hard on his side.

Motherly instincts kicked in, but before Dani could do more than stand, Mark jumped up and threw the ball in Derek's direction, who headed the soccer ball to Tommy Hendricks. The Tiger Sharks raced for the opposite end of the field.

Forty-five minutes later, the refs blew their whistles to indicate the end of the game. The Tiger Sharks went into full celebration mode. Derek and Tommy hoisted Brittany on their shoulders since she scored the winning goal.

Surprisingly, Kenny ran to the bench to help Justine out to the field to join in the antics. Apparently, being taken hostage by the Devil himself had changed the boy as well as his mother. Or maybe Kenny decided to be a little nicer after seeing Penny in action.

"Dani?" Courtney Lasser waved and approached Dani's family as they headed for the gate. "Do you have a minute?"

Crap, she forgot she promised to consider running for OPA president. Dani plastered on a civil smile. "Do you mind if we speak at Rusty Rat's after we get the team fed? Once they're distracted, we will have a quiet moment to talk."

Courtney smiled and nodded. "No problem. I was about to suggest the same thing. It's too cold to do this in the parking lot." She strode toward her own minivan, only to slide on a patch of slushy snow. Her arms flailed.

Dani raced over and caught Courtney before she landed on the concrete.

She gasped and clung to Dani. "Thank you! I could have broken something."

"It's okay. You're okay." She awkwardly patted Courtney's back. "Take it easier going through the parking lot."

Courtney nodded, but she stepped a little more gingerly as she crossed the parking lot to where her gold minivan was parked.

"Wow," Heath murmured in Dani's ear. "I haven't seen you move that fast since Mark tried to stick a knife in a kitchen socket."

She looked up at him. "Saving people. It's what I do these days."

He kissed her lightly on the lips. "I'm seriously impressed with the new you."

"Aww, man!" Mark blurted.

They both turned to look at their son.

"Can you two stop kissing for five minutes?"

"Be nice, Marcos," Mom said. "You'll understand when you get older."

He groaned, stalked toward their green minivan, and yanked open the side sliding door.

Heath held out his free elbow for Mom and she took it. "What was that about?" he said as he escorted Dani and Mom to the minivan.

Dani chuckled. "You came home just in time for him to turn into a teenager."

"I'll drive," Heath said.

"No thanks." She smiled at him. "Nothing personal, but Verde doesn't like anyone else driving her."

"You named your minivan?" He paused as they reached the vehicle and stared.

"It's her horse, silly." Mom playfully slapped his arm before she climbed into the rear seat with a muddy Mark.

"Should we run home so Mark can change?" Heath asked as he and Dani climbed in the front seats.

"Our stains are a badge of pride, Dad," Mark said.

"But you brought a change of clothes like I asked, right?" Dani eyed him in the rearview mirror.

He rolled his eyes. "Of course, Mom. Hey, is it okay if Justine comes over after the party?"

"What happened to you going over to Derek's?"

"His dad is picking him up at Rusty Rat's." Mark shrugged, but his cheeks glowed. "Justine got the latest Blood Oath game, and Brittany isn't into FPS games."

Dani tried to keep a neutral expression. Mark and Justine had been inseparable since first grade, but obviously, something had changed. Another puberty challenge was something she didn't need right now.

"It's fine with me if it's okay with Penny and Gene."

"Is it okay if Justine stays for dinner, too?"

"You need to ask her mom."

"We always do, Mo-o-om."

And the attitude was back.

Gritting her teeth, she started the minivan, threw the gear in reverse, and tapped the accelerator. A jolt shuddered through the frame, and she stomped on the brake.

Mark slid open the side door before she could shift to park and he jumped out of the vehicle. "Oh, my god!" His shout held more panic than when they'd been in the accident with her pickup three months ago.

It took precious seconds for Dani's numb fingers to unbuckle her belt. She jumped out and ran to the rear of her minivan/horse. Soccer balls bounced and rolled everywhere, but her eyes were drawn to her son kneeling beside an unconscious man. Coach Cordero lay on the damp, cold asphalt, blood streaming from his head.

Mark looked up at her, his brown eyes wide. "Mom! You killed my coach!"

Chapter 25

Dani covered her mouth with her mittened hands, frozen in place. This couldn't be happening. She'd killed him. Sure, she'd argued with Jesus yesterday, but she certainly hadn't wished him dead.

Wila raced over to the prone form, her first aid bag in hand. "Dani, call 9-1-1."

Except she couldn't move. Horror twisted her heart. Had she just destroyed all her sisters' efforts to stop the Apocalypse? Had she triggered the end of the world?

A scream rang out. Maria ran to her husband's side. Heath joined Mark and Wila.

Wila glanced at Dani before she turned to Heath and handed him her phone. "Call 9-1-1 for me, Heath." She pulled out her stethoscope and listened for a heartbeat.

Francine, the two off-duty police officers who acted as security, and the demon hunters kept the other spectators out of the way. The silence in the parking lot was deafening.

"Dani! Get your ass over here now!" Wila's bellowed order shook Dani out of her paralysis. She rushed over and crouched next to her friend. "I need you to do mouth-to-mouth while I do compressions.

"B-but—"

"The dispatcher wants to know your badge number," Heath reported. Wila rattled it off before adding, "Crap! Where's my gloves?"

"Should I be moving his head?" Dani asked. That had been one of the things she remembered from the CPR class Wila had made her friends take.

Wila pulled off her coat and packed it around Coach Cordero's head. "Maria, brace his head between your knees to keep his head as still as possible. You understand?"

Tears streamed down the other woman's face, but she did as Wila instructed.

"Go, Dani."

Pulling on the information from the class Wila had taught, Dani pulled open his mouth and checked the coach's airway. Clear. She sucked in a deep breath, pinched his nose shut, and covered his mouth with hers.

She didn't want to do this. She wanted to run away like she had when she demanded to see Heath's body after the accident. She needed to hide from what she'd done to Jesus, but she couldn't.

A second deep breath, and blow. The air came out, but there was no inhalation on his part.

A third breath. Dani felt a tingle of power race through her, like when she was Death. This time, Jesus inhaled on his own. His big, brown eyes fluttered open, and he gave her a puzzled look.

"I don't think my wife will be happy about you kissing me, Dani."

Dani slumped in a hard plastic chair in the ER waiting room. Heath had driven Verde to Rusty Rat's after Dani had given the mare a lecture about keeping her family safe. Derek had gone to the end-of-the-season party with her family.

Francine had taken her family to the pizza party joint and picked up Penny, who had already arrived at Rusty Rat's. Maria was the only one allowed back with Jesus in the treatment area of the ER. She had ridden with Wila and Dani to the hospital. Maria had said over and over that it was an accident, and it wasn't Dani's fault.

But it was her fault. She hadn't checked her mirrors before backing out. Verde hadn't indicated anything. Except Dani couldn't blame her minivan.

Was she expecting too much from Verde? Or had Verde picked up on Dani's anger with Jesus and allowed Dani to run into the man?

So, everyone except Wila sat in the waiting room drinking really crappy coffee. Wila paced like an angry lion. But lions didn't mumble about taking Verde to a glue factory for not watching Dani's back, and thereby ruining her winter coat.

Penny nudged Dani's arm. She looked up to see two Oakfield police officers walk through the sliding glass doors. Rafe Estrada and Deshauna Keyes. Dani's face heated as they approached her. It didn't help these cops were people she knew.

"Hey, Rafe. Deshauna." Dani pushed to her feet. "Can I put my coat on before you put the cuffs on me?"

"You shouldn't have taken off from the scene of the accident." Rafe took off his cap and rubbed the back of his head. "Where's your minivan?"

"At Rusty Rat's with my family for the post soccer season party." Dani sighed. "Neither Maria Cordero or I were in any shape to drive, so Wila brought us both to the hospital."

Penny inserted herself between Dani and the cops. "Have you talked to the witnesses at the park? They'll tell you it was an accident."

"We did talk to the witnesses," Deshauna said. "But the D.A. wants to question Dani."

"Not without an attorney present," Francine protested sharply.

"This wasn't our idea or Chief Wright's, Ms. Coy-Astin," Rafe said. "I know you four can beat the crap out of me and my partner, but if you interfere in official business, we will have arrest you. Have you heard how the coach is doing?"

Rafe's concern about Jesus was to be expected. He started coaching when Rafe was in high school. Jesus's guidance kept a lot of the poorer kids like Rafe out of the juvenile system and gave them a good start in life.

"Not yet," Wila interjected. "But he was awake and talking when McDonald and Fuller loaded Cordero into their rig."

"Guys, stop arguing with Rafe and Deshauna. They're just doing their jobs." Dani reached behind her for her coat and shrugged it on before she held out her wrists.

"C'mon, girl." Deshauna shook her head. "We're not going to ruin a good pair of cuffs by putting them on you."

"I wouldn't—" Dani protested.

"If we run into demons on the way to the station, you damn well would, and we both know it." Deshauna grinned.

"Dani, don't say a word to D.A. Benson until your attorney arrives," Wila ordered.

"But—" Dani sagged at the glares from the other three Soccer Moms. "Fine, I'll wait."

Her acquiescence didn't stop the flood of heat to her face as Deshauna and Rafe led her out to their patrol car. The morning started more normal than her days had in years.

She should have known her good fortune wouldn't last.

Chapter 26

The interrogation room at the Oakfield Police Station had a funky smell the disinfectant couldn't disguise. Deshauna was kind enough to bring Dani a cup of joe while she waited. Somehow, the coffee at the station was even worse than the coffee at the hospital.

Dani wanted to pull her hair out. Too much was happening. And the only thing she could have controlled was the one thing she hadn't controlled. Now, Jesus Cordero lay in the hospital, and she had no idea how he was doing. And there was no idea how long she would be here. Most attorneys didn't hang out in their offices on a Saturday afternoon this close to Christmas.

What would Heath think when he found out she'd been arrested? Mom would be outraged. The worst thing Dani had ever done in her life was punch the bully who made fun of her Mexican heritage.

And if Jesus died, what would happen to the world?

The lock of the interrogation room clicked before the door opened. A tiny woman with a gray pixie cut stormed into the room. She wore a red cardigan, black turtleneck, and blue jeans beneath her gray wool coat.

Dani stared. "Ms. King? What are you doing here?"

"Wila called me." She tossed her tote bag on the table and shrugged off her coat before she faced the officer in the doorway. "Get out, and tell Art and Warren they damn well better not be recording this conversation."

"Yes, ma'am." The young officer meekly closed the door.

"Ms. King—" Dani started.

"Call me Lilah, sweetheart." She sat down and pulled a yellow legal pad and a pen from her tote.

"Lilah, you just had a heart attack," Dani blurted. "What are you doing here?"

"Dani, sweetheart, that's the great thing about modern medicine." The older woman grinned. "The docs didn't have to crack me open from stem to stern like they did with my father. Couple of small cuts on my thigh. Two days in the hospital, some tests to make sure my blood's flowing like it should, and a couple of days rest at home, and I'm practically as good as new."

She clicked her pen. "Now, tell me your side of the story."

An hour later, Dani felt as tired as she had been when she waitressed through high school and college.

"Let me go have a little talk with Warren." Lilah jumped to her feet with her notes and pen. "I'll be right back." She charged out the door. At least, it wasn't locked this time, but then Dani technically wasn't under arrest.

Yet.

She sipped the dreadful coffee. When she got her phone back from the police, she'd call Mark, have Heath come get her, and stop at Java's Palace for a decent double mocha.

A few minutes later, Lilah came back with Chief Wright and a man in a tailored suit.

Make that a possessed human in a tailored suit.

Power flowed over and through Dani. She launched herself over the table and slashed with her scythe. The demon inside screamed, but it didn't die in the flashes of white as she'd become accustomed.

The possessed man collapsed. Black smoke poured from him to form a figure with wings. Holy crap. It was one of the Fallen.

And she didn't have her sisters to back her up.

"Lilah! Chief! Get out," Dani screamed.

"None of you are going anywhere." The fallen angel grabbed both conscious people and flung them across the interrogation room. Chief Wright's heel hit the table, and coffee spilled across the surface and splashed on the linoleum floor.

The Fallen tried to kick Dani, but she blocked his leg with the handle of her scythe. Wings batted her shoulders and inhibited her movements. So she jabbed the angel in the chest with the tip of the snath. He jumped back out of the range of her blade and stopped whacking her with his wings.

It gave her a moment to examine the angel. Like Crucifer, he had pitch black hair, eyes, and feathers on his wings. His skin had the same pearlescent sheen. Black smoke shifted around him from his neck to his ankles like an ever-moving toga.

"What do you want?" Dani demanded.

"For you to honor your deal with Crucifer," the angel spat.

Why the hell was every fallen angel trying to cut a deal with her? Penny was the de facto leader of the Soccer Moms. Why weren't any of them talking to her? Except Penny was a smart cookie with lots of business negotiating experience.

Anger rose inside of Dani. So, the Fallen considered her the youngest and dumbest of the quartet.

"Crucifer is dead." She shifted her scythe so the edge of the blade faced the fallen angel. "Who are you, and why did you send a mere demon to assassinate me and my sisters yesterday?"

"I am Buer." He cocked his head. "But what demon are you talking about?"

"He didn't stop to introduce himself," she said dryly. "You're not Crucifer, so I'm not about to trust you. Especially when you're hurting humans."

"I wouldn't have touched them if you hadn't attacked me first." Buer sneered.

"Oh, honey, you possessed the D.A. before I attacked you." Dani would have smiled sweetly if she had the skin to do so."

"It was the only chance for us to talk privately," he replied.

"Death get out of the way," Chief Wright snarled from behind her. "Let me shoot the bastard."

Dani didn't move. "It's not going to work. He's not an average demon. He's a fallen angel."

"A what?"

She didn't have to turn around to know the police chief's mouth was hanging open. An image of Verde galloping flashed through her mind along with the assurance the other three mares were with her.

"Spit out what you were going to tell me and get out, Buer. My sisters are on their way."

"There are those of us who agree with Crucifer's plan," the Fallen said. "We would like to adhere to the same terms."

"Why?" Dani snapped.

"We want to go home," Buer said. "As the Favored Warriors of the Son, you could help us negotiate an end to the war."

Maybe the leaders of Hell didn't view her as stupid and naïve after all. Maybe they were simply that desperate. The more-than-proverbial prodigal sons.

"I'll have to discuss renewing the deal with Him and my sisters. Have you discussed this with your prince?"

The angel smirked. "Much as Crucible did prior to the prince killing him with Pestilence's arrow."

This whole situation was starting to get very, very messy.

"Fine. You've delivered your message to me." She gestured at the door. "I suggest you leave while you can."

Buer flapped his wings and disappeared in a puff of black smoke. Dani whirled around, rushed to Lilah's side, and prayed she wasn't responsible for another death.

Chapter 27

Dani sat in Chief Wright's office, sipping yet another cup of terrible coffee, while the police took pictures of Verde. Her horse was once again a minivan, except there were no signs of where she bumped into Jesus.

Ambulances had come and gone with Lilah King and D.A. Benson. The paramedics suspected Lilah had a broken arm. The district attorney suffered from post-possession catatonia.

Francine sat beside Dani and reassured her that Jesus was fine. Just needed five stitches to seal the cut in his scalp. Maria took her husband home after she chewed out Sergeant Park when he dared to suggest that she and her husband file charges.

Meanwhile, Penny and Wila stood over Chief Wright's desk and chewed him a new one for dragging Dani down to the police station.

"Stop it," Dani finally snapped. "It's not his fault a fallen angel used the D.A. to get close to me."

Penny and Wila abruptly shut up and stared at her.

Francine laid a hand on Dani's arm. "What are you talking about?"

Chief Wright watched her with narrowed eyes.

Dani sighed. "Buer wants to cut the same deal we had with Crucifer."

"That's suicide," Wila muttered.

"Chief Wright, is there any reason I need to stay here?" Dani pushed to her feet. "I'm happy to cooperate, but I need something to eat after two cups of the station's coffee."

"The Soccer Moms of the Apocalypse don't want the lowly human to know what's really going on, do they?" However, he said the words with a teasing tone.

"Sir, you already know too much, and I worry about your safety," she replied.

"I know when to play stupid, Ms. Elante." He chuckled. "You don't survive public service without knowing when to keep your mouth shut."

"Thank you." Dani smiled and collected her coat. She tossed the bad coffee and cup in the trash as she and her sisters left.

When they exited the police station, the wind had picked up though most of the snow had melted beneath the day's bright sunshine. What she really wanted was to go home and curl up in bed with Heath. Instead, she turned to the other Soccer Moms.

"We need to talk," Dani said. "There's more than what even the chief knows."

"We kind of figured that one out for ourselves." Penny pulled out her phone to check the time. "Java's Palace doesn't close for another three hours, and we all have extra people at home these days. What if I pick up pizza and salads and we meet at Java's Too?"

"The renovations are already done?" Wila asked.

"My project got moved up." Penny laughed and shook her head. "My contractor's other jobs were cancelled or delayed because the Apocalypse has started. Everyone's waiting to see if we can stop it."

"I need real coffee after the sludge I drank at the hospital and police station," Dani said. "If you don't mind, I'll run through the original Java's drive-thru."

"Give me the keys to the new café." Francine held out her hand. "I've got extra boxes of Long Johns in Sable, and Wila can pick up some plates and napkins at Arrow." Penny handed over a ring of keys with the new café's logo dangling from the set.

"Thanks for volunteering me," Wila growled.

"You want to trade?" Francine held out the keyring to Wila.

"No, just—" Wila pursed her lips for a moment. "Everyone needs to watch their backs if we've got more fallen angels running around in addition to regular old demons."

"Are you saying we shouldn't split up?" Penny frowned.

"Would you listen to me if I said we shouldn't?" But Wila's tone hold none of her usual snark. She was dead serious.

And every time a demon or fallen angel had approached Dani lately, she had been alone.

"Wila's right," Dani said. "And it will take more than one of us to kill one of the Fallen. I sliced through Buer. My scythe caused him enough pain to leave the D.A.'s body, but that was the extent of the damage."

"But Lucifer used one of my arrows to kill Crucifer," Penny pointed out.

"The prince has his own power," Wila said.

"And he managed to kill Crucifer using the combination," Francine added.

"I'll ride with Penny if it's all right with Silver," Wila said.

"Same with me, Dani, and Verde," Francine added.

It didn't take much convincing of their minivans/horses either. Sable and Scarlett shifted to their four-footed modes and galloped off together to wait at Java's Too.

When Dani climbed into Verde's driver seat, she got a sense of—well, the green minivan wasn't pleased. More like satisfaction that Dani was coming clean with her sisters. However, Francine remained quiet as they headed for the coffee shop and focused on her phone.

"Do you think I ran into Jesus on purpose?" Dani asked softly.

"Hmmm, no." Francine pulled herself from whatever she was doing. "No, I know you didn't hurt him on purpose." She sighed. "I'm more concerned about how you brought him back. And that's assuming it was your abilities as a Horseman and not some foreordained craziness."

"All I did was perform mouth-to-mouth while Wila did compressions," Dani protested.

"Did you look at his soul?"

Francine's gaze felt like a couple of lasers burning through Dani's skull, but she kept her attention on the road. She couldn't afford any more vehicular mishaps today.

"No," Dani admitted. "What did you see?"

"Coach Cordero was dead, Dani. I could see the energy bands holding his soul to his body dissolving. But the third time you breathed air into him, you fixed the bands because they were still partly there."

Dani considered Francine's words. Her friend had no reason to lie about which she saw, but Dani doubted she had anything to do with Jesus recovering so quickly. He was the Son of God after all.

"You sure it wasn't Jesus Himself?" Dani said. "He did heal Father McAvoy after he had that stroke the week before Thanksgiving. Or maybe it was God?"

"Have you asked Verde about her version of the incident?" Francine asked.

"Really?" Dani shot Francine a look. "When have I had a chance to talk to my horse since I hit Jesus?"

"Guess I'm not the only one who's developed an attitude since we became the Soccer Moms," Francine retorted.

"We said you developed a potty mouth," Dani pointed out as she turned into the Palace's parking lot. From the number of vehicles, Penny's café had a lot of post-shopping customers picking up a hot drink and a bite to eat before heading home to hide and/or wrap their presents. "Not an attitude. There's a difference."

"Pull into the drive-thru and ask for my order," Francine gestured at the specific lane.

"You already ordered?"

"Yes," Francine said. "We need to have that talk. I don't get why Buer focused on you, but we need to figure it out."

"Oh, brother." Dani groaned. "Wila reminded Crucifer of his wife. I really hope that's not the case here."

"Especially since Heath is back." Francine giggled. "So have you and he . . . you know?"

"That's a rude question!" Dani snapped, but she could feel her cheeks heat.

"I would have, too," Francine said. "It would kill me if I lost Neal, but if he came back to me, I'd hang on for dear life."

As Dani pulled up to the drive-thru window, she had to wonder. What if the only way to keep Heath was by sacrificing the universe?

Chapter 28

Scarlett and Sable were minivans once again and parked in front of Penny's new, soon-to-be café. Dani pulled Verde next to Sable, and she and Francine went inside.

The new place looked more like a jazz nightclub than a coffee shop. The walls were a cool light blue with electric art deco sconces. The small round tables were made of a dark wood, and each had four matching chairs currently stacked upside down on top. It would be a perfect little spot to end a romantic date for those who didn't indulge in alcohol. Maybe Dani could bring Heath here when Penny opened the place for business.

Dani and Francine had finished placing chairs on the floor from one of the tables when someone pounded on the door. Dani went to answer it, but it wasn't Penny and Wila with dinner.

A young woman with a wild mane of brunette hair and turquoise highlights stood outside. She was bundled in a parka the same color as her highlights, which set off her olive skin, with jeans and a pair of nice black leather boots. A matching large tote was slung over her shoulder. When she spotted Dani, she smiled and waved a mittened hand.

Dani cracked the door open. "I'm sorry, but Java's Too isn't open yet."

"Oh, I know." If anything, the woman's smile brightened a few more watts. "When I saw the lights on, I was hoping to catch Ms. Hudson."

There was something odd about the stranger. She definitely wasn't a demon, but Dani had the impression she wasn't quite human either. Dani took a look at her soul.

It wasn't a jewel like how a normal human appeared. No, it seemed to be a ball of swirling sea water, but it was connected to her body with the same ribbons of energy like a humans.

The young woman gasped and took a step back. "Th-the rumors are true. You're a Horseman!"

Dang it! Of course she could see Dani's soul, too.

"I'm sorry," Dani said. "I had to make sure you weren't a demon or a fallen angel."

"I beg your forgiveness, Lady Death." The woman inclined her head. "I am Jenna Descant. I heard Ms. Hudson, ur, Lady Pestilence planned to open an evening version of her coffee shop with music. I wanted to apply for the position of music director. I can run karaoke nights, act as a DJ, and line up local talent for live acts."

Francine joined them with a frown on her face. "First, you need to tell us what you are."

Of course, she'd been listening to the entire conversation.

The younger woman's confidence faltered. "I'm, well, uh, I'm a siren."

"A siren?" Dani cocked her head. If she hadn't looked at Jenna's soul, she would have assumed Jenna was feeding them a truckload of cow cookies. "Aren't your people a saltwater species?"

A bit of the siren's confidence returned. "Actually, we can live anywhere there's storms, rocks, and a large body of water. My great-great-grandmother immigrated to Chicago from Algeria in the late eighteen-hundreds."

"Do you have a resumé or something with your contact information for Ms. Hudson?" Francine asked.

"Yes, ma'am." Jenna fished a folder from her tote and pulled a piece of paper from the folder. "Here's my resumé. My phone number is the best way to get a hold of me."

Dani took the paper. "May we have two copies? Both Ms. Hudson and her manager will interview you if they haven't found someone already."

"Do you mind if I ask the name of the manager?" Jenna handed another copy of her resumé to Dani. "In case, she calls first."

"Valerie Simmons," Dani said.

Jenna bobbed her head. "Thank you for your time." She turned and strode toward a cute little electric blue VW Bug.

Once she climbed in and drove away, Dani relaxed. "Do you think she was telling the truth about being a siren?"

"You tell me," Francine said. "You're the one who looked at her soul."

"It definitely wasn't a human soul." Dani closed the door and locked it. "I never thought mythological creatures would show up on our doorstep."

"Really?" Francine grinned. "We fought Lucifer, you're having sex with your resurrected husband, and Jesus Christ coaches our kids' soccer team. I'm just surprised she wasn't one of the Greek Muses."

"That's a little sacrilegious." Dani shook her head as they walked back to the table they'd cleared.

"Said one of the Four Horseman to another."

"Soccer Moms," Dani automatically corrected.

It was over a half hour after Jenna left before Penny and Wila arrived with dinner.

"Papa Mario's was insane tonight," Wila complained as she shrugged off her coat.

"It's almost Christmas," Penny responded. "Everyone's too busy to cook."

Dani and Francine filled them in on Jenna's visit while they dished out the pizza and salads.

"A siren, huh?" Penny took a bite of pizza and chewed. After she swallowed, she said, "As long as she doesn't seduce the customers. I'm fine with it."

"Doesn't it bug you fairytale creatures are showing up?" Wila blurted.

"Depending on someone's point-of-view, we've had fairytale creatures trying to take our businesses, invading our houses, and attempting to kill us for nearly three months now." Penny sipped her coffee.

"What is wrong with you?" Dani demanded. "All of you? You're acting like other deities exist. What happened to the First Commandment?"

"And that's coming from the Fourth Horseman after she ran over Christ earlier today." Francine smirked.

"Soccer Mom," Dani said in unison with Penny and Wila.

"What did you want to talk about?" Francine stabbed a forkful of veggies in her salad bowl.

Dani gulped her double mocha. Time to come clean, but it meant admitting she hadn't been straight with her sisters.

"Buer isn't the first fallen angel to approach me about cutting a deal."

"Well, duh." Francine rolled her eyes. "Crucifer—"

"Approached me at Arrow." Wila's eyes narrowed as she turned back to Dani. "Who and when?"

"Lucifer sent a demon to set up the meet while I was on my way home Thursday night." Dani stared at her plate while her guilt sipped on her stomach acid. "I spoke with him Friday morning."

"What did he want?" Penny asked.

"He wants us to join forces and allow the Apocalypse to continue." Dani took another sip of her mocha. "He said it was the only way for him to go home and for Heath to stay with me. Then he added if I didn't believe him, I needed to ask Jesus."

"Is that what the fight between you and Coach Cordero was about on Friday morning?" Worry filled Francine's face. "He knew you talked to Lucifer?"

"Yeah, to both questions," Dani mumbled.

"What did Coach Cordero say to you?" Penny asked.

Dani's eyes stung. "If we stop the Apocalypse, all the dead go back to their graves."

Wila let loose a stream of curses that would blistered the ears of every priest currently in Oakfield. She jumped out of her chair and paced, her fists punching at the air.

"You put any holes in anything in my café, and so help me, I'll whack you with your sword," Penny threatened.

"Oh, sweetie." Francine reached over and hugged Dani, which actually helped a little. "You should have told us. That's an awful thing to carry for the last two days."

Wila stalked back to the table. "Wait a minute. What about the demon in Joey at Andy's offices?"

"Another messenger demon waited for me at the entrance to my subdivision after we did the PSA." Dani grabbed a piece of pizza from the box. Suddenly, she was starving. "After the incident with Joey, I killed the demon rather than listen to it."

"Smart move." Wila dropped back on her chair.

"Except I ended up with Lucifer and five demons in my backyard at three in the morning." Dani bit into the slice of pepperoni and extra cheese. "He said he didn't send the demon who possessed Joey. He claims there's someone else behind the scenes who wants to see the world destroyed."

Penny leaned back in her chair. "Does he think it's Coach Cordero?"

"He says he doesn't know," Dani said around a mouthful of pizza. "But he doesn't think so. He said it wasn't the Kid's style."

"He is the Prince of Lies." Wila grimaced.

"But Edward says demons prefer to use truth to manipulate humans," Penny said.

Francine tossed her fork in her remaining salad and pushed the bowl back. "You could say the same thing about Coach Cordero and the Vatican taskforce."

Dani swallowed. "How did you find out about my argument with Jesus?"

"Karen told me." Francine shrugged. "It's not like there's any secrecy at Saint Michael's right now."

I don't like this," Wila said. "We have no idea who's manipulating us or why. Maybe we need to assume everyone is until proven otherwise."

"And what do I tell my son if to save the world in the end, I have to send his father back to his grave?" Dani asked.

The other three Soccer Moms looked at each other, and for the first time since Dani met them, none of the women had a clue.

Chapter 29

Dani felt a little better after confessing her secrets to her sisters. Even her minivan/horse seemed pleased she'd come clean with the other Soccer Moms. Dani hated missing dinner with Mark, but tonight's session with the other Soccer Moms was a necessity. Besides, she already texted Mark to raid the cash in the cookie jar and order pizza for anyone who was at the house.

Penny hadn't said anything about Justine being at the Elante house though. Dani tapped the button for voice control. "Call Penny."

A second later, Penny said, "Don't tell me you forgot something at Java's Too."

"No," Dani replied. "Mark had asked if Justine could come over this afternoon. In the chaos of the accident, I forgot. Did she ask you and Gene if it was okay?"

"Yeah, she mentioned it. Laura bought her a video game, claiming she was making up for the last two Christmases." Penny chuckled. "Edward had a hissy fit. He claimed Laura was implying he couldn't buy his own granddaughter appropriate gifts. Anyway, let me call Gene and check. Call you back in two."

Dani braked to a stop at a red light. She wasn't sure exactly how she felt about Justine and Mark's budding attraction. To her, Justine was still the little tomboy who played trucks with her son. A glimmer of sadness hit her. The kids were growing up too fast.

Two minutes later, Penny called back as promised. "Yes, Justine is at your house right now. You want me to swing by and pick her up?"

"No, if the kids are having fun, I'll bring her home later."

"You sure?" There was a hint of worry in Penny's voice.

"Girl, this is the most normal thing that's happened with my family over the last two days." Dani laughed. "I'm going to take it as the win it is."

"If you're sure?"

"If Mark read my text, he already ordered pizza for the family and demon hunters," Dani said. "But if not, I'll make sure she has some dinner before I bring her home."

"All right," Penny said tentatively. "We'll be home for the rest of the night."

"You hope." Dani laughed again. "See you later."

As she tapped the control to end the call, she realized she hadn't said anything about the angels hanging around Saint Michael's or her house. Taking Justine home would give her the opportunity to check out Penny's house for any extra visitors. Not to mention, it would be better to relay this news in person.

No surprises waited for her when she pulled into her subdivision. Only the handful of angels sat on her roof when she guided Verde into the garage. The craziness of the day caught up with Dani as she pushed the button to turn off the engine. Verde sent an image of Dani going to bed.

She patted the dashboard of the minivan/horse. "That sounds like an excellent idea, girl. Hopefully, we can both get a good night's sleep for once."

Verde answered by sending snoring sounds.

Dani chuckled and climbed out of the driver's seat. By the time she reached the door to the kitchen, she wondered if the couch was a better idea. Raucous laughter and shouts came from the living room.

But Mom sat at the kitchen table with a scowl on her face and her arms crossed. For an instant, guilt washed through Dani. She promised to spend time with Mom, but the insanity of the last couple days had interfered with her best intentions.

Despite her fatigue, she smiled. "Hey, Mom." She gestured at the two remaining pizza boxes on the table. "Is there any left?"

"Yes," Mom bit out.

Uh-oh. Something had definitely crawled up Mom's butt. Dani hung up her coat and retrieved a plate from the cupboard before she sat across the table from Mom and grabbed a slice of double pepperoni.

"I thought you were in jail."

"Is that what's bugging you?" Dani got up and retrieved a can of grapefruit-flavored sparkling water from the refrigerator. "I was at the police station for questioning because I accidentally hit Coach Cordero. I wasn't in a cell. And I'm damn lucky the coach is okay other than a few stitches."

"Is that why Mark has a girlfriend?" Mom said in a low, nasty tone. "Because you are too busy at the *policía* to pay attention to your son's friends?"

Ah, crap. Mom only slipped into Spanish when she was truly pissed off. Dani sat down, open the tab, and took a sip before she addressed Mom's crazy.

"Mark and Justine have been friends since they were in first grade," Dani said. "She's been at our house hundreds of times and vice versa. You insisted the Hudsons come to your house for Thanksgiving after Laura's death because you said they shouldn't be alone for their first major holiday without her. So what's really wrong?"

"I caught them kissing," Mom hissed.

Dani kept her own emotions in check only by sheer force of will. Mom can and did blow things out of proportion, as shown by Carmen's broken arm.

"Kissing where?"

"In the living room." Mom gesture at the doorway to the aforementioned area.

Dani took another sip of flavored water to stop herself from screaming at her mother. "I meant did she kiss him on the cheek."

"Well, yes." Mom blushed.

"They are only twelve. If they aren't kissing on the lips—"

"My friend Esmerelda had a baby when she was thirteen!"

Dani heard this story too many times when she was growing up, but she never understood the context until she hit her teen years herself. "Because her parents were stupid enough to let a twenty-one year old man date their twelve-year-old daughter!"

"I thought I heard you, sweetheart." Heath strode into the kitchen with an empty plate. "Did you leave me some pizza?"

Mom clamped her jaws shut. Dani was beginning to see what her sisters saw in her mother. And that was the weird thing. If Dani kept her meetings with Lucifer secret, her mom would have lectured her mercilessly. The other Soccer Moms had accepted her confession with only a few questions to clarify a few points. Not even Wila bitched her out for doing something stupid.

"There's plenty of pizza, sweetheart." Dani smiled at Mom. "And you might want to run out and buy some condoms in case Justine spends the night. Mom's a little worried about Mark knocking up his best friend.

"Uhhhh." Heath looked at Mom and back at Dani. "What am I missing here?"

Mom shoved back her chair and rose. "You need to read your Bible and beg forgiveness from God for disrespecting your own mother."

"Mom, I ran over Jesus Christ this morning," Dani snapped. "If the Lord was going to strike me down for anything, it would have been that."

Mom's mouth fell open, and her whole body shook. Finally, she closed her mouth with a click of her teeth and stomped out of the kitchen.

Heath stared at Dani. "I've never heard you talk back to your mom. Ever."

"I'm sorry—"

"No, sweetie." He grinned at her. "You've needed to stand up for yourself for a long time." He bent over and kissed her forehead. "And I'm sorry for not respecting the fact you've had to do that on your own since I died. However, is Coach Cordero really, uh—?"

"Yes," Dani murmured.

"That explains why you freaked out," he said. "But it was an accident, sweetheart. And God knows it was."

"But—" She tilted her head to look at him. His head dipped, and his lips met hers. The kiss was as passionate as their first one all those years ago. And she wasn't sure she could literally trade him for all of the world.

Chapter 30

"Oh, gross!"

Dani pulled back from Heath and glared at Mark.

Justine stood behind him and smirked. "Dude, chill." She elbowed him in the ribs. "Parents do mushy stuff."

"But-but not my parents!" Mark appeared as if he were about to get sick.

Dani looked up at Heath. "And now you know why I haven't dated since your accident."

Father Rodriguez and Ellen, one of the new demon hunter trainees, entered the kitchen.

"Wait until you're older, little dude." Ellen ruffled Mark's hair. "You'll change your mind about kissing."

Mark's cheeks flushed a brilliant rose color, but Dani wasn't sure if he was embarrassed by Ellen's gesture or by wanting to kiss Justine. And she wasn't about to ask her son in front of so many witnesses.

"Senorita!" Father Rodriguez shot her an appalled look. "You are a representative of the Church! You do not encourage children to sin against the Lord!"

"Calm down, Father," Dani shook her head. "No one is encouraging anyone to sin."

"Senora Olivia is right," Father Rodriguez said. "People in this century are far too permissive with themselves and their children."

"I wouldn't take my mother as a paragon of virtue," Dani replied. "Ask her when she got married and when my brother Marty was born. He was a healthy eight pounds for allegedly being born three months early."

The priest stared at her while everyone else, including the two twelve-year-olds, snickered. Dani stared calmly back at Father Rodriguez.

Finally, the priest said softly, "Honor thy father and mother."

"Thou shalt not bear false witness," she calmly replied. "Father, I'm not looking for an argument, but a little humility when you've screwed up goes a long way. I screwed up with my sisters this week, and I had to be honest with them tonight and fix things. Mom wants to pretend she never screws up, and the weird thing is if she admitted her faults, I would love her more for acknowledging her sins and trying to be a better person."

She gestured toward Mark. "I've tried to teach my son to be kind and respectful, but he's as human as I am."

"I'm not sure about that these days," he mumbled under his breath.

Dani ignored Mark's comment. She had enough of her own concerns over what she was becoming. "The point being, he's going to make the occasional mistake." She smiled at him. "But I will always love you, Mark, and I hope you do what you have to in order to correct that occasional mistake."

Father Rodriguez nodded. "You're words are wise, Lady Death. I see why our Lord chose you as one of His Horsemen."

"Soccer Mom," everyone else in the kitchen, including Heath, said in unison.

A hint of a smile quirked the corners of the priest's mouth. "Forgive me for my misstatement."

Dani pushed to her feet. As much as Father Rodriguez's self-righteousness irritated her at times, he was right about one thing. She needed to talk with Mom.

"Don't clear the dishes," Dani said. "I'll be back to finish my pizza." She walked through the living room and up the stairs. This was going to be hard, but not as hard as losing Heath. Deep down, losing a parent was expected. It was the cycle of life after all. Losing a husband before she reached thirty had made her question a lot of things, including the plan of the Almighty.

Dani sucked in a deep breath and knocked on the door of the guest room. There was no answer. She considered going back downstairs.

Which is exactly what the old Dani would have done. Don't rock the boat. Don't cause a fuss. Be a good little girl. And where had that gotten her?

She knocked again. A faint "Come in" came through the door, so she opened it.

Mom sat at the foot of the twin bed, the one Dad had bought for the nights when Marty did something stupid and one of his wives had kicked him out for the night.

Or the week.

"Hey, can we talk?" Dani murmured.

"About my many sins?" Except there was no bite in Mom's words.

Dani sat next to Mom, but she didn't try to touch her. "You heard me?"

"I was about to come downstairs to apologize to you," Mom said. "I—I didn't realize you knew—"

"Mom, I was a business major before I got pregnant with Mark." Dani laid her left hand on Mom's right. "I can count. And it's not like you and Dad weren't in love."

Mom sniffed before she looked at Dani. "That was the problem. We weren't."

"Oh." Dani wasn't sure what to say. One thing she thought was truth broke.

Mom patted Dani's left hand with her left. "By the time we conceived you, your father and I had grown to love one another. But I sometimes wonder if Martin isn't cursed with our sins."

"What are you talking about? You wouldn't be the first couple who had a condom break on them."

"I—made love to Carlos out of revenge."

"Revenge against who?"

"You don't know them." Mom seemed lost in the past for a moment. "My boyfriend at the time and your father's girlfriend cheated on us." She emitted an odd chuckle. "Ironically, discovering their infidelity is how I met your father."

"Mom, you were eighteen," Dani said. "Hormones can seriously mess with a teenager's cognitive abilities."

"That's no different than saying the devil made me do it."

Dani laughed. "He'd be the first to say he doesn't make a human being do anything against their will."

Mom froze. "Have-have you—"

"We've run into him a few times." Dani shrugged. "One of the hazards of my new job. You don't want to know what we did to Courtney Lasser's house the first time we battled him."

Mom shook her head. "I don't know how you do what you do, Daniella. I would cower in fear if I had to face the Devil himself and his demons."

"Actually, I can do it because of you." Dani smiled at her. "I just thought what would Mom do, and I knew you wouldn't tolerate Lucifer's shit for one moment."

"Language, young lady." But Mom smiled back even as she said it.

Dani couldn't stop her own trembling, but Mom would be honest with her no matter how much the words might hurt.

"M-Mom, what if the only way to stop the Apocalypse is for me to return you and all the other resurrected to their eternal sleep?"

Mom cupped Dani's face in both of her hands. "If it meant protecting you and your brother and allowing you the life you were meant to lead, then yes, I would do what I have to."

Dani swallowed hard. "I don't know if I could do that."

"Because of Heath?"

Dani nodded.

Mom sighed. "I can't tell you what to do, but if Heath cares anything at all for Mark, he'll understand why you must do this." She kissed Dani's forehead. "And for the record, I understand, and I do not blame you. I'm sorry, so, so sorry, the Lord put this much weight on you, my little one."

Dani's own tears cut loose, and Mom held her for a very long time.

Chapter 31

Once Dani could finally compose herself, she went to her own bedroom, closed the door, and locked it. Outside her window, two angels perched in the oak tree. She closed the blinds before she sat on her bed and stared at her phone for a few moments. Then she started dialing.

Once all her sisters were connected on a conference call, she started with the subject she'd forgotten to mention when they met earlier.

"Angels?" Wila said. "You mean the heavenly variety?"

"Yes, but I mean how they're described in the Old Testament," Dani replied. "All feathers and eyeballs. Not the blond kids in white robes with wings."

"I haven't seen anything like that," Francine added.

"Check my roof when you bring Justine home." Penny didn't sound pissed.

Exactly.

"Look, I'm sorry I keep forgetting them," Dani said. "Honestly between the time Verde and I pulled into the garage until I looked out my bedroom window a moment ago—"

"Maybe they have some effect on humans," Francine suggested. "Maybe you aren't supposed to remember them when you're not Death. We could have seen them, too, but we can't recall."

"According to most Biblical accounts, these are Watchers," Penny said. "Maybe it doesn't matter because we're supposed to lead the fighting angels."

"Which brings me to another issue. I think I know how to stop the Apocalypse," Dani blurted.

Silence ruled for a ten long seconds before Wila asked, "How?"

"I need to put the resurrected folks back in their graves." Another long silence followed Dani's statement.

"That's why Lucifer has been trying to cut a deal with you and keeping the rest of us out," Penny said.

"I believe so," Dani murmured.

"Do you realize what you're saying, girl?" Wila protested. "Laura, Gammy, Olivia, Heath. We lose all of them."

"They aren't supposed to be here," Francine said softly.

"You don't have a say in this," Wila spat. "You don't have someone at home you'll lose if Dani does this."

"I dare you to say that to Rose's face," Francine bit back.

More guilt raged through Dani. Francine's daughter Brittany was treating resurrected Rose Dorchester like the little sister she never had. Of course, Francine and her family would be affected by laying the dead back to rest, too.

"Would you prefer I raise the rest of the dead?" Dani asked. "The aid organizations are running out of money, supplies, and places to house those who don't have living family to take them in or living family who can't take them in."

"All our arguing is moot," Penny said. "The Sixth Seal could break at any moment. We're talking catastrophic earthquakes. Add in the landslides and tsunamis generated by those quakes. We're talking massive loss of life and enormous suffering for the survivors, living and resurrected."

"How do you think the demon hunters are going to handle this?" Francine said. "As far as the resurrected folks are concerned, they are here to fight on Heaven's side."

"You think they might rebel if Dani tries to put them back in their graves?" Penny said.

"Some of them will," Wila murmured. "Not to mention, more than half of them flew here from Europe. Where do we put them? Also, who's going to watch our backs while Dani's putting everyone to rest? She's going to need our help to do it. The demons and humans who want the Apocalypse to happen aren't going to stand idly by while we do this."

"There's angels who feel the same way," Dani added. "They want the Apocalypse to happen, too."

"That would explain the angels all over your roof," Penny said.

"What about Coach Cordero?" Wila asked. "Which way will He jump?"

"He's said from the beginning He picked us as the Soccer Moms because He knew we would do our damnedest to save the world." Francine sounded like she was on the verge of crying. "That means we need to watch out for our living children."

"So that's it, isn't it?" Dani's eyes watered, and she sniffed back the snot clogging the back of her throat. "We have to choose between our living family and our resurrected family."

"W-we grieved once for those we lost." Penny muffled a sob, but it was still obvious with Dani's enhanced senses as Death. "We were given a very special second chance to talk to them and hug them once again. No one can take that away from us."

"All right." Dani swiped away the tears that escaped and trickled down her cheeks. "Let me bring Justine home. I'll swing by Francine and Wila's places and check for angels."

"Drive by the Cordero place, too," Wila suggested. "If you need back up, girl, don't waste time using your phone. You have Verde yell for our horses."

"Okay." Dani chuckled weakly. "Let's see how fast I can get the kids into the minivan."

Her bedroom doorknob rattled as she signed off on the call. Next came a knock.

"Sweetheart?" Heath knocked again.

She rushed over and unlocked the door. He took one look at her face and pulled her into his arms. She sunk into his embrace. God, she didn't want to lose this feeling again.

"You want to tell me about it?" He whispered against her hair.

"I need to take Justine home first," she replied. "Once we're home and Mark is in bed, I'll tell you what's going on."

And it was going to kill her when she did.

Chapter 32

In the end, Heath and Mark came along with Dani and Justine in Verde. The kids sat in the back seats, rattling on about scores, best weapons, and the number of dead zombies from the video game Justine had received from her grandmother. In the driver seat, Dani glanced at Heath next to her. He didn't seem bothered by the zombie talk. She sucked in a deep breath and tried not to worry about it.

When she turned down the Hudsons' street, sure enough, angels perched in the twin oaks in the front yard of Gene and Penny's home. Dani parked along the curb behind an older model truck belonging to one of the new demon hunter trainees. She could hear Edward and the new recruit talking in the back yard. Instead of leaping out of Verde, Justine remained buckled in her seat.

Dani turned to look at her. "What's wrong, sweetie?"

Fear distorted the girl's features.

"You can tell my mom, Justine," Mark murmured. "She's not going to think you're crazy."

After a long pause, Justine blurted, "C-can you see what's in the trees, Dani?"

"You mean the Watcher angels?" At Justine's nod, Dani added, "Yes, I can see them, too."

Relief spread through the girl, and she relaxed. "I-I thought I was imagining things. I don't want to end up in the hospital like Dad did after he was possessed."

"You're not going to end up in the psychiatric ward," Dani assured her. Thankfully, Heath and Mark kept their mouths shut on the topic. "I can see them, too. I made the mistake of assuming your mom could see them like me, but she does know about them. It's safe to talk to her about it."

Justine nodded. "I just . . ."

"Don't want to be different than the other kids?" Dani said.

"Yeah."

"Adults don't want to be different than the other adults either, so I understand the feeling." Dani unlatched her seatbelt. "Heath, I'll be right back. I want to walk Justine into the house."

"I can do that." Mark hit the release on his own seatbelt.

Dani opened her mouth to protest, but she didn't want to hurt her son's feelings.

Heath picked up on her hesitation. "Mark, stay here with me."

"But—"

Heath turned to look at Mark. "You got your squirt bottles with holy water right? I forgot mine. It's your mom's way of trying to spare my feelings."

"Your dad is kind of new at the whole demon thing," Justine whispered.

"All right, I'll watch Dad for you, Mom," Mark said.

"Thank you," Dani murmured. Heath winked at her, and she couldn't help smiling. "I'll leave the engine running to keep you two warm."

While she slid out of the driver seat, Justine exited through the sliding side door. The girl didn't look as nervous as she had a moment before her confession, but she wasn't totally at ease either. Even Dani was starting to wonder at the Watchers' real reason for hanging outside the Soccer Moms' homes.

Justine unlocked the front door, practically leapt across the threshold, and yelled, "I'm home."

"Hey, sweetie." Gene appeared in the doorway to his office. "Did you have a good time?"

"Yeah, I did." Justine shot a nervous glance at Dani before she added, "Where's Mom? I need to talk to you both."

Gene shot a look at Dani, searching her face for a clue. She shrugged. It was Justine's tale to tell. He turned back to his daughter. "She's reading in the family room."

Justine hung up her coat, but Dani kept hers on. She didn't want to leave Mark and Heath alone any longer than she had to. They followed Gene down the main hallway.

Laura sat at the kitchen table with a notepad. Her headset was connected to her cell phone. From her conversation, she was guiding a Vatican taskforce team through what sounded like a particularly nasty exorcism.

The trio continued through the kitchen into the family room. Penny was curled up on one end of the couch with her tablet. She looked up at them and smiled. "Hey, sweetie!"

Justine rushed into her mother's arms, and her words spilled out between sobs. "I'm sorry. I should have told you. I didn't want to lie. But I don't want to be crazy!"

Penny whispered calming words to her daughter.

Gene leaned closer to Dani. "What happened?"

"Give her a chance to tell you," Dani whispered back. "You need to take care of your family. I need to take care of mine tonight. Tell Penny I'll call her in the morning."

Dani left the room as Gene joined his family on the couch. She waved to Laura who was still on the phone.

She reached the front door when Laura called out softly, "Dani. Wait. Please."

She paused until Laura reached her.

"Justine can see the Watchers, can't she?" Laura shoved her hands in her jeans pockets.

Dani nodded. "You can, too?"

"All of us dead can." A wry smile tilted Laura's mouth. "We didn't want to scare anybody. The demons are bad enough. It makes sense why you can see them, but Justine?"

"The cancer," Dani said softly. Crap. Gene and Penny probably hadn't told his parents about the night of Justine's seizure.

The younger Hudsons had been such a huge help after Heath's death. When Justine was diagnosed with leukemia nine months later, Dani and Mark would bring dinner over on the weekends. But three months into chemo, Justine had a seizure in the middle of one of those meals. Again, Dani shouldn't be the one telling Laura.

"Does Penny know about you being able to see the angels?" Dani asked.

Laura shook her head. "Gene would have a fit, and she tells him everything."

"They need to know so they can help Justine deal with this." Dani pulled the older woman into a fierce hug. "Go take care of your family, Laura."

She turned and left the house. Singing came from above her. When she reached the driver-side door, she looked up, and the music abruptly stopped. At least a dozen new angels perched on the Hudsons' roof and the surrounding oaks.

Despite her faith, Dani had had enough of the Watchers. "I don't know if you're trying to scare Justine on purpose, but it's a lousy way to treat an innocent kid. I hope you guys realize that if you're here to make sure the Apocalypse happens, I've got a scythe with your names on the wrong end of the blade. You feel me?"

They remained silent.

She climbed into her minivan/horse and shut the door.

Heath watched her, but he also remained silent.

"Were you talking to the angels, Mom?" Mark asked.

"Yes." She buckled her seatbelt.

"Is Justine okay?"

"She will be," Dani replied as she pulled away from the curb.

"This is because of the time she had that seizure and stopped breathing, isn't it?" Mark said.

Of course he wasn't stupid. None of the Soccer Mom's kids were. She angrily swiped at the tear that escaped.

"I'm afraid so, baby," Dani said.

He remained silent for a few blocks before he added softly, "I just wanted to help her."

"You did, baby. A lot more than you realize." Dani sighed. "I need to drive around town for a quick angel survey. You guys up for that, or should I drop you off at home first?"

"I'd like to see how much Oakfield has changed," Heath said.

"Can we get milkshakes at Wilson's?" Mark asked.

"When it's this cold?" Heath said.

"Hey, I don't know how many more shakes I will have in my life, and I'm trying to work my way through all the flavors!" Mark protested.

"Thanks for the vote of faith, dude." Dani said.

"Mom, I'm counting on you and the other Soccer Moms to stop the Apocalypse." Mark patted her shoulder. "It's why I'm leaving the orange cream shake for last."

Another tear trickled down Dani's cheek. The orange cream flavor wasn't going to make a difference. Mark was going to hate her for the rest of his life for taking away his father after he just got Heath back.

Chapter 33

The tour around town didn't help Dani's mood. Not only were angels camped out at Francine, Wila, and the Corderos' houses, they flocked at all the places of worship, including the tiny storefronts housing an independent Christian congregation and a Pagan group in a strip mall. When Dani pulled into their subdivision, nearly every oak had a pair or more angels.

She took it as a sign the Soccer Moms were running out of time.

Mom was asleep when they got home, so Mark stuck her plain vanilla shake in the freezer. Ellen appreciated her banana shake, but Father Rodriguez wasn't quite sure what to make of his chocolate marshmallow shake when Dani handed it to him.

"It's flavored ice cream mixed with milk so it's drinkable," Dani said.

"What's ice cream?"

Crap. She'd totally forgot he died nearly five hundred years ago. She didn't keep a lot of junk food in her house.

"Trust her, Padre," Ellen said. "Suck the straw like the one on the juice box Rose had you try."

"But this straw is so much bigger," the priest protested.

"You liked hot chocolate when I make it for you, right?" Mark said. "This is the cold version."

"Oh." Father Rodriguez took a long pull through the straw, swallowed, and grinned. "It's very good. I think I like cold chocolate even better. However, you should finish your treat, Marcos. You need a good night's sleep before we go to Mass."

Mark turned to Dani with a pleading expression.

"Father, I already told Mark we could skip Mass tomorrow," she said. "It's been a very long, stressful two days already for my family, and we need a break."

Instead of the fight she expected from the priest, he nodded. "I did not mean to intrude on your parental authority, Lady Death. I fall into many of my old habits—" Grief and pain flashed across Father Rodriguez's face before he regained control. "I will patrol the block before I finish the milkshake. Thank you for thinking of me, Marcos." The priest set his milkshake on the table, grabbed his coat, and headed for the back door.

Ellen muttered an obscenity under her breath. "You wanna stick his milkshake and mine in the fridge for us, please. I'll go keep an eye on the padre." She grabbed her own coat and trudge out into the cold night.

"What happened?" Heath murmured.

"Father Rodriguez was burned at the stake by the Inquisition," Mark said bitterly.

"That would make him . . ." Heath's eyes widened.

"And he's not the oldest of the resurrected," Dani said gently. "The world's kind of screwed up right now."

"No foolin,'" he muttered.

While Ellen and Father Rodriguez ostensibly patrolled around the neighborhood, the Elantes finished their milkshakes while watching a sitcom episode. Mark announced he was going to bed, but Dani didn't miss him grabbing his phone on the way upstairs.

Maybe she was worrying over nothing. He had no one else to talk to other than Justine, Derek, and Brittany. None of his other friends understood what it was like to have a Horseman for a mom. And worse, the other three kids still had both parents around and alive.

"You did a great job raising him," Heath murmured. "I'm so sorry I wasn't here for you both."

"Stop apologizing." She snuggled against his chest. He wrapped his arm around her. She needed to tell him the truth, but she didn't want to lose this moment.

"Can I ask what's going on with the police?"

"My questioning was a con job by the fallen angel possessing the Oakfield D.A." She sighed. "It's not just demons pouring into town. We're seeing a huge uptick in angels."

"That explains the Soccer Mom meeting this evening." He kissed her forehead. "You and your friends have any bright ideas on how to stop the Apocalypse?"

She should tell him. She really should. But she found she couldn't.

"We're working on it," she said. "We know we're running out of time. But we're looking at the potential of a lot of blowback from everyone, including the Vatican taskforce, over our plan."

"You need to put us resurrected folks back in our graves," he stated flatly.

She pulled away from his comforting chest and stared at her husband. The husband she had wished desperately would come back to her. And now that he was here, she had to send him back.

"Yes." She waited for the rage. The recrimination. The blame for the unfairness of the entire situation.

"What will happen to Mark if we all go back to our graves?"

"Nothing." Dani stared at her hands clutched together on her lap. "It will end the Apocalypse."

"I don't suppose you can make an exception for me."

She looked up at him. A wry half-smile tilted his mouth.

"It's all or nothing," she said. "I can't break the rules, honey. If I do, I break the universe, and our son will cease to exist." She wasn't lying. She knew the truth deep in her gut. Had known since the first time she saw a demon consume the soul of a resurrected.

Heath's half-smile faded. "Then there's no choice. Mark's well-being takes priority."

"Please don't think I don't love you," she choked out the words.

"If I were in your position, I would make the same decision, sweetheart." He reached over and covered her hands with his. "Would you hate me for making that choice?"

Her eyes burned. "God, no! How could you think that?"

"You told me to stop saying I'm sorry," he said. "Then stop doing your version of it to me, sweetheart." He gently wiped the tears from her cheeks. "We had two nights together we weren't supposed to have. We still have tonight, right?"

She nodded.

"Then let's make the most of tonight." He pulled her close. His kiss was as sweet and tender as the first night they made love.

Her sisters were right. She had put her life in hold since the night of Heath's accident. Yet, time marched on. She needed to seize what she had in front of her while she could.

Dani drew back from Heath's kiss and cupped his cheeks. Stubble tickled her palms, and she smiled and asked him the same question she had all those years ago.

"Would you care to adjourn to my boudoir, Mr. Elante?"

"I thought you would never ask, Ms. Hernandez." He grinned.

They stood and held hands as they climbed the stairs to their bedroom.

Chapter 34

A weird squeaking woke Dani. It was followed by the glass cosmetic bottles rattling on their mirrored tray. Then she realized it was the bedframe making the squeaks as her phone jiggled to the edge of the nightstand. She caught the phone as it fell.

Just in time for the emergency alert to blare from the phone's speakers.

Heath bolted upright. "What the hell is going on?"

"Earthquake!" Following his bellow, Mark burst into their bedroom. "What do we do?"

Even though weak sunlight filtered through the curtains, the vibrations didn't slow. They grew worse. Outside, car alarms bleated. A crack formed on the ceiling. Downstairs, glass shattered.

More footsteps pounded up the stairs. "Mark, where are you?" Ellen shouted. A second later the demon hunter poked her head in the main bedroom. "Dani, get your family's butts downstairs!" She darted toward the guest bedroom and pounded on the door. "Mrs. Hernandez!"

"Mark, grab your shoes!" Dani scrambled out of bed and slipped on her own running shoes. Mark raced out of their bedroom. On the other side of the bed, Heath put on his own shoes.

Dani stood, and the floor shook. Together, she and Heath made their way out of the room.

"I got your mom," Heath said. "Get Mark."

Dani reached her son's room, and the shivering and shaking of the house faded.

"Is it over?" Mark stopped and looked around. The shelf holding his Lego sets had fallen. The couple of model planes hanging from the ceiling swayed on their wires. Books had tumbled off his desk.

"Let's go downstairs for now," she said.

Heath and Mom paused at the top of the stairs and looked around them.

"Was that it?" Mom asked. "Was that the Sixth Seal?"

"I don't think so," Dani murmured. "Everyone downstairs while I make some calls and some coffee." Together, they trooped downstairs.

When they reached the bottom of the stairs, Ellen was dragging the garbage can into the living room. "Everyone have footwear? There's quite a bit of broken glass down here."

A handful of family photos had been shaken from the hooks on the walls. Some of Mom's crystal menagerie had been knocked off their little display shelf. Only the mouse's golden tail had broke. The rest managed to land on the carpet. Dani set the critters on the end table.

"Get my gardening gloves, Ellen," she said. "They're hanging on the back porch. I don't want you to cut up your hands. The ER's going to be crazy enough as it is."

Dani headed into the kitchen for coffee to find Father Rodriquez crouching on the floor. He picked up pieces of mugs and what was left of the coffee maker's carafe.

"I apologize, Lady Death." The priest wore a forlorn expression. "I had retrieved your dishes to make coffee during Ellen's planned trip to buy pastries when the ground trembled. In my shock, I dropped everything."

"Don't sweat it, Father." Dani smiled gently at the priest. "If Ellen was planning on heading to The Bake Shoppe, I'll give her some money to pick up coffee for us at Java's Palace." When she grabbed for her purse, her phone sang "Nine to Five".

She sat down at the table and pressed the answer button. "Hey, Penny. How much is broken at your place with this morning's quake?"

"Three broken picture frames, a broken mirror, and one of the family room windows is cracked," Penny reported. "It's my heart that's the real problem."

"No trumpets yet, girl." Dani winced at the nasty look from Father Rodriguez. It was hard to believe he wasn't considered a proper priest back in his day.

"Laura said it was a four-six or a four-seven." Penny sighed. "She thinks it's a foreshock."

"The Lord's way of letting us know we're running out of time?" Dani pulled out her wallet. Crap. She forgot she gave all her cash to Heath yesterday for the pizza party at Rusty Rat's when she headed for the hospital.

"Yeah," Penny said. "From the description in Revelation, she thinks the main event will a nine-point or greater—shit!" Tires screeched in the background.

"Penny?" Dani's heart leapt into her throat. "Penny, answer me!"

"Sorry, didn't mean to scare you." Penny made a disgusted sound. "Traffic lights are out, and everyone seems to have forgotten how to drive when all the lights are blinking red."

"Where are you?"

"On my way to Java's Palace. The earthquake brought down a couple of trees at the campus. Unfortunately, one of them landed on Josie's car. Any damage at your place?"

"Same as you," Dani said. "Broken glass, including the pot to my coffee maker. Can I give you my credit card for an order? I've got a couple of tired demon hunters and a cranky Soccer Mom who desperately need some caffeine."

Penny chuckled. "It's on me. Text me your order."

"I can't—"

"Sweetie, let me do this small thing, "Penny murmured. "You're going to have to do the hard work."

"Thanks. I'll send Ellen over. Some of us need showers."

"We'll have your drinks ready when she gets to Java's," Penny assured her.

Dani signed off and started tapping in the list of drinks. "Can I talk you into trying a mocha, Father Rodriguez?"

"No, thank you." The priest dumped the smaller broken bits into the smaller trash can from the utility room. "I thought the coffee would make my heart explode. I shall continue to drink hot chocolate in the mornings."

"One hot chocolate it is." Dani grabbed her credit card, got up and headed into the living room with her phone to get everybody else's orders.

"Ellen, here's my card for The Bake Shoppe," Dani said. "Please get a half dozen chocolate Long Johns."

"That won't be enough—" the demon hunter started.

"That's just my order." Dani gestured to indicate her family. "Get everyone else's requests. What do you want at Java's Palace? Penny will have our drinks ready by the time you're done at The Bake Shoppe."

"A peppermint mocha, please. And thank you!" Ellen peeled off Dani's gardening gloves. "Here you go."

"Thanks," Dani said.

Mark dragged the vacuum into the room. Dani headed for the stairs.

"Daniella, where are you going?" Mom said.

Dani paused on the stairs and resisted the urge to roll her eyes. "I have not had a shower since Thursday morning. I need a shower."

"You should sweep the carpet—"

"Mom, Mark knows how to use the vacuum cleaner, and I promise not to use all the hot water. But frankly, I need five minutes to myself that does not involve kids, resurrected people, or demon hunters." Dani continued up the stairs, leaving silence behind her.

Chapter 35

Wrapped in towels, Dani stepped out of the main bath to find Heath sitting against the headboard of their bed. He looked up from the book he held. It was the thriller he'd been reading before the accident.

"Sorry for ruining your privacy." He grimaced. "The bedroom was safer for Olivia than if I stayed downstairs."

Dani's shoulders sagged. "I'm sorry for whatever she said."

"Are you joking?" He chuckled. "I wanted to cheer you on when you were telling her off, but I doubt it would have helped. However—" He put the bookmark on his current page. "I like the woman you've become."

"But Mom doesn't." She grimaced as she grabbed her bottle of lotion from her nightstand.

"You want some help with your back?"

She looked over her shoulder at him and smiled. "Yes, please."

Heath set his novel on his nightstand and scooted across the mattress. Dani flipped up the cap and squirted some lotion in his waiting palm. He untucked the ends of the bath towel to expose her torso and began smoothing lotion across her skin. She dispensed a dollop in her own hand, pressed the cap back in place, and rubbed lotion across her chest and belly.

"Mind if I ask a question?" he said.

"Sure."

"If it's been six years, why have you kept all my stuff?"

She froze. It was a question her sisters brought up once a year.

"Dani," he said softly. "The bookmark was exactly where I left it before

I drove into the city for that last business trip. All of my clothes are where I left them." He chuckled. "Except for the dirties in the hamper."

"Mom thought she was helping and washed everything, including the sheets." Dani concentrated on applying lotion to her arms. It was the only way she wouldn't cry.

"Sweetie—" He rested his hands on her shoulders. "I'm going to have to leave you again. It's not my first choice, but I'm so proud of you for making the world and all eight billion living people your priority. But I need to know you'll be okay."

She reached up and patted his hands. "I admit I was a mess after losing you the first time. The girls got me through it. They will do it again."

Her phone rang, and they both jumped.

Dani leaned over and grabbed her phone. She didn't recognize the number, but the last three digits were six-six-six. Damn, Lucifer had a warped sense of humor.

She pressed the answer icon. "What do you want?"

"It's time for you to make a decision, my dear Death," Lucifer purred. "Are you joining me, or are you siding with the Kid?"

"I don't see how I have much of a choice if I want to keep my husband," she said. "What do you want me to do?"

"I want you to kill the Kid and his wife."

Cold rushed through Dani. "No."

"No?" Lucifer actually sounded surprised.

"You heard me the first time," she spat. "I'm not committing fratricide for you."

"I can kill your family—"

"Let's be straight here," she interrupted. "You want Him dead, but you're afraid Daddy will strike you down if you do. If you want to be the big man in Heaven, maybe you should act like it. Otherwise, you wouldn't have so many of your cronies like Crucifer wanting to stab you in the back. Just like you did with them."

"You have no idea what you're talking about," he snapped.

"Then why were you so desperate to kill a fellow fallen angel?" she mocked. "If you want me to join you, Lucifer, you need to prove yourself to me." She ended the call and blocked the number before Lucifer could call her back.

"Was that really . . ." Heath stared at her.

"The devil himself? Yes."

"Who does he want you to kill?"

"Christ."

"Now is not the time for swearing at me," Heath protested.

"No." Dani laughed bitterly. "The Devil wants me to kill Jesus Christ."

"But you already killed him yesterday." Heath spread his hands in a warding off gesture. "Though technically, it was an accident."

"I know." She pressed the speed dial icon for Karen Longstreet's phone number. She caught the sounds of people at a meal until the new head of the U.S. demon hunters spoke.

"What's up, Dani?" Immediately, silence reigned on the other end of the line.

"Can you assign extra security on the Corderos?"

"Already did last night," Karen answered. "Just a sec. Neal's banishing the kids to the basement so Francine can join the conversation."

In the background, Brittany and Rose protested, but Neal had the last word by joining the kids downstairs in their game room.

"Okay, we're on speaker," Karen said.

"I just got a call from Lucifer." Dani repeated the conversation she had with the Devil.

"You think he'll try to kill Jesus and Maria?" Francine asked.

"If he wants my help, he might."

"But you sort of killed him yesterday," Karen said. "Are you sure his soul was disconnected then reattached? What if your power works like the demons, and you can't do anything to someone who has been resurrected?"

Francine swore. "That would put a major crimp in our plan to stop the Apocalypse."

"What plan?" Karen asked.

Heath motioned for Dani to mute her phone. "Test your plan on me."

Her heart pounded so hard it felt as if it would break through her ribs. "Sweetie—"

He grasped her free hand. "We knew you would need to do it eventually. If it works, I'm out of your way, and you can focus on your job. And Lucifer can't use me against you."

"H-how did you know he threatened you and Mark?"

"Because the only other time I've seen you this scared was the night we rushed Mark to the ER when he had that awful flu, and he was having trouble breathing." Heath gently squeezed her hand. "And the last thing I want is to hold you back." He smiled. "Besides, you're on a mission from God. All you need is your sunglasses."

Dani stared at him for a moment before she burst out laughing. "You are worse than Penny and Wila. And I'm really beginning to hate that movie."

She tapped the icon to unmute her phone. "You ladies feel like joining me at the Oakfield Cemetery?"

Chapter 36

Dani's stomach protested while she dressed and Heath changed into one of his other suits. Her phone buzzed, and she read the text from Francine. Penny, Laura, and Wila were joining their little expedition.

"You're going to need to talk to Mark," she murmured.

"I know." He fumbled with his tie. Maybe he wasn't as sure about this as he pretended.

"We don't have to—" she began.

He paused in his struggle with creating a proper knot. "Yes, we do. I'm not supposed to be here. We both know that. I don't want to hurt you or Mark again, but you need to know you can do this."

He sucked in a deep breath and unraveled his tie. Slowly releasing his breath, he created a perfect Windsor knot. "How's that?"

"You look very handsome." She smiled and gestured at her jeans and sweatshirt. "I feel a might under dressed."

"After you, my dear." He swept his arm to indicate her to proceed him down the stairs.

Dani steeled herself as she went downstairs.

As she hit the bottom step, Ellen entered with an armful on pink boxes. "Breakfast is here!" She stopped and stared at Heath. "You going to Mass after all, Mr. Elante?"

"No, I—"

"No!" Mark's voice cracked on the syllable, and he jumped up from the couch. "You can't leave us!"

Father Rodriguez and Mom rushed into the living room from the kitchen. Their attention switched from the shaking Mark to the dressed up Heath.

"Mark, don't be mad at your mom." Heath stepped closer to Mark, but he didn't try to touch him. "This was my idea."

"B-but you can't—" Mark's voice cracked again, but the last syllable ended on a sob.

"Daniella, what is going on?" Mom twisted a kitchen towel in her hands.

"I'm taking Heath back to his grave," Dani said. "The Devil just called me. He threatened to kill Heath. The only sure way to protect his soul is to send it back to Heaven."

Mom's mouth fell open, but the priest frowned.

"What happens if you put all us who were resurrected back in our graves?" Father Rodriguez asked. "Would it stop the Apocalypse?"

"I don't know for sure, Father," Dani said.

"But that's what you and the other Soccer Moms believe, correct?" he asked.

"We're not going to know for sure until I try to put someone back, but after what happened with Coach Cordero yesterday—" She shrugged. "If I can bring someone back from the dead, then I should be able to return a resurrected person to their grave."

The priest nodded thoughtfully. It wasn't the reaction she expected, but given the torture he went through at the end of his life, she could understand why the priest might want the peace of Heaven back.

"What if I volunteer in Heath's place?" he said.

"No!" Mark shrieked. "Mom, you can't kill anyone. I won't let you."

"I appreciate the offer, Father," Heath said. "But the Soccer Moms need you demon hunters—"

"And Marcos needs his father more," Father Rodriguez replied.

"Stop it, you two," Mom barked. "Just stop it." She stepped closer to Dani. "Is it true? If we go back to our graves, will it stop the Apocalypse?"

"We're not sure, but it's the only reason we can come up with to explain why Lucifer is trying so hard to recruit me to his side." Dani wished she hadn't said anything to any of the resurrected people in her home. The last thing she wanted was to hurt them or her son.

"Abuelita?" Mark looked at Mom with a stricken expression. "You'd leave me, too?"

"If it means saving you, then yes." A tremulous smile tilted her mouth. "It's the same reason your father volunteered, cupcake."

"But-but—" Mark's tears started falling in earnest. "If you have to go, please let me come with you. At least to the graveyard."

As much as Dani wanted to say no, she couldn't. Mark was hurting as much, if not more, than she was.

"Yeah, kid, you're going," Ellen bit out. "And so am I." The demon hunter glared at Dani. "You were afraid of the backlash from the resurrected, weren't you?"

"Yes." She lifted her chin. "Yes, we were."

Ellen shook her head. "Don't you get it? There's a reason the righteous dead are the ones that came back. They'd be the ones who would sacrifice themselves to save the world. And God choose you as Death because you could do the hardest thing of all. Send them back."

Chapter 37

Ellen handed one box of doughnuts to Mark and doled out the Elantes' coffee and hot chocolate while Mom changed into a good Sunday dress. Dani and her immediate family climbed into her minivan/horse while Ellen and Father Rodriguez followed in the demon hunter's ancient Saturn.

"I cannot argue with my last meal being Long Johns from The Bake Shoppe." Heath took a huge bite from his chocolate delicacy.

"How can you be happy about this?" Mark whined from behind Dani.

"This was what your mom craved when she was pregnant with you," Heath replied. "I'm surprised you're not eating Long Johns every day."

"Brittany's mom lightened up on her sweets rules." Mark groaned. "Francine now buys a couple of dozen Long Johns every day. We're all pretty sick of them after the last two months."

"Two dozen? Every day?" Heath said. "How is she not three hundred pounds?"

"Because she's Famine," Dani and Mark said at the same time.

"When she first became Famine, she unconsciously turned her power on herself to keep from harming the people around her," Dani added. "In a way, we all did."

Heath froze in place. "You killed yourself?"

"That's a sin, Daniella," Mom protested. "You'll never go to Heaven."

"I did it accidentally, Mom." Maybe putting Mom back in her grave wouldn't be as difficult as Dani thought it would be. "It's not like God gave us instruction manuals when He made us the Soccer Moms of the Apocalypse."

"What happened?" Heath asked.

"I was at Wila's for our girls' night—"

"Wila doesn't like being alone when Derek stays with his dad on Wednesdays," Mark volunteered.

"Where do you go on Wednesday nights?" Mom asked Mark.

"Since you died, Mom takes me over to the Hudsons' house," he said. "If Justine and I get our homework done, Gene takes us to the movies or bowling. In the summer, we go over to Brittany's house and swim while Neal and Gene have intense manly discussions about the proper way to barbeque."

"Why don't you go see Papa or Uncle Marty?" Mom asked.

"Mom's worried they're a bad influence on me because of their serial dating."

Dani didn't need to glance at the rearview mirror to feel Mom's glare boring into her skull.

"Daniella? You would keep Marcos from his own family?"

God help her, she couldn't stand Mom's sing-song voice, the one she used when she was mad but they were in front of witnesses. "Marty can't keep his pants zipped, and we both know it. He's got two different baby mamas, and maybe even three. I honestly question little Luca's paternity."

"Daniella!" Mom protested.

"And I have no question Dad was faithful to you while you were alive," Dani continued. "However, he's gone through more girlfriends than Marty has since you passed away."

"Would I be able to spend time with my own son on your girls' nights?" Heath asked.

Ouch. In ranting at Mom, Dani had accidentally stepped on her husband's feelings.

"If you were here, sweetie, I wouldn't be worried about other male influences." She flashed him a smile. "In fact, you could probably teach Gene and Neal a thing or two about proper grilling."

Heath chuckled. "I don't know. You know how stubborn gringos can be."

"Mom, can't you please make an exception?" Mark murmured in her ear.

Like she wasn't feeling terrible enough. Dani gritted her teeth and flipped the right turn signal. She guided Verde through the gates of the Oakfield Cemetery.

"Mom?" Mark urgently whispered.

She slammed on the brakes hard enough Verde squealed via the serpentine belt. She shifted into park and thumbed the buckle to release her seatbelt so she could turn in her seat and face her son.

"What about Justine?" she demanded.

Mark blinked. "What about her?"

"If we let the Apocalypse happen, if I don't return the dead to their graves, do you have any idea of what will happen?"

"The Bible says after the war, we all go to Heaven." The timidity in his voice was so unlike her son.

"What's going to happen during that war, Mark?" she pressed.

"I-I don't know."

"Penny, Francine, and Wila will have to unleash their powers on Earth," Dani said softly. "That means Justine's cancer will come back. We don't get to pick and choose who we affect."

Mark swallowed hard. Mom gaped at her. Even Heath remained completely still, the box of doughnuts forgotten in his lap.

"I-I didn't know," Mark whispered.

"I know, baby. I know." Dani squeezed her eyes shut to keep the tears from falling. "I tried to protect you from what we're facing. I keep forgetting how old you are. To me, you're still the tiny baby your dad and I brought home from the hospital. I should have been honest with you, but frankly, I wasn't being honest with myself. I'm sorry I wasn't honest with you either."

Mark reached out and squeezed her shoulder. "I'm sorry I was whining like a little kid."

She patted his hand. "It's okay to be sad. We all are going to be sad for a while, but it'll be okay."

Behind them, Ellen honked. Before Dani could respond, the minivan gear flipped out of park, and the vehicle rolled down the lane that meandered through the grounds. Ellen's Saturn followed them.

"Verde!" Dani barked.

The fan jumped to level three then back to one.

"Everyone beat us here?" Dani asked.

The hazard lights flashed twice.

"I'm assuming there aren't any other witnesses in the cemetery." Dani wanted to cross her fingers. The PSA would go live online later tonight and air in the television stations tomorrow morning. But they didn't need another confrontation in the graveyard like what happened to Francine back in October.

Verde flashed her hazards once.

"Your minivan can talk?" Mom shrieked.

"Yes," Dani bit out.

"You were the one who said Verde is actually Mom's horse," Mark volunteered.

"I-I was joking," Mom murmured.

Heath chose the safer option. He took another large bite out of his chocolate Long John.

"Yeah, she's is a totally awesome zombie horse when she's not a minivan."

"But-but the Bible says Death rides a pale horse," Mom protested.

"It's a translation issue," Dani volunteered. "The word in the original Greek of the New Testament refers to the pale green of a rotting corpse."

"We-we—" Mom made a gagging noise. "We're riding in a rotting horse?"

A raspberry noise came through the sound system speakers.

"Mom, please don't insult Verde," Dani said. "She's proud of her job, but she's a little sensitive about her looks compared to her sisters."

"Um, I'm sorry, Verde." Mom cleared her throat. "I didn't mean to insult you. I'm still getting used to all the changes since I died."

Verde honked her horn.

"She accepts your apology, Mom," Dani translated.

Verde pulled off the little lane into the grass and stopped behind Scarlett. When Dani slid out of her seat, she spotted the other three Soccer Moms, their families living and resurrected, plus their Vatican taskforce bodyguards and Father Perez.

Dani strode over to the priest. "Why aren't you at Mass?"

His right eyebrow rose. "I could ask the same thing as you."

Wila leaned close to Father Perez and pseudo-whispered, "Now's not the time, padre."

"Father Mbaye is covering for me at the church," the priest said. "Penny picked me up on her way here."

"I figured it might help if someone could perform Last Rites," Penny explained.

Gammy Wilkinson swatted Wila's arm. "Why didn't you call Reverend Sanford for me?"

"Because a person of the cloth is a person of the cloth, no matter the denomination, Gammy," Wila snapped. "In case you hadn't noticed, none of the Soccer Moms attended the same church."

Dani realized Gammy, Laura, and Rose were dressed up. "I wasn't expecting an audience, much less extra resurrected people."

Francine crossed to Dani and hugged her. "I think at some level we knew you would have to be the backbone of any solution. Especially after the dead started rising."

They parted, and Dani waved in the direction of Father Rodriguez and a couple of other resurrected taskforce members. "But a lot of these folks were buried in Vatican City."

Father Rodriquez smiled. "It doesn't matter where our bodies rest, Dani." He looked around the cemetery. "However, this is a very nice place."

"I've already talked to the cardinal," Karen said. "We've made arrangements to buy plots here and in a couple of other local cemeteries rather than fly the—" She swallowed hard. "To fly our non-American members back to their countries."

"None of them object?" Penny asked.

Brother Giuseppe rattled something in Italian. Or maybe it was Latin.

Sister Joan chuckled before she repeated the monk's words in English. "None of us are very happy with the way the Pope has treated the Soccer Moms. We all would prefer to stay here with Laura."

Dani faced Penny's mother-in-law. "Laura, are you sure?"

"If this is what it takes to save my granddaughter and the rest of the world, so be it." Laura shrugged. "We weren't meant to be here if it weren't for the damn Apocalypse."

Heath laid his hand on Dani's shoulder. "She's right, sweetie. Put us back, and everyone can move on with their lives."

"Wait." Wila cocked her head. "You guys don't feel that?"

"Feel what?" Penny's father-in-law Edward demanded.

The scuzzy impression of something crawling under Dani's skin made her want to claw at her flesh. "Demons."

Chapter 38

Silver crosses and squirt bottles came out of people's pockets and purses. Demon hunters raced to retrieve Super Soakers and paintball guns from the trunks of their cars and load them with holy water.

Dani closed her eyes and let Death's power flow over her. When she could see again, her sisters had donned their Horsemen, too.

"We need to get the civilians out of here," Penny said.

"We're already surrounded," Wila murmured.

"How'd they find out what we planned to do?" Francine asked.

"Shit!" Dani rattled. "Lucifer must have put a tail on me after I pissed him off this morning."

"You pissed off Lucifer?" Edward stared at her.

"Kids, spouses, and ancestors, get in the middle," Karen ordered. "Resurrected demon hunters, surround the noncombatants. Living demon hunters, intersperse between the Soccer Moms in the outer circle. You can't let any of these demons get by us."

They were in the middle of the cemetery with only a handful of oaks randomly placed in this section. Most of the graves around them were the simple horizontal slabs. There wasn't any place to hide. No place that was defensible.

Wila had already mounted Scarlett. From the way her eyes narrowed, she wasn't happy about their odds either.

"What?" Dani asked.

Wila shook her head. "I don't like playing Custer in the Battle of Little Big Horn."

Her words twisted through Dani, but maybe everything wasn't lost. She chuckled as she swung up into Verde's saddle. "Then let someone without any guts play decoy."

Wila grinned before she pulled her balaclava up over her nose. "Hey, Penny! Dani and I will be right back. We're going to do a little snipe hunting."

Dani bent low over her saddle as Verde galloped after Scarlett. Then the horses did the weirdest thing they'd done since Dani and her friends became the Soccer Moms of the Apocalypse.

They dove into the turf.

Dani lost sight of Wila. Verde raced through the soil and rocks as if she were swimming through water. It must be an aspect of their phasing ability. Dani didn't breathe when she wore Death, so the effect wasn't too bad. She wondered how Wila was doing.

Or how long her sister could hold her breath.

Verde burst from the sod and dormant grass. Dani would have gasped if she could. The black-painted steel cemetery fence stood right in front of them. Verde launched into a tight left turn before she slowed to a trot. They joined Wila and Scarlett behind a large family mausoleum.

"Ready to play decoy?" Wila whispered.

Dani nodded.

"Keep their attention on you. I'll take them from behind."

"Let's go, Verde," Dani murmured.

The mare bolted from behind the mausoleum. She shrieked with the same bone-on-bone grating sound Dani's voice had as Death. The demon-possessed humans jerked around at the horse's cry.

Dani didn't recognize any of the faces of the armed group. These people definitely weren't local, and they weren't carrying typical hunting rifles. They looked like cover models for some mercenary-for-hire magazine.

She and Verde charged the small crowd. They scattered like a flock of pigeons. She managed to catch two of the demons with her scythe. The human puppets collapsed with the demons dead.

Shouts of fury followed as Verde galloped away from them. Dani glanced over her shoulder. The demons' attention was focused on her and her horse. They raised their firearms.

Shots rang out. Holes appeared in her tattered robes. Bullets sheared off bits of Verde's rotting flesh. The blade of her scythe clanged when it was hit.

Ahead, a cluster of vehicles sat along the berm of the paved road. Dani leaned over in her saddle. Verde felt the shift and veered toward the vehicles. If the horses could exist in different planes, Dani's weapon should be able to as well. She concentrated.

Tires popped as her scythe slashed through them. Dani glanced behind her once again. True to her word, Wila had taken out the remaining demons with her flaming sword. The bastards probably hadn't even realized what had hit them. Verde wheeled around and galloped up to Scarlett.

"Nice bit with the tires." Wila grinned.

"I'm finally getting the hang of forcing the blade to be in our reality." Dani said. "What's our next plan?"

"We need to clear a path to either the north or south gates."

"Humans generally go out the way they came in," Dani said. "We entered from the south gate. The demons will expect us to go out that way."

Wila tilted her head. "What's your source for that tidbit?"

"Reading too many analyses of disasters where the insurance company had to pay out because people stampeded and crushed each other attempting to flee through the entrance instead of paying attention to the exit signs."

Wila laughed. "Forget what Penny said about finishing your degree. You need to stay in the insurance game. Now, let's plow the road at the north gates so our families can get the hell out of here."

Verde galloped after Scarlett, but something nagged Dani. It wasn't her usual anxiety. More like a premonition. Someone wasn't going to make it out the Oakfield Cemetery alive.

Chapter 39

Near the north gates to the graveyard. Dani pulled the same distraction techniques as before. Once she and Wila dispatched all of the demons and sabotaged the possessed peoples' vehicles, Dani pulled out her phone and dialed Penny.

"The lane to the north gates is clear," Dani said. "I'm circling back to meet you. Wila's staying to keep the way open."

"We'll get everyone loaded into vehicles," Penny replied.

Verde took off for Heath's grave where they left everyone. Unfortunately, there were still groups of mercenary-riding demons running around the huge cemetery. It would be a race to get everyone out before the demons caught up with them. The dang things could sense the Soccer Moms just like they could sense the demons.

Normally, Dani would have prayed for help in such dire circumstances, but she was beginning to understand Penny's feelings of abandonment by the Lord. Especially since the Soccer Moms had no idea of who was playing what game.

A white minivan led a stream of vehicles speeding towards the north exit.

"Please tell me that's Silver," Dani whispered in Verde's ear. The mare neighed and nodded.

Dani nudged Verde off the pavement to give the vehicles space. As soon as the last car, Karen's blue sports car, passed them, Verde galloped after the family members and the demon hunters.

Screeching came from above and behind Dani. She looked over her shoulder. A flock of angels followed the Soccer Moms, their families, and friends. Dani concentrated on the record scratching/singing sounds they made.

Abominations! Kill them! Kill the living! Give the dead to the demons!

Holy crap! Lucifer hadn't been joking about some of the angels wanting the Apocalypse to happen. And odds were the demons in the cemetery could hear the angels, too.

The angels were too high for her to hit with her scythe. She needed someone with a little more reach.

"Verde, we need to catch up with Silver."

The mare jumped back on the grass and increased her speed. Dani pulled out her phone and touched the icon to call Penny.

"What's wrong?"

"We got angels following us, screaming for our blood and telling the demons exactly where we are," Dani said. "I need your Olympic level shooting ability. Tell Silver to keep going, and you come with me."

She tucked her phone away as Verde caught up with Silver. From the ripples of hair appearing along the body paint, the other horse was struggling to stay in minivan mode. Mark flashed a thumbs up from the third row seat of the minivan.

Penny rolled down the driver side window. "How am I supposed to shoot angels when I can't see them?"

"Mom!" Justine shrieked from the third row. "You can see them if you admit they're real!"

"They aren't fairies!" Penny yelled back.

"Justine's right! Now, get on Verde!" Dani shouted. "Silver, get to Wila and Scarlett! We're depending on you to keep our families safe!"

"Wait a minute!" Edward roared. "Who the hell's driving?"

"Silver is." White poured over Penny to turn her into Pestilence. This time, her cape was missing. She flipped over the center console to the second row. Gene opened the sliding door. She laid a kiss on him as she edged past him.

Dani switched her scythe from her right hand to her left and kept Verde's reins loose. She held out her arm. "Ready!"

Penny leapt out of the minivan. Dani caught her and swung her onto Verde's back. Gene slammed Silver's door shut.

"Scootch a little forward in the saddle," Penny yelled in Dani's ear.

She complied and went further forward than she expected. It made sense. She was literally just bones. Penny shifted her weight. Dani looked over her shoulder to see her sister crouched on the saddle. Penny turned so she faced Verde's tail and resumed her seat.

"Holy shit," she murmured under her breath. "Those aren't the angels I grew up with."

"Can you see and hear them now?" Dani asked.

"Yeah." Penny's bow of horn appeared in her hand. She drew an arrow.

Verde slowed and leapt over Ellen's car without any warning. Dani spotted why. A bright yellow Hummer roared over the graves without any regard for the dead still sleeping, and it was headed straight for their little convoy.

Sirens wailed in the distance. Hopefully, someone had called the police. The Soccer Moms definitely needed a little help.

Behind Dani, the bowstring twanged. A shrill cry reminiscent of Marty's first attempt at playing the violin rattled her bones.

"One down," Penny said. "Where you going—oh, crap!"

"Get down and hang on!" Dani concentrated and prayed she could do her tire trick left-handed. Verde raced for the Hummer, which turned directly toward them. People poked their heads and guns out the windows.

"Half of the angels are chasing us!" Penny yelled.

Crap. A quick glance over her shoulder confirmed her sister's observation. If Dani still had a stomach right now, she'd be vomiting all over herself.

Flashes came from the gun muzzles. Dani could literally see the metal coming toward her. Normally, she wouldn't fret about getting shot, but Penny was with her, and Pestilence was still made of flesh as well as bone. Dani twirled her scythe to deflect the bullets, a little amazed at what she could do.

The Hummer tried to swerve to hit them, but Verde phased through the vehicle. Dani managed to slice through three of the demons inside the vehicle, including the driver. Verde galloped in a tight circle and charged after the out-of-control vehicle.

Dani swapped her scythe back to her right hand as her mare gained on the Hummer. She swung. Tires blew out on the left side of the vehicle. The Hummer started to tip, but Verde pulled ahead of it before it rolled over on the dormant grass and remaining splotches of snow.

Behind her, Penny adjusted herself so she was facing forward again. "Stay low over Verde's neck."

Dani ducked. A series of twangs vibrated through her bones. Angels exploded into balls of white feathers as each arrow hit one. The rest of the flock scream-sang, *Treason!* They whirled and fled towards the rest of the angels and demons who were attacking the Soccer Mom convoy just short of the gate.

Verde tore in the direction of their family and friends. Silver and Sable remained in minivan mode to protect their occupants. The angels and demons ignored them, instead focusing on the more vulnerable normal cars. Their foes smashed windows and attempted to drag out the drivers and passengers.

Holy water and bullets did nothing to the angels, so the hunters focused their unconventional ammo at the demons. That left the angels to Wila and Francine. Most of the angelic assholes where smart enough to stay out of range of the Soccer Moms weapons.

Until Wila retorted to throwing her flaming sword at one.

With a *whoosh*, the angel disappeared in a ball of flame.

When an angel dragged Heath from the backseat of Ellen's Saturn, Dani and Verde both screamed, but they were too far away to help. The angel tossed Heath to a demon. And like the incident with Pence's resurrected grandmother, the demon started sucking Heath's soul out of his body.

Chapter 40

Pestilence's arrow whizzed by Dani's skull and hit the demon who was eating Heath's soul. White light flashed as the demon died. Both the freed human and Heath dropped to the ground.

Mom opened the back door and jumped out. She tried to drag Heath back into the car, but she didn't have the strength.

A fire truck roared through the open north gates of the cemetery and screech to a halt.

Dani leaned forward and whispered in Verde's ear, "Obey Pestilence like you would me while I help my family."

A wave of agreement came from the mare.

Dani jump from Verde's back and swung her scythe as she landed. The two angels didn't know what hit them as they exploded into a pile of white feathers.

Father Rodriguez launched himself out of the front passenger seat. "Get inside, Olivia!"

Mom scrambled into the backseat, and together, she, Dani, and the priest wrestled Heath's limp body beside her and slammed the door shut. Thank goodness, he was still breathing.

From the other end of the cemetery, police cars raced toward their party, siren wailing and lights flashing. They were followed by paramedic rigs.

Dani pushed Father Rodriguez back into the car just in time. The fire truck sprayed the vehicles and their attackers with one of their hoses. To her amazement, the possessed humans collapsed in the jet of water, and white light flashed as the demons died.

More screeching came from above her. She looked up to find the angels fighting amongst themselves. Or had a new group come to the cemetery? There were a lot more in the air than there were before Penny started shooting them.

One of the angels landed on top Ellen's car and sang, *Forgive us, sister. We did not realize there were those in our ranks who would interfere in your mission.*

As fast as it all began, the fight was over. The firefighters turned off the hose. Police officers approached and cuff the formerly possessed humans. Chief Wright walked over to Penny.

I am truly sorry your mate is dying, the angel on top of the Saturn sang.

"Dani!" Mom shrieked. "There's something wrong with Heath!"

His eyes fluttered open. "Dang, Olivia. You could wake the dead with that voice." He started to chuckle, but it turned into hoarse gasping.

Harvest his soul, Death, the angel sang. *We will return him to Heaven.*

"What do you mean harvest his soul?" Dani yelled.

Look at the soul, the angel sang. *It is leaking. If you don't harvest it soon, there will be nothing for us to return to our Father.*

Dani laid her hand on Heath's knee and shifted her vision. His soul was no longer a brilliant electric blue. More like the dull institutional blue paint the Oakfield Hospital used on its walls. Like the angel said, there was a rip on his soul and bits dripped from the opening. Someone laid a hand on Dani's shoulder.

"Can't we repair it?" Wila said.

No, the angel sang.

"Sweetheart, this was the plan," Heath whispered. "Let me go back to Heaven. Please."

Dani felt like her own soul was disintegrating. She knew she would lose him in order to stop the Apocalypse, but not like this. Oh, God, not like this.

She whistled. "Verde!"

"What's going on?" Chief Wright demanded. "Who the hell are you talking to?"

"Death's talking to the angel sitting on the roof of the car," Penny snapped. "Mount Verde, and I'll hand Heath up to you." She ducked her head into the rear of the vehicle. "Come on, big guy. Just one last trip."

Scarlett trotted up to Wila as Dani stepped into Verde's stirrup and swung her other leg over the saddle.

"I've got her back." Wila mounted her own horse. "Get everyone home, Pestilence."

When Penny held Heath up to Dani, she forced her scythe to disappear and pulled him into her lap. His life was leaking away with his soul.

"Come on, Verde," she murmured. "Back to his grave."

Her horse took off for the middle of the cemetery. Scarlett and Wila raced beside them. Heath's breathing became more labored as the seconds ticked away.

Hurry, an angel sang.

Dani looked over her shoulder. Yep, one of the flying sets of eyeballs clung to the edge of her saddle. Three more angels flew escort behind them.

"Are you the one who told me to check his soul?"

Yes, it sang.

"I'm trusting you here," she said. "Don't mess with me, and don't you dare do something awful to my husband."

No, it sang. *We would not trick one of the Lord's chosen generals.*

"Yeah, some of your buddies did," Wila grumbled.

You and Pestilence punished most of them, the angel warbled. *Our Lord on High will deal with the rest.*

"You could have told me I had an angel stuck to my ass," Dani complained.

Before Wila could respond, their horses slowed and stopped. Right at the grave Dani visited every Wednesday before their girls' night.

The ground in front of the tombstone was disturbed. The truth hit her harder than she expected.

Wila jumped out of her saddle. Dani lowered Heath to her sister's waiting arms before she dismounted.

"Where do I put him?" Wila asked.

"Lay him on the spot where he climbed out."

The angels landed on the torn turf around the gravesite.

Once Wila set Heath on the ground, Dani knelt next to him and took his hand in hers. "Sweetie, the next part won't hurt. I promise. I love you."

He opened his eyes. "Let me see your face one last time."

Dani dropped the power of Death.

Heath smiled at her. "Always beautiful inside and out."

She bent over and kissed him lightly on the lips. Unlike six years ago, she knew this was their last kiss.

When they parted, he whispered, "I love you, Dani."

"I love you, too. Close your eyes, sweetie," she murmured. "I want you to remember this face."

He complied. She sucked in a deep breath and pulled the power of Death around her.

"You take good care of him, and get him back to Heaven," Dani said to the angels. "If I found out you didn't—"

"They will," Jesus said.

Dani looked up to see him and Father Perez walking over to them from the lane. Behind Jesus's pickup, a police car sat. Officer Rick Graham and his partner Simmons climbed out, nodded at her and Wila, and removed their caps.

Father Perez began the prayers of Last Rites. At least, Heath would have proper rites this time.

Dani shifted her sight, and with her scythe, she delicately cut the energy strings holding his soul to his body. She cradled the huge gem against her breast and blew into it. The sparkling electric blue gem glittered in her hands.

". . . in the name of the Father, the Son, and the Holy Ghost. Amen," Father Perez murmured.

The angel perched next to her held out two of its wings.

"You remember what I said," Dani warned.

We do, all the angels sang.

Dani handed her husband's soul to the angel beside her. "Take good care of him."

We will, the quartet sang. They took off, flying higher and higher until not even Death's vision could see them anymore.

Wila cleared her throat. "Uh, do we need to call cemetery management for a backhoe?"

Dani looked down at Heath. Not Heath, his corpse, she reminded herself. The same way she had six years ago. Without the power of God, the body looked shrunken and desiccated as it should.

She closed her eyes and gently pushed the corpse back into its coffin. When she was done, she opened her eyes. The gravesite looked exactly as it had on last Wednesday afternoon. And the numbness she felt for the last six years dissolved. In its stead, the grief bubbled and poured out of her.

Dimly, she heard Wila tell the guys to get lost before she held and rocked Dani while she sobbed.

Chapter 41

An hour later, Dani was a little surprised at the sight of Francine's house when she, Wila, and their horses arrived at the home. The Coy-Astins' yard was tastefully decorated with large plastic red-and-white-striped candy canes and enough white tiny lights to illuminate the entire neighborhood. Another reminder Dani hadn't even pulled their artificial tree from the attic and set it up yet.

She wasn't sure if she could deal with Christmas again after losing Heath for a second time.

All of the cars from their group that had been at the Oakfield Cemetery were parked along the street. Jesus's pickup was there as well. Verde halted at the end of the line of vehicles. She waited for Dani to dismount before she shifted into a minivan.

Wila parked at the other end of the line and joined Dani at the beginning of the Coy-Astins' driveway. Dani hated to admit how comforting Wila's arm was around her shoulders as they walked up the concrete drive. Part of her wished she could throw away her responsibilities as Death.

The other part didn't want Heath's second passing to be in vain.

When they reached the front portico, Wila pressed the doorbell. Brittany opened the door. To Dani's surprise, the girl threw her arms around Dani and started sobbing.

Which of course triggered another round of Dani's own weeping.

"Brittany, honey, let us get inside before you and Dani both have icicles hanging off your noses," Wila said gently.

The girl released Dani and retreated inside before she wiped her face on her sleeves. Dani entered the house, and Wila followed, closing the door against the cold.

"Pretty much everyone's in the family room talking or playing pool down in the basement," Brittany said. "Mark's upstairs in my room with Derek and Justine. He couldn't handle being around everyone. He keeps saying he should have made his dad ride with Mom or Penny."

Part of the ease of Heath's first death was Mark being too young to really understand what had happened. But this time . . .

"I'll go talk to him." Dani fished a couple of tissues from her purse, one for Brittany and one to dry her own eyes. "Thank you for being his friend, sweetie."

The girl nodded. "I wish there was more we could do."

Dani hugged the girl again before she climbed the stairs. The walkway overlooked the Astin's family room. The hardest part was the silence when the people downstairs spotted her. She ignored them and followed the sounds of Derek and Justine's voices.

She knocked on the partially closed bedroom door before she pushed it open. "Derek, Justine, do you mind if Mark and I talk alone for a few minutes?"

"No problem." Derek rose from Brittany's bed where he sat next to Mark. "We'll be downstairs if you need us, *ese*." He clapped Mark on his shoulder before he strode out of the room.

Justine sat on the other side of Mark. She said nothing, merely squeezed his hand before she rose and followed Derek downstairs.

Dani closed the door behind them.

"Did it hurt?" Mark whispered.

"Did what hurt?" Dani crossed the room and sat next to her son.

"Did Dad feel any pain when y-you had to kill him the second time?"

"No." Dani swallowed hard. "I made sure of that."

"I don't think I could have done that." Mark swiped at his face.

"I'm glad you didn't have to."

"I'm just so angry." He clenched his fists. "None of this is fair. Me losing Dad again. Derek and Justine are going to lose their grandmothers. "And Rose is the younger sibling we all wanted."

"You're right," Dani said softly. "It wasn't fair when we lost your dad the first time around either. And I am so sorry you had to go through it again." She brushed Mark's hair back from his face. "I can say you were his priority. He made me promise to do whatever I had to in order to keep you safe."

Mark finally looked at her. "Did Dad go back to Heaven?"

"Yes, an angel took his soul back to Heaven." She smiled even though her own heart was shattered. "And Coach Cordero vouched for the angel who returned your dad back to the Lord."

Mark threw his arms around Dani, and she hugged him tightly for a long time.

Dani was a little relieved when Mark declared he was hungry. Thank goodness for preteen appetites.

However, when they went downstairs, everybody abruptly quieted. Mark ignored them and headed straight for the platter of sandwiches from Goldberg's Deli on the kitchen counter.

On the other hand, Dani shook her head at Francine and Neal. "You can't keep feeding everyone like this. Even you two will go broke."

"If you ladies stop the Apocalypse, it'll be worth every penny," Neal said. He wrapped his arm around Francine's waist and kissed her cheek.

"Did I hear someone take my name in vain?" Penny charged into the kitchen with an empty paper plate as Mark headed downstairs to eat with the rest of the kids.

"We were talking the copper kind." Neal grinned. "Would you like a scoop of ice cream on your peanut butter fudge brownie?"

"Yes, please." Penny dumped her used plate in the trash before she walked over to Dani and hugged her. She said nothing more. There wasn't anything to be said.

Wila entered the kitchen from the Coy-Astins' patio, followed by Jesus. "Ladies, we need to talk." She eyed Dani. "If you're up for it, that is."

Old, familiar numbness cocooned Dani. She welcomed it because she was going to need it to get through what she would have to do next. She nodded.

"Mind if we use the home office, honey?" Francine asked Neal.

"Go right ahead." He kissed her again on the cheek. "I'll make brownies a la mode for all you and bring them in."

"Thanks, babe." She pecked him lightly on the lips.

Dani's phone rang. Fearing it might be Dad or Marty, she pulled it out of her pocket and checked the caller ID. This time, caller ID showed an area code of six-six-six. Of course, it was Lucifer. She tapped the answer icon.

"What do you want?" she said coldly. Her sisters, Neal, and Jesus watched her.

"I wasn't behind the attack at the cemetery."

"Why should I believe you?" Dani said. "You threatened to kill my husband this morning, and a demon succeeded."

"Because I need you, and someone's trying very hard to alienate the one ally I have." Lucifer actually sounded upset.

"What about your fallen angel buddies?"

"They plan to overthrow me regardless of whether I win this war. Can we please meet and talk?"

Her sisters could hear Lucifer's side of the conversation, and from the expression on Jesus's face, he could, too.

"Fine. We'll meet, but on my terms," Dani said.

Lucifer hesitated a moment before he asked, "What are they?"

"We're going to work out a deal between just you and the Kid." She eyed Jesus, but he remained quiet. "And by we, I mean the Four Soccer Moms of the Apocalypse."

"Do you have any idea how ridiculous you sound by calling yourselves that?"

She could hear the sneer he was no doubt wearing. "My terms or no deal, Lucifer."

"Go on," he said much more calmly.

"Just the six of us will meet at Miles Pence's home in one hour. Alone. No one's at his house right now, is there?"

"No."

"Anymore snarky comments?" Dani demanded.

"No, m'lady."

"And, Lucifer, remember one thing," she continued. "Everything dies. Even angels. You renege on this deal, you won't live to see the next sunrise, much less Heaven. Do we have an agreement?"

"Yes, m'lady."

Dani tapped her phone to end the call. "I'm starving. You got any turkey sandwiches on that platter, Neal?"

Chapter 42

Once Dani fixed a plate for herself, she said, "Neal, I appreciate you offering your office for privacy, but let's stay in the kitchen. Everyone needs to be involved in this discussion."

She and the Soccer Moms sat down at Francine's kitchen table along with Jesus. Neal prepared dessert for everyone. Gene wandered in and joined them since Penny hadn't returned to the Coy-Astins' family room.

When Penny told Gene of Dani's plan, he looked at her with some concern. "A suicide mission isn't going to restore Heath to you."

"He never was supposed to be here to begin with," Dani said around a mouthful of turkey and cheddar. "If we can cut a deal between Heaven and Hell, all of this is over, and the resurrected can return to Heaven where they belong. And you're going to provide some free therapy for this dysfunctional family."

"I'm going to what?" Gene stared at her with an expression of horror.

"Are you trying to get my husband killed?" Penny protested.

"If either side harms Gene, then they'll pay the price." Dani swallowed and turned to Jesus. "Neither side is innocent. Those were angels who tried to kill us this morning."

"I know." He bowed his head briefly before he looked at her with sad eyes. "You have every right to be suspicious of me. But I believe your plan is better than Wila's."

"What was Wila's plan?" Dani took another bite of her sandwich as they all faced Wila.

She shrugged. "I figured you could lure in Lucifer, and we'd kill him."

"Not we," Francine said. "Dani. We can hurt him, but she could take him out permanently. That's why he's been trying so hard to woo her to his side."

"You and Penny could make him so damn miserable he'd beg for death," Wila pointed out.

"The thing Lucifer wants the most is to go back to Heaven." Dani eyed Jesus. "What would it take for the Lord to agree to that?"

"True repentance. On both sides." Jesus considered the matter a moment longer before he added, "It may take time, but with Gene's help, I think it's possible to accomplish a reconciliation amongst Our Family."

"What about—" Penny inclined her head toward the family room.

"We say our goodbyes—" Wila sniffed. "—negotiate this deal, and then Dani will do what she has to do."

"But can you do this on a global scale?" Penny asked softly.

"I have to," Dani replied. "For the rest of the world to live, I have to."

After the Soccer Moms finished their peanut butter fudge brownies a la mode, Dani waited outside while the other three said their goodbyes to their resurrected loved ones. She tapped her toe bones on the concrete sidewalk. It was weird how they didn't make a sound. Why hadn't she noticed before now? She should ask her sisters if they had.

A familiar gold minivan pulled to a stop beside her and Verde. The passenger window rolled down, and Courtney Lasser smiled. "Dani?"

"Hey, Courtney."

Her husband Rick and their daughter Kimberly stared at Dani. On the other hand, Kenny actually waved enthusiastically at her.

"Sorry, we didn't have a chance to talk at the party yesterday," Courtney continued. "Since you're on your way to your second job, give me a call when you have some time."

It took Dani a few seconds to realize what Courtney was talking about. "The OPA presidency. Oh, dear, I apologize. Between accidentally killing Christ yesterday and my husband Heath dying for the second time a couple of hours ago, my head's been a little floofy."

"I totally understand," Courtney said brightly. "You do have a lot going on, but I still think you'd make a super president of the OPA for the next term. Call me later!"

She rolled up the window, and Rick continued driving down the street. They passed Scarlett and Wila, who responded to Courtney's wave with a salute. Scarlett trotted up to Verde, and the two horses nuzzled each other.

"What was that all about?" Wila asked.

"Courtney's been trying to recruit me to run for president of the Oakfield Parents Association next year."

"Since when?"

"Since Friday." Dani shook her head. "Do you think she's losing it? She didn't even flinch seeing me in broad daylight like this." She gestured at her black robes and bones.

Wila shrugged. "From what I hear, she's been a nicer person to everyone since we saved her ass from Lucifer. On the other hand, maybe she thinks she'll get brownie points from Saint Peter when she arrives at the Pearly Gates by sucking up to the Four Horsemen."

Dani mounted Verde before Wila added, "You sure this plan of yours will work?"

"It will if we don't give the angels or the demons a choice."

Wila shook her head. "That's an awful lot of enemies to make in one day."

"Or we reunite a family that's been fractured since the beginning of the human race," Dani said. "Isn't that worth the risk?"

"You're awfully forgiving for someone who's lost the love of their life for a second time."

"Maybe I want our sons to have a chance to find their own loves." Dani chuckled. "And when this is over, you need to call Chance Paxton and ask him out."

Wila inhaled as if to say something, but she didn't. Dani suspected Wila was about to bring up Ramon, one of her fellow paramedics. She'd been trying to fix them up for the last four months.

Before the Apocalypse.

"If you go out with Chance, I'll go out with Ramon," Dani said softly. "Maybe we could double date. After New Year's. There'll be too much pressure before that."

"Sweetie, you just buried you husband for a second time literally hours ago," Wila murmured.

"No, I buried an illusion of someone I loved a long time ago. I knew from the beginning it wouldn't last." Dani glanced around the neighborhood. The quiet unnerved her. "If we can pull off stopping the Apocalypse, that's how the world will regard it. A mass dream."

"Maybe that's for the best," Penny said as she and Francine rode up to join them.

"Maybe," Dani replied.

"You guys notice something weird?" Wila said.

Penny and Francine looked at each other before they shook their heads.

"There's no angels perching on Francine and Neal's roof," Dani said.

Penny urged Silver to an angle where she could see the back of the house. "None in the trees behind the house either."

"Where's Jesus?" Dani asked.

"The coach is on the phone with Maria," Francine said. "He'll be here in a second."

As if on cue, Jesus burst out the front door of the Coy-Astin home and jogged over to the quartet. "Do you want me to follow you in my pickup?"

"No, you're riding with me." Dani held out her free arm and kick the left stirrup off her foot bones. "I have no ass as Death so there's room for both of us on Verde's saddle."

Jesus chuckled as he climbed up behind Dani. "Thank you for the ride. I can't afford the increase in my insurance if something happens to my vehicle."

"If we pull this off, call me at the office tomorrow," Dani said. "I'll see what we can do to lower your rates."

"When we pull this off," Jesus said gently.

"When," she replied.

He clung to her waist as Verde galloped after the other three horses.

Chapter 43

They passed no one on the Oakfield streets on the way to Pence's house. A shiver ran up Dani's spine. This close to Christmas, more people should be about even with this morning's earthquake. Outside of the city limits, the horses cut across fields in a beeline for their destination.

They reached the back fence line of the acre of land where Pence's house sat. The place looked even more forlorn than it had the last time they were here. But then, the real Miles Pence hadn't lived here in weeks.

The horses leapt over the board and post fence and trotted to the back deck. Wila and Scarlett broke off and circled the house. Francine and Sable followed them. When they came around the other side, Wila shook her head.

"Pence's Harley is the only thing in the garage," she reported. "There's a couple of notes from neighbors, saying they'll help him if he turns himself in."

Penny muttered a few imprecations under her breath. "We're on time. Personally, I don't feel like waiting around for an ambush."

"If this is supposed to be a civil negotiation, why don't we try knocking?" Dani slid off Verde, walked up the deck steps, and did just that. The curtain on the back door window shifted, and Pence's, or rather Lucifer's, face peered out. The sound of the deadbolt sliding back was followed by the door opening.

"Come in, ladies, Brother." For once, there were no leers, no sarcasm, no smarmy comments. Lucifer stepped back and held the door open.

Dani waited for Jesus and her sisters before they entered the house. Amazingly, it smelled like the house had been recently cleaned.

"I made coffee for our discussion," Lucifer said. "It's the Kona blend from Java's Palace. Freshly ground."

"No, thank you," Dani said politely. "It makes a bit of a mess if I try to drink it in this form."

Her sisters also politely declined, but Jesus said, "I would gladly accept a cup of coffee, Lucifer."

Once two cups were poured, Lucifer gestured toward the living room. "Shall we have our discussion in there?"

"That is acceptable," Jesus said.

The whole thing was rather bizarre, but with the underlying tension between the two men, the brittle manners was much better than yet another battle with demons or angels.

"Lucifer, you've indicated you wish to go home to Heaven," Dani began. "Jesus has said everyone needs to apologize for that to happen."

Both men opened their mouths, and Wila slashed the blade of her hand through the air. "Don't restart your argument. Is what Dani said a fair assessment of each of your desired results?"

"Yes," Lucifer muttered.

"It's accurate," Jesus replied.

"On our side, we need two things from you and one thing for yourselves," Dani continued. "The Apocalypse has to stop. We know how to do it, but we need you to keep the demons and angels who want the end of the world off our backs while we accomplish this."

"May we ask what our actions entail?" Jesus asked.

"Kill 'em if you have to," Penny snapped. "But if they get by you, we definitely will kill them after what they did to Heath today."

"I know the priests have been keeping you ladies and the Vatican taskforce supplied with holy water to fight the demons, but that isn't going to work on the angels," Lucifer said.

"We know." Dani faced Jesus. "You gonna spill?"

"I'd prefer not to get anyone else killed," he said.

"*Ese*, you'd better cough up a way to stop the angels because they're not going to have one damn problem with killing the six of us," Wila snapped.

"Other than My Father and your weapons, there is no way to kill an angel," he said softly.

"But they can be harmed." Lucifer glared at Jesus. "With a scourge."

Jesus's jaw muscles twitched a few times before he said, "Yes."

"Any scourge?" Dani asked, but even as she said the words, she knew it was the specific one he used on the moneychangers at the temple in Jerusalem.

Jesus produced a small scourge from his jeans pocket and set it on the coffee table. It was made of strips of brown leather, woven together at one end to form a handle. The free tassels at the other end were knotted. The individual pieces were about the width of a shoestring.

"Are you willing to use it?" Penny raised her right eyebrow.

"To stop the disobedient angels, yes." But he didn't look happy about it.

"What's the second thing you need from us?" Lucifer asked.

"You leave Miles Pence here," Dani said. "We know damn well you can take physical form."

"You're putting him in danger by leaving him here alone," Lucifer said.

"Nope, I texted a taskforce person and a cop we trust to come out and pick him up before we left to meet you." Francine held up her phone. "They should be here in five minutes."

Lucifer's eyes narrowed. "What is the thing we have to do for ourselves?"

"You and Jesus are going to attend family counseling with Penny's husband Gene," Dani said.

Lucifer burst out laughing. He laughed so hard he fell out of Pence's recliner, and tears ran down his face.

Jesus let out an exasperated sigh. "How am I supposed to allow you back into Heaven if you're not willing to rebuild our relationship?"

Lucifer gasped. "Did you hear what they want us to do?" He roared and rolled on the floor. "Like any human could possibly understand us."

"Technically, I am human," Jesus said dryly.

Lucifer abruptly stopped laughing and stared at the ceiling. "I knew there was a reason I hated you."

"You can attend counseling, get your shit together, and go home," Dani said. "Or you can face your fellow fallen angels who hate your guts for not helping them save their human families and the Heavenly angels who hate you for defying the Lord. What's it going to be?"

Lucifer pushed himself into a sitting position and heaved a sigh. "All right. I'll do the counseling."

"Who decides when the guys have had enough counseling?" Wila asked.

"Since we need an objective third party, Gene should make the decision." Dani eyed each man in turn. "He's an atheist. You're not going to get anyone else this even-handed."

Lucifer and Jesus watched each other.

"Gene would be the perfect choice outside of Heaven." Jesus cocked his head. "Unless you have an objection?"

Lucifer made a face to make all adolescent expressions of disgust with the family forever obsolete. "He's going to take your side because Gene let the demon Gakeel possess him."

"If anything, Jesus should be complaining," Penny said. "Gene knows what it feels like to have a tough father and a younger brother who gets away with everything. He may have an unconscious bias in your favor."

"I suppose we both need to trust our therapist to deal with us evenly—" Jesus started.

"You just said Gene was perfect," Lucifer snapped.

"All you do is complain." Very human irritation glinted in Jesus's eyes. "Everything's unfair. Everything's stacked against you. But you're asked to do something that will give you exactly what you want, and you bitch for the sake of bitching."

Lucifer smirked. "I wondered if you could lose your temper outside of those money grubbers at the Temple." He turned to Dani. "I accept your terms."

"Swear to me in the name of the Lord you will follow our directions and you will not harm Eugene Crawford Hudson, the husband of the Horseman Pestilence by any means whatsoever," Dani demanded.

Lucifer climbed back onto Pence's La-Z-Boy chair and reclined. He closed his eyes, and black smoke poured from every orifice.

Dani didn't remember Crucifer's smoke as quite so . . . sparkly. Like black diamonds. The glittery, ebony mist coalesced into a male shape with huge wings. He looked a lot Crucifer. The same dark shaggy hair, but his eyes were a blue so pale the irises edged into white. The mist settled into replicas of the jeans and blue and green plaid flannel shirt the unconscious Pence wore.

Lucifer sang his oath in the angelic song language. The more Dani heard of it, the more she understood. But she'd never be able to replicate the sheer beauty of their tongue in either her human form or as Death.

When he finished, she inclined her head. "Thank you, Lucifer Morningstar."

He smirked. "So, ladies, who do I get to ride with?"

Chapter 44

Once the unconscious Pence was safely cuffed and tucked in the back of Rick Graham's squad SUV, Ellen approached Dani. "With all due respect, Lady Death, you need backup."

"You guys will be in the middle of a supernatural battle," Dani said. "If I fail, the human race is going to need you and your fellow taskforce members."

Ellen opened her mouth to protest, but she decided against whatever she'd been about to say. Instead, she hugged Dani. "Break a leg, girl."

After the Oakfield Police SUV disappeared down the township road, Dani and Penny politely asked their mares to switch to their van modes. Wila rode with Dani and Lucifer in Verde. Francine accompanied Penny and Jesus. Scarlett and Sable raced beside the two minivans.

Despite his oath, Lucifer had trouble keeping his mouth shut. Kind of like Dad and Marty, and the ridiculous macho stories they told Mark. Dani almost missed the silence of her son listening to his music and ignoring the world.

"Death, do you really think War could stop me with her pigsticker?" Lucifer said.

"I'm not here to protect her," Wila drawled from the back seat. "I'm here to keep her from killing you."

That comment silenced Lucifer for a few miles on their way back to the Oakfield Cemetery. Some instinct told Dani she needed to do this at the grave of the first person she put back.

Which meant she had to go back to Heath's resting place. But she need-ed to check on one other thing first.

🔥 ☠ 🔥

With a quick call to Penny, Dani guided Verde to Riverside Cemetery. She parked along the berm, and Penny pulled in behind her. Everyone stared at the tombstones and sculptures marking the graves.

"Well, that's different," Wila murmured. "Now we know where they went."

One angel sat on the marker of each of the disturbed graves they could see from the street. None of them were singing. Dani rolled down her win-dow to make sure. Nope, not a peep from any angel.

"It's like they're waiting for something," Wila said.

"They know Death's plan," Lucifer said. "They're waiting for the resur-rected humans to come back to their coffins so they can return the souls to Father."

Dani's phone rang, and she tapped the answer button on her steering wheel. "Yeah, Penny?"

"Jesus says the angels are waiting for you to do your thing."

"Lucifer said the same thing." Dani glanced at the Prince of Hell. It was weird not seeing him in Pence's body. But she could totally understand Wila's crush on Crucifer now. "These guys aren't going to interfere with us, are they?"

"They are here only to return the souls if you succeed," Lucifer said.

"All right, we're heading straight to Oakfield Cemetery," Dani said. "Francine, call Chief Wright. Ask him to set up a perimeter around the place."

"How big?" Francine wheezed.

"Tell him to evacuate any humans within two blocks of the cemetery." Dani ended the call before she shifted into drive and pressed the accelerator.

"Why don't you call your police chief yourself?" Lucifer mocked.

"Have you heard my voice?" She cackled. "I sounds like bones rattling in a clothes dryer. It freaks people out. Plus, Francine has been helping to coordinate between the Oakfield first responders and the Vatican taskforce to protect the citizens of our town. She's got a better rapport with them."

"Why evacuate the area?" This time, Lucifer was totally serious. "If you fail, there won't be any safe place in the universe."

"Then I can't fail," Dani shot back.

Dani didn't blame Verde when the minivan/horse hesitated at the north entrance of the Oakfield Cemetery. She could feel the presence of the demons, too. It was a good thing Francine alerted the police.

Like Riverside, angels perched on the tombstones of the disturbed graves, but the Soccer Moms couldn't rely on them for assistance.

"Wila?"

"Already pulled them out of the back, girl."

Dani glanced in the rearview mirror. Sure enough, Wila poured a large bottle of holy water into the two Super Soakers Dani kept in the minivan's hidden compartment in the storage area.

"You're the strategist, Wila. Drive or ride?" Dani asked.

"Frankly, I'd feel better on Scarlett, and the girls can move faster as horses than they can as minivans," Wila answered.

A surge in the tachometer indicated Verde's agreement.

Dani opened the driver side door. "All right. Everyone out. And Wila, give Lucifer one of the Super Soakers and a refill bottle."

Penny chewed her lower lip when she exited Silver. "Please tell me you can feel them."

"If you mean the demon, yes, we all do." Dani looked at Jesus. "You sure you can't get these angels to help us?"

He shook his head. "No, they are obeying our Father's commands."

"Not even if the new rebel angels attack them?" Penny asked.

"No," he said softly.

Francine closed Silver's rear hatch. She approached with the Super Soakers and holy water sacks Penny had stored in the minivan. Silver shook and shifted into her horse form again.

"Can two of you take the Dynamic Duo here?" Dani said. "I'll be the demons' primary target. I don't want either of them killed because the demons are taking potshots at me."

"Jesus, you're with Francine," Penny ordered. "Lucifer you're with me." She narrowed her eyes and deliberately stepped into the fallen angel's personal space. "And if you mess with any of my shots, I will end you."

"Now, now, Pestilence." The grin on Lucifer's face was somehow creepier than when he possessed Pence. "You're much too beautiful to imitate Liam Neeson."

Dani manifested her scythe and twirled it. "You're right, Lucifer. But I'm just the right amount of crazy to get rid of you permanently if you decide to mess with us. So, you'd better do what the boss lady says."

The fallen angel's grin faded. "My apologies for teasing you, Pestilence."

Dani mounted Verde, and the mare tensed beneath her. "Mind if I take the lead on this one, boss?"

"It's all yours, girlfriend."

"Let's go, Verde," Dani murmured. The rotting horse took off for Heath's grave, leaping over angels and markers with ease. Dani hoped the rest of her job would be easy, but she resisted the urge to pray.

She wasn't sure she'd like God's answer.

Chapter 45

The demons seemed to come out of nowhere as the Four Horsemen, the Devil, and Christ raced across the cemetery. However, the possessed humans wore brown camouflage that the area deer hunters wore during white-tail season except without the bright orange hats and safety vests.

And they definitely weren't carrying hunting rifles. The demons must have hit one of the National Guard units. As Dani expected, they were focusing their stolen weapons on her.

A couple of bullets nicked her ribs, but most passed harmlessly through her except for tearing holes in her robes. Verde wasn't so lucky. The automatic weapons ripped off chunks of her rotting flesh, but the mare didn't slow down.

Scarlett swung to Verde's left. Wila wielded her flaming sword in one hand and a Super Soaker in the other. The pair made quick work of the demons attempting to cut Dani off from her sisters.

"Dani, grenade launcher!" Wila screamed over the multiple guns firing.

Dani glanced to her right. One of the demons had a huge black tubular device pressed to its shoulder. Crap. Those might actually do real damage to her and Verde.

The demon fired. Dani swung her scythe and knocked the grenade back toward the demons. Their scrambling for cover would have been hilarious if the situation wasn't so dire. The grenade exploded, knocking over headstones and angels and showering dirt over demons and horses alike.

Verde slid to a stop in front of Heath's headstone, and Dani jumped off.

Wila and Francine exchanged Super Soakers in mid-gallop, and Scarlett raced for the idiots who'd launched the grenade.

Sable's hooves dug up the dormant grass as she also skidded to a stop. Francine dismounted and dragged Jesus away from her horse. "Get down and stay down," she ordered. "We need you for the second wave."

Overhead came the discordant song of some very angry angels.

Dani did her best to ignore the cacophony around her. She sat cross-legged in front of Heath's grave and held her scythe across her lap. Beneath her, she could hear the heartbeat of the planet. Focusing on that, she extended her senses.

The wrongness of the resurrected flooded her very being. She'd spent the last two months ignoring the feeling when she was around the undead. Now, she grabbed onto that awareness and started to sing herself. An old lullaby in Spanish Abuelita Hernandez sang to her when she was little.

The song matched the rhythm of Earth. The tune and the planet throbbed, and the wrongness answered because it, too, wanted to join. As Dani began the song over, something hit her in the face and knocked her backward.

A whistle and a crack preceded an unholy screech of pain. The weight on her head disappeared. Jesus helped her into a sitting position. But the sight of what was going on around her made her want to run home and bury herself under the covers forever.

The demons were attacking the resurrected drawn to the cemetery by her. Her sisters attempted to protect her and the defenseless undead from the demons and the rebel angels.

Lucifer spread his wings, covering the righteous from the demons conventional weaponry, while wielding his own fiery sword. He sang a song of combat and honor and passion. The sky suddenly filled with black wings of the rest of the fallen angels. They charged into the fray against their former siblings.

Despair filled Dani. All hers and her sisters' efforts were for nothing. Heaven and Hell battled around her, the beginning of the end.

"I can't do this," she wailed.

"Your song is working," Jesus murmured as he held her. "You've got to keep going, Dani."

"But all I did was start the Apocalypse!"

"This is nothing compared to what will happen if you don't finish what you started." He smiled gently. "Or don't you have faith in me?"

"I don't know anymore." Everything was so mixed up, and what wasn't chaotic was simply terrifying. She would be crying if she had tear ducts. "I shouldn't have told Heath to spend the night in Chicago. All of this is my fault."

Jesus reached over and cupped her skull in his hands. "Think of Mark. You promised Heath you would protect your son."

Mark. Who was at Francine's house with the rest of their families. He needed his own chance to grow up. To have his own children. And Dani could tell her grandchildren stories about Heath, and they would cherish her husband as she did.

She nodded. "All right."

The choked words of Abuelita Hernandez's lullaby forced their way from Dani's throat. Years from now she would tell her grandchildren how Christ and the Devil guarded her while her sisters fought the beings who wanted all life to end.

Earth sang with her, a deep tone of caring for the righteous dead's bodies, while the Watchers warbled their promise to return the souls to Heaven where they belonged.

Love poured from the souls as they were collected. Some were stronger than others. Father Rodriguez asked for Mark to light a candle for him at Saint Michael's. Rose wanted to thank the Coy-Astins for being her family for this short time. Mom whispered in her ear, asking her to tell Marty how much she loved them both, and gave her blessing for Carmen and Dad's happiness. The singing died away as the last body was put to rest and the last soul was carefully carried to Heaven.

Dani blinked. Her face was wet, and everything hurt, but her scythe still rested across her knees. Only it was gripped by her very human hands.

With Jesus's help, she carefully stood. The possessed humans were all unconscious, she hoped. Black and white feathers covered the ground and markers for yards in every direction. The Watcher angels were gone.

And the Soccer Moms, Lucifer, and Jesus were surrounded by some very angry-looking fallen angels.

Chapter 46

Dani swallowed hard. She should have known Buer and the rest of Crucifer's buddies would show up at some point.

"Thank you for you assistance—" she started.

But the fallen angels weren't in the mood to play nice. "Give the Morningstar to us. We will deal with him," Buer demanded.

She shot a quick glance at Lucifer. For once, he actually looked worried.

"Who the hell are you?" Penny demanded.

"That's Buer," Dani said. "The one who visited me at the police station."

"You mean the one that put Lilah back in the hospital," Wila snapped. She stepped forward, her flaming sword in hand. "She was no danger to you, asshole."

Buer didn't bat an eyelash. "She was merely a pawn to get Death's attention and subsequently her sisters.'"

Dani grabbed Wila and pulled her back before she started another battle. "Lilah is our friend, and you hurt her. It doesn't make us want to help you."

"Crucifer was a fool to trust the Horsemen," Buer spat. "And you were fools to trust the Morningstar."

"Then why did you help us?" Penny asked in a gentle voice.

Buer remained silent. So did all the other fallen angels, even Lucifer.

"The fluff balls that attacked us were some of the same jerks who killed your wives and children, weren't they?" Wila ventured.

When the fallen angels didn't speak, Jesus said, "Yes, they were."

Francine eyed Lucifer. "So what's the real reason they hate you?"

"I'm the only one of the Fallen who didn't have a mate and children," Lucifer said. "And I promised I would protect them after Our Lord commanded me to kill their families."

Dani exchanged glances with her sisters. That put a very different spin on the story of the Fall.

"Is Lucifer telling the truth, Jesus?" Penny demanded.

"Yes." Jesus stared at the ground. "We didn't understand what We did until We had a human wife and a human child."

"It's been nearly two thousand years since You died," Dani said. "You couldn't forgive the Fallen in that time?"

"We should have." Jesus raised his head. "I apologize, My Children."

"Are you going to make the same deal with them you did with Lucifer?" Penny asked.

"Yes." Jesus nodded.

"And what deal is that?" Buer sneered.

"Family counseling to work out your issues to prevent additional problems when you return to Heaven," Penny said.

"And if we don't agree?" another fallen angel piped up.

"Then you need to go back to Hell," Wila said. "But I suggest you talk it over amongst yourselves before you make any hasty decisions."

"Uh, maybe we should have our own conversation," Francine said. "Could you gentlebeings excuse us for a few minutes?"

Buer and his comrades nodded before they gathered twenty yards away and sang softly to themselves. The Soccer Moms retreated twenty yards in the opposite direction, leaving Jesus and Lucifer in the pile of black and white angel feathers by Heath's grave.

"What's wrong?" Dani asked.

"What happens to all the demons if all of the fallen angels go back to Heaven?" Francine said.

Penny and Wila exchanged worried looks.

"Crap," Penny muttered. "I didn't even think about that."

"Is there any way we can redeem them?" Francine suggested.

"No." When all the sisters looked at her, Wila held up her palms. "I'm not being negative here, but let's face it. Demons lost their humanity by the choices they made in life. They would have to change their ways and want forgiveness. Some people just can't do that."

"If we end up cutting a deal with the rest of the fallen angels, we probably won't have our Soccer Mom abilities anymore either since technically, the Apocalypse is done," Penny said. "That could put our families in danger."

Dani shrugged. "It's simple really. The Vatican taskforce still exists. We tell the surviving demons on earth to go back to Hell and stay there or their existence is forfeit."

"And why are they going to listen to us?" Francine said.

Dani grinned and twirled her scythe. "I think they'll take me quite seriously."

Penny nodded. "Sounds like a plan. Unless anybody else has a better one."

Both Francine and Wila shook their heads. Dani and her sisters walked back over to Jesus. The fallen angels were still discussing the deal. When one of them sang too loud, the angel next to him batted the noisy one with his wings.

"Is there a problem, ladies?" Lucifer asked.

"Nope," Penny answered. "Jesus, how soon do you take back the Horsemen and what happens to our minivans when you take the horses home?"

Jesus smiled. "I'm afraid it doesn't work that way. You ladies will be the Horsemen, sorry, Soccer Moms for the rest of your lives."

"What?" Wila exclaimed. Buer and the other fallen angels looked at her, and she lowered her voice. "What do you mean we'll be the Soccer Moms for the rest of our lives?"

Jesus shrugged. "Someone has to deal with the remaining demons if Lucifer, Buer, and the others return to Heaven. That leaves you four and the Vatican taskforce. Since you will remain the Soccer Moms of the Apocalypse, your horses will continue to disguise themselves as conventional vehicles."

"We didn't ask for this," Francine protested.

"And I didn't ask to be crucified the first time around." He shrugged again. "Destiny and free will can coexist, but it's up to us to find the balance."

Buer and the other fallen angels approached them. "While we accept Your forgiveness, Lord, we do not wish to return to Heaven. Nor do we want to return to Hell."

"You want things to go back to the way they were?" Jesus cocked his head. His expression of disbelief would have been comical under other circumstances.

"We enjoyed life with human beings." Buer almost looked embarrassed. "We understand your position, Lord. You must have compassion for all of creation, but we are individuals, just like humans, and learned why they pursue love so passionately."

Jesus turned to Dani and her sisters. "What say you, ladies?"

Penny, Francine, and Wila looked at Dani.

"You're the one who lost her husband for the second time today," Penny said softly. "It's your call."

Dani's eyes stung at the reminder. She understood why her sisters were leaving the decision to her. She was in the same position as the fallen angels. Six years of holding onto her grief was terrible enough. She couldn't imagine being tortured by her failure to protect Heath and Mark for thousands of years.

"Fine," she said. "You can stay on earth under two conditions."

Buer and the fallen angels immediately tensed up. "What are these conditions?"

"First, behave yourselves," she said sternly. "No miracles. No supernatural shit. If you start to get serious with someone, tell them the truth about what you are and what your potential children might be."

"And the second?" Buer relaxed a little, but he was still concerned about what she would say next.

"Teach your children how to control their abilities if they have them and how to stay off the humans' radar. The people who have the potential to be demons will come after your kids." Dani smiled. "And I understand your distrust of Heaven, but if you run into a problem you're not sure about, I hope you'll call me or one of the other Soccer Moms. We'll do our best to help you."

Buer and his group bowed to her. "We will heed your terms, Lady Death."

Their figures blurred, but their smoke forms were no longer black. Their gray mist faded into white clouds as they left.

"When's my first appointment with Doctor Hudson?" Lucifer asked.

Penny pulled out her phone and texted Gene. She smiled a few seconds later. "January 2nd, ten a.m. at our house. And, Lucifer, if you do anything to my husband—"

"I know, I know." The former Prince of Hell sighed. "You'll send Dani to deal with me."

"Damn straight she will," Dani growled.

He spread his wings. Like the other Fallen, his feathers were no longer black. His form blurred and the puff of cloud rose into the sky.

Chapter 47

As the Soccer Moms of the Apocalypse expected, the news media chalked the rising dead up to a worldwide hysterical delusion. All kinds of accusations flew between nations and extremist groups, but even the officials' half-assed explanations made no sense.

The last full week of school before the winter break passed uneventfully. For the most part, their families settled back to their old routines, except for the first time in years they skipped their weekly girls' night. It didn't seem right with Laura, Gammy, and Sister Joan gone.

Thankfully, Gene and Penny were pretty laid back about letting Mark go home with Justine after school while Dani finally packed up most of Heath's clothes and donated them to the homeless shelter. She and Mark kept a few of Heath's t-shirts and sweatshirts as keepsakes.

Dave Simmons dropped by the insurance agency and thanked Dani for sparing Pence. He was alive but in a coma. Simmons' theory was his former partner couldn't deal with the Devil being nicer than him, so Pence retreated from reality. The police officer might have been right. It wasn't like the doctors at Oakfield Hospital had a clue.

Ten days after laying the dead to rest, the Soccer Moms met at Wila's for girls' night, but it wasn't quite the same without the extended group.

"So much for filming those damn promos," Dani said.

Wila chuckled. "A day late and a dollar short as Gammy would have said."

"They're still useful," Francine protested. "Not all of the demons will obey the truce. People need to know how to defend themselves."

"That's assuming they listen to us and not the media pundits accusing us of being part of the hoax," Penny said while she poured the wine. "By the way, where's Karen? I though she was coming with you tonight."

"I took her to O'Hare this morning." Francine accepted her glass. "She's headed to Rome. The pope appointed her the new head of the Vatican task-force. With everything that happened, the cardinal formerly in charge will be lucky if he doesn't get excommunicated for the way he handled the impending Apocalypse."

"Jesus and Maria left town this morning, too," Dani added. "They sold their house and his carpentry business, but they stopped by our place to say goodbye. By the way, Maria's pregnant."

"Mark told Justine, didn't he?" Penny grimaced at Dani's nod. She dipped a potato chip in the French onion dip. "That explains Justine's foul mood when I picked them up at school."

"Why would Justine be upset?" Wila sipped her wine.

"Because she respected him as a coach. She's now threatening to quit soccer." Penny rolled her eyes. "I tried to offer her some hours at the Palace for spending money over the holidays, but apparently, working in a coffee shop is too boring."

"Speaking of which, when is the grand opening at Java's Too?" Dani asked as she shuffled the deck of cards.

"New Year's Eve." Penny reached into her purse. "By the way, here are your invitations."

Dani handed the deck to Francine to cut before she examined the envelope. The heavy cream paper and glossy black ink were classy without being pretentious. The logo for the new coffee house had music notes coming out of the cup instead of steam.

"I still think you should get a liquor license." Francine passed the deck back to Dani deal the cards.

"I like the idea of a coffee place that's open late for those of us on swing shifts," Wila proclaimed. "And the new logo's adorable."

"Plus, I don't need my father-in-law drinking himself silly," Penny said.

Dani frowned. "He's not dealing with Laura second death well?"

Penny shook her head.

"Brittany won't admit it, but I hear her crying herself to sleep in Rose's room," Francine said sadly.

"All of our house are too quiet right now," Wila admitted. "Derek's even moping about here. It's not like him."

"And you aren't?" Francine raised an eyebrow.

"Why do you think I wanted our girls' night?" Wila snapped.

"We all are dealing with our loved ones' second deaths." Dani finished dealing and turned up the nine of clubs as trump.

"How's Jenna working out, Penny?" Leave it to Francine to change the subject when things got uncomfortable. "Pass."

"So far, Valerie and Jenna are working well together." Penny picked up her cards and examined them. "I was a little surprised when Jenna confessed to Valerie that she's a siren. But overall, they each have their own area of responsibility and are respecting each other's strengths. Pass."

"Pass. That's before you open, girl," Wila said. "Everything could change once you're dealing with real customers."

Dani looked at her hand. To her shock, she had a perfect solo hand. Left and right bowers, ace, king, and queen. She turned down the nine of clubs.

"Do you always have to be so negative?" Francine complained. "Pass."

"Pass," Penny said.

"Pass." Wila glared at Francine. "And I'm not always negative."

Dani never thought she'd miss those two bickering, but in a way, it was nice things were getting back to normal. "By the way, ladies, I expect your votes next month at the OPA meeting."

Penny blinked. "You're going to run for president?"

"Yep." Dani nodded. "Helen was the one who actually convinced me. She said the board needs some new blood."

Wila snorted. "I just hope it's not yours. Courtney's not the type to let go of power."

"I don't know," Francine said. "Her personality has done a one-eighty since we saved hers and Kenny's butts. Everyone in the subdivision is talking about it."

Maybe not everything was back to normal, but their lives were definitely a little better.

Dani grinned at Penny. "Stay home, partner. Hearts are trump, ladies."

Chapter 48

The only Christmas worse than this one for Dani had been the first one after Heath died the first time. This year, none of the Soccer Moms or their immediate households could handle their extended families. At least, the ones who were living. The extra grief and exhaustion was simply too much.

Francine insisted they gather at her house. The only exception to the no-extended-family rule was Karen Longstreet. She'd become as much of a sister as the rest of the Soccer Moms during the Apocalypse, especially after she went to bat for the new Chicago recruits against the cardinal she'd replaced as the head of the taskforce. She flew back to Illinois for a few days, but she couldn't stay long. She simply had too much to do in Rome.

Surprisingly, Wila's ex-husband Deion relented when Derek begged him to let him join Wila and the Soccer Moms for Christmas Day. According to Derek, his dad and stepmom had changed a lot after the talk Wila had with Deion right before Thanksgiving. Both of them acted calmer and were even including Derek in decisions regarding the baby girl Deion and Rashida were expecting.

Even more surprising was when Mark insisted on attending Midnight Mass at Saint Michael's. He lit candles for Heath, Mom, and Father Rodriguez. Father Perez approached Dani and said if she needed to talk, his door was always open.

Dani also learned Ellen took over the position of the church's secretary while Father McAvoy was staying as an advisor to both Father Perez and Lucas Manewell. The local demon hunters elected Lucas as their new leader for Oakfield.

With New Year's Eve coming up, the kids conspired to stay with Edward to keep him entertained. When Dani asked Mark why, he said with the gravitas of someone much older, "Papa has Carmen, but Justine's grandpa lost both his wife and his girlfriend. He thinks he has no one. You can see it in his eyes. Justine's worried his grief might kill him."

"But you're not worried about me?" Dani tried to tease.

"Of course, I am," Mark retorted. "But you have the other Soccer Moms. All of Grandpa Edward's friends like that are gone except for Father McAvoy. And it's hard to talk about girl stuff to a priest."

Dani bit her tongue to keep from laughing because her son was totally right.

🔥　☠　🔥

Java's Too was already packed from the massive number of vehicles when Dani pulled into the Waterford Crossing Shopping Center's parking lot. All of the other businesses were closed except the pizza joint of a certain nationwide franchise. It was on the other end of the strip mall, and the only traffic on that side were the delivery drivers rushing in and out of the store.

When she entered, she was amazed at how nicely the coffeehouse had been decorated. With the navy velvet tablecloths, the electric candles, and the strings of tiny, white lights, it looked like a classy nightclub. And as she expected, the place was full.

At the opposite end of the café, a stage had been set up with navy carpet to match the tablecloths. Jenna joked and laughed with the audience before smoothly introducing the next karaoke contestant.

"Do you have your invitation, ma'am?" A girl Dani didn't recognize stood inside the door.

"Yes." Dani pulled her envelope from her coat pocket and handed it to the girl.

She signaled one of the waitresses. "Please escort Ms. Elante to the VIP table."

The waitress turned out to be Melody from Java's Palace. She grinned and said, "How are you doing tonight, Dani?"

"I'm doing good." It had become her standard answer over the past three weeks. With everyone assuming they had imagined the dead rising from their graves, she couldn't deal with saying she'd lost Heath a second time.

Melody accepted the small menu the hostess handed to her. "This way."

Dani followed Melody through the crowd. Three tables with "Reserved" signs had been pushed together. Wila, Francine, and Neal sat at two of the tables. All three got up to hug Dani, and she took the seat next to Wila.

"Where's Penny?" Dani asked.

"Micromanaging the kitchen staff," Melody pseudo-whispered.

"So where's Gene?" Dani had a suspicion, which Melody confirmed.

"Trying to stop her from micromanaging the kitchen staff." The waitress/barista grinned. "What can I get you, Dani?"

She glanced at the menu. "I'll take the Kahlua coffee milkshake."

"Be right back." Melody scurried through the crowd.

"What are you drinking?" Dani asked Wila.

"The banana peanut butter espresso shake." Wila held out her glass. "Want a taste?"

"No, thank you." Dani was about to tease Wila about her weird tastes when her face fell.

"Oh, crap," Wila muttered.

Dani looked over her shoulder in the direction Wila stared. Chance Paxton walked toward their table, but this time, the attorney wasn't possessed by any demon.

He stopped at their table, his eyes only on Wila. "Excuse me, but have we met before?"

"I don't think so," she lied.

Dani curled her toes to keep from stomping on Wila's foot with her own spiked heel.

Chance cocked his head. "Then why do I keep dreaming of you?"

Wila's voice jumped an octave. "Dreaming of me?"

"Yeah." He ran his hand over his hair. "I-I'm sorry. I know how weird it sounds. I've dreamed of sitting on a stone patio and talking to you for the last month. I-I'm sorry for bothering you." He turned to leave.

"Wait," Dani said.

He paused.

She looked at Wila. "If I need to get on with my life, so do you." She turned back to Chance. "You two met during the craziness last autumn. If you remember each other, then you made an impression. Would you like to go out on a double date? There's a co-worker of hers Wila wants to set me up with. Can you handle bowling?"

Chance smiled. "It's been a while, but I remember the basics." He looked at Wila. "Maybe I should start with those same basics. I'm Chance Paxton." He held out his palm.

Wila smiled, too, as she shook his hand. "I know."

He gave an odd look. "Then why did you say you didn't know who I was?"

"You probably don't remember, but you stopped my ex-husband from taking my son last month when Lilah King was in the hospital for emergency heart surgery." Wila sighed. "I embarrassed myself by kissing you. I apologize for being inappropriate and lying about knowing you."

His expression turned wry. "Wila Ardale. That explains both my dreams and the case file I didn't recognize."

"If you want to forget the whole thing, I totally understand," she murmured.

"No." He chuckled. "I've forgotten quite enough." He turned to Dani. "Which bowling alley and when?"

"Saturday night at eight," Dani said. "Great Lakes Lanes over on Washburn."

"It's a date. I'll see you then, Wila." He sauntered off with a pleased smile on his face.

"I can't believe you did that," Wila hissed.

"I can't believe you lied to him." Dani shook her head. "Don't you know lawyers write everything down?"

Francine nudged Dani's shoulder. "Scoot over."

Dani slid her chair over so Francine could fit her chair next to Dani.

"So what are we gossiping about under our breath?" Francine whispered.

"Wila insisted I needed to go out with her work buddy Ramon, so I set her up with Chance Paxton." Dani rubbed her hands together and cackled evilly.

"About time you two joined the living." Francine sipped her drink.

"Hey!" Dani and Wila protested at the same time.

Jenna approached their table. "Francine, you and Wila are up next. Shall I sign you up for karaoke, Dani? Name your song."

"Thanks, but not tonight." Dani smiled at the siren.

Wila and Francine followed Jenna up to the stage where a couple were doing a half-way decent rendition of Bon Jovi's "Livin' on a Prayer".

Neal set a tray in front of Dani and placed her drink on the table. "Your milkshake, madam."

On the stage, Francine and Wila launched into Paul McCartney and Michael Jackson's "Ebony and Ivory".

She chuckled while Neal set other drinks at everyone's places. "Did you get drafted?"

"Sort of." He grinned. "The staff is a little afraid of Penny right now."

As if to emphasize the point, Gene was literally shoving his wife past the partying guests.

"But Valerie needs help," Penny protested.

"No she doesn't," Gene said. "And you were causing more problems than you were solving."

"But—"

"Honey." Gene rested both hands on her shoulders. "Valerie asked me to get you out of the kitchen before she killed you. Now, please sit down, and enjoy the evening."

Penny's phone rang and she pulled it from her suit jacket pocket. "I have to answer this." She stepped aside to speak, but Dani could hear everything both she and Police Chief Wright were saying.

Gene must have understood Dani's grimace. "How bad?"

"Hostage situation," Dani answered.

He groaned and sat down beside Neal. "I'll stick around and help Valerie with the cleanup."

"Me, too," Neal added.

"Thanks, guys." Dani got up to join Penny.

"We're on our way, Chief." Penny ended the call.

Dani shook her head. "There's always some asshole who's got to ruin the holiday for everyone."

"Tell me about it." White shimmered around Penny, but Dani doubted anyone but Jenna and the other two Soccer Moms could see it.

Wila and Francine finished their duet to a round of applause. Wila nudged Francine and whispered something to her as they left the stage.

Jenna stepped up to the microphone. "Thank you, ladies. Let's give another round of applause to Wila and Francine. Next up, we have Brian and Maggie with "Don't Go Breaking My Heart." Dani felt the slight wave of the siren's power keep the crowd's attention on the stage. She was definitely a good addition to Penny's staff. Jenna handed Wila's paramedic partner and his stepmom microphones, and they launched into the Elton John/Kiki Dee classic while Wila and Francine made a beeline for Penny and Dani.

"Tell us on the way," Wila said as she grabbed her coat before she rushed past Dani and out the door. The other three followed as they donned their coats, and once outside, Penny explained the situation. Despite the brightly lit parking lot, one security lamp was out next to a couple of oaks. Beneath the shadows of the trees, their horses waited. By the time the quartet reached their mounts, all four women wore their horsemen personas.

"What a way to ring in the New Year," Penny said as she stepped into Silver's stirrup.

"Almost as good as Halloween," Francine answered.

Dani exchanged a look with Wila.

"Race you there," Wila said.

"You're on!" Dani cackled as the women and their mares galloped into the night.

Turn the page for a thrilling sneak peak of
Spells and Sleuths!

Spells and Sleuths

When the dark cherry front door of Aunt Jo's coffee shop slammed open, Kirsten Wilson jumped. The coffee pot filled with the day's special, a fresh, hot Jamaican Blue blend, slipped from her damp hand. She watched in slow-motion horror as the glass pot dropped toward the red and white tile floor.

Instinctively, she reached out with her powers. Unfortunately, her elemental specialty was water, not earth. The pot shattered against the ceramic tiles, but the java swirled and steamed in midair. Freezing wind blew through the doorway as Rose Gleason struggled to close the coffee shop door against the mid-morning autumn storm. Aunt Jo rushed over to help the elderly lady.

Kirsten grabbed a clean, empty pot. She concentrated a bit more and shifted the hot coffee from her bubble of magick into the new pot. Thank goodness, no other customers were in the shop. Even though the existence of supernaturals had been exposed due to their efforts to save the Normals who couldn't evacuate Puget Sound when the former Mount Rainier had erupted twelve years ago, there was still a lot of suspicion and fear among the Normal community.

Not to mention, Mom and Dad always said not to show off.

Rain splattered even harder against the coffee shop's huge plate glass windows. The edges of the forest green awning over the entrance and windows danced and rippled from the storm's gusts. A few people hurried into the courthouse across the way, but no one treaded the sidewalks on this side of Jackson Street in such a blustery, wet, cold morning.

"I'm so sorry, ladies." Miz Rose panted. "Darn wind." She turned seventy last month, and from the way her fingers curled, her arthritis was getting worse. Between that, the drop in temperatures, and the fierce wind, no wonder she lost her grip on the brass door handle.

"What can we get you, Miz Rose?" Kirsten dumped the broken glass into the trash and wiped her hands on her orange apron as Jo helped their only customer out of her coat. Rose Gleason had been their 4-H Club advisor when Kirsten and her twin Kaley joined. She insisted her club members call her "Rose" because "Mrs. Gleason" was her mother-in-law. Holmes County, Ohio, was far too conservative not to have an honorific, so "Miz Rose" had stuck as her name forever.

"A cinnamon latte, please." A frown creased Miz Rose's face. "But I'm not here for just coffee."

"A Tarot card reading? A little gossip?" Jo grinned. Even though both women were the same age, the life expectancy for witches was one hundred-thirty years. Jo could have passed as Kirsten's older sister with the right hairstyle, clothes, and makeup. No gray marred Jo's mahogany braid, the same mahogany both Mom and Kirsten had. Thank goddess, Jo didn't wear elastic-waist polyester pants, but sometimes, she said something incongruous with her physical appearance.

When Kirsten's twin Kaley teased Jo about being old enough to see the first moon landing live on TV, their great aunt said the Rainier Outing was the best thing that ever happened. Otherwise, she would have had to sell her coffee shop and move to another town by now to avoid the scrutiny of Normals. And she could stop dying gray streaks in her hair.

Miz Rose toddled to her left, checking the matching cherry tables and chairs past the service counter and the hallway leading to the restrooms. There was nothing on that side of the store but the framed paintings and photos by local artists that hung on the off white walls. Once Miz Rose made sure they were alone in the coffee shop, she shuffled to a table closest to the radiator.

Kirsten started the espresso brewing while she kept an eye on their visitor. Despite Miz Rose knowing about the supernaturals long before the Outing, she and folks who were Mom's age or older still had a problem talking about woo-woo stuff in public. And if Miz Rose checked for privacy, that's exactly what she wanted to talk about.

Their elderly customer turned back to Jo. "Actually, I think I have a ghost problem." An even deeper wrinkle appeared above Miz Rose's bright orange glasses that matched her Halloween sweater. She gestured for Jo to join her before she carefully lowered herself into the wooden chair.

This month's coffee shop seat covers featured black cats and pumpkins appliqued on cream broad cloth. Mary Levy made them in addition to working the early morning shift at the coffee shop. She was currently in the back of the shop putting together salads and sandwiches in preparation for lunch.

Kirsten never quite understood why the Amish community were more accepting of the supernaturals than the rest of the Normals in Millersburg. Maybe because they were used to being outsiders, too. Though in Mary's case, her great-great-aunt Anne had been a vampire until the cure for the disease had been discovered.

Jo took the chair beside Rose where she could keep an eye on the front door. "Sweetie—" She reached over and patted Rose's hand. "—I told you before. Your mom has passed on. She's not there."

"I don't think it's Mother." The elderly woman's eyes glistened behind her thick lens. "I think it's Dick. Wouldn't his death count as unfinished business?"

The giant picture windows at the front of the store shivered from a harsh blast of wind. The perky scent of the espresso mixed with the warm spice of cinnamon, though neither completely blocked the sweet odor of fresh baked pastries in the well-lit glass case on the right side of the register and counter.

Kirsten listened intently to the women as she steamed the milk for Rose's latte. Rose's brother had been murdered by the Millersburg Monster before Kirsten and her twin Kaley had been born.

Except there wasn't really a monster. Just a trapped Native American water spirit forced to kill against its will. But the monster version sounded cooler, and one of the Normal farmers used the idea for his cornfield maze every year. The event drew so many people from Cleveland and Columbus it drove Sheriff Birkheimer a little crazy trying to find extra help for traffic control for the month of October.

"What makes you think it's Mister Dick?" Kirsten asked. "If he was still hanging around, wouldn't he have made himself known long before now?"

At Jo's pursed her lips and glare, Kirsten ducked her head and retrieved the can of whipped cream from the mini-refrigerator under the counter.

"Rose, maybe it's time to think about—" Jo started.

Kirsten rolled her eyes. Sometimes, her great-aunt wasn't the most subtle person on the face of the planet. Miz Rose's explosion of temper would have been expected by anybody else who dared suggest she was too old to be living alone in a giant Victorian.

"I am not moving!" The elderly woman's frail body shook. "That house has been in my family for six generations! I am not leaving!"

Kirsten set the hot cup in front of Miz Rose. "What if I come over after the lunch rush?"

This time, both Miz Rose and Jo glared at her.

"Shouldn't you be in school?" Miz Rose said, patting her damp, iron-gray locks back in place.

"Teacher in-service day." Kirsten squared her shoulders and faced Jo. "I can check out Miz Rose's house. If there's nothing, it'll relieve your mind. And if there's something—"

"You'll come get me." Jo leaned back in her chair and crossed her arms. "The last thing we need is a ghost possessing you, young lady."

Oh, geez! Like she'd be stupid enough to let a ghost kick her out of her own body. But somehow, Kirsten squelched the urge to roll her eyes again. If she did, Jo would forbid her from going to Rose's house.

Right before Jo tattled on her to Mom.

"If there's something in Miz Rose's house, I'll come straight back here and let you know." Kirsten shut up and waited, a trick her twin never understood. She knew the I-just-turned-seventeen argument wouldn't fly with her great-aunt.

Finally, the crinkles around Jo's eyes eased, and her nostrils flared as she exhaled. "Fine. But I want you to call me before you go home, and let me know either way."

"Yes, ma'am."

Jo inclined her head toward the kitchen. "Tell Mary to take it easy on the salads. A dozen will do." She turned to watch the street. A couple of minivans rolled by, but no pedestrians. Raindrops fell sideways in the fierce wind and smacked the huge picture windows with sharp little reports. Jo shook her head. "I don't think we'll get much business with this weather."

Turned out, Jo was so very wrong on that count. Between the cold wind and spitting rain, half of Millersburg decided they wanted something hot, whether it be soup or coffee, to go with their salad or sandwich. In fact, it was nearly three before business died enough for Kirsten to clock out.

"You still going to Rose's house?" Jo eyed Kirsten.

"Yes, ma'am, I am," she answered as she slung on her burgundy waterproof jacket.

Jo inclined her head toward the back of the shop and lowered her voice. "There's some white sage sticks in my desk. Bottom drawer on the right."

"Thanks, Aunt Jo." Kirsten grinned and headed toward the storeroom cum office. Once she secured two of the sage sticks, a pack of matches, and a Ziploc bag of salt in a larger Ziploc to keep everything dry inside her backpack, she returned to the front to find Kaley leaning against the pastry display case. Her twin wore her varsity jacket and jeans.

Like cheerleaders should get to wear a varsity jacket.

"I don't get your fingerprints all over that," Kirsten snapped. "I just cleaned the glass."

"Be nice to me if you want a ride home in the rain," Kaley shot back, flipping her bottle-blond hair over her shoulder in the process. "Mom sent me to get you."

"Fine. But I have a stop first." Kirsten turned and waved. "See you Saturday morning, Jo!"

Their great-aunt waved absently before turning back to Augusta Wright who was ordering pastries for next week's Ladies Auxiliary meeting. Once they were outside, Kirsten could feel her sister's eyes on her despite them both ducking their heads against the wind and the rain.

"Where do we need to go?" Kaley yelled over the ropes slapping against the flagpole in front of the courthouse. "I've got some time before I need to be at Tina's."

Kirsten shook her head. "Babysitting again?"

Kaley shrugged. "After her ugly divorce, I don't blame her for wanting to go out for some stress relief."

Despite having a good job in the Pomerene Hospital administration department, Tina Eisler's idea of stress relief involved sleeping with every eligible male in Holmes County, plus a couple of ineligible ones. She really needed to pay more attention to her two kids, who were hurting just as bad as she was. However, Kirsten kept her mouth shut on that topic. Mom treated Tina like her little sister no matter how bad Tina screwed up at life or magick.

"What?" Kaley said as they rounded the shop and crossed the parking lot. "No smart ass comments about Tina?"

"Not today. I need to get over to the old Miller Mansion."

"Miz Rose's place? Why?"

"I just need to check out a problem she's having."

"What kind of problem?" Kaley tapped the key fob to unlock the doors of Mom's little sedan. When Kirsten remained silent after they climbed inside, Kaley waved the fob. "Spill unless you want to walk there in the rain."

Kirsten sighed. No, she didn't. It was only spitting rain now, but more gray clouds darkened the sky to the west. If she walked, she wouldn't make to Miz Rose's house before the next wave hit.

On the other hand, she wanted to prove to both Mom and Jo she could handle things on her own. Kaley didn't take her magick studies as seriously, and their older relatives assumed her lack of focus applied to Kirsten as well. It irritated the hell out of her.

"Miz Rose thinks she has a ghost."

"Awesome!" Kaley flashed a maniacal grin before she pressed the button to start the car. "I'm coming with you if you're going to bust a ghost."

"What about Tina's kids?"

"I don't have to be there until seven." Kaley back out of the spot. "Plenty of time."

Kirsten leaned back in the passenger seat. Part of her was annoyed by her sister tagging along. But another part was glad to have backup.

Just in case there really was a ghost haunting Miz Rose's house.

Acknowledgements

As always, the utmost respect and thanks go to my cover designer Elaina Lee of For the Muse Design and my formatter JW Manus. These ladies go above and beyond the call when it comes to making my books look fabulous.

Thank you to my sprinting partners Tracie, Kate, and Candi for helping me stay on the writing track for this book.

A huge thank you and a ginormous hug to the Kickstarter backers who helped me bring this series to life.

Love and thanks to Darling Husband and Princess Bella for keeping my head on straight after the death of my mother while penning this volume.

And much love and appreciation to my readers for allowing me to entertain you.